Praise for *The Spectacular Visio*

'Dark, beautifully crafted ... hilarious ... Highly recommended for young adults and grown-ups alike'
— **Fiona Parker, former panellist on the WHSmith Children's Book Awards**

'Insightful ... moving ... on a par with *The Curious Incident of the Dog in the Night-Time*'
— **Linda Townsend**

'Written with enormous humour and compassion, Oskar and his supporting cast live well beyond the pages of this highly imaginative and haunting tale. Hugely thought-provoking, this would be a fantastic book to read and discuss with young adults'
— **Sarah Quigley**

'Original and interesting'
— **Judith Webster, ReadandReview**

'Unique, absorbing, complex and absolutely unforgettable'
— **Raminta Raj, Book Inspector**

Praise for *Cinema Lumière* by Hattie Holden Edmonds

'A magical, thought-provoking and uplifting tale ... one of this year's must-reads'

– Daily Mirror

'A stunning debut. Made me laugh out loud, cry ... and ache with recognition'

– The Huffington Post

'An extraordinary, funny, soul-warming book'

– Sainsbury's Magazine

THE
SPECTACULAR
VISION
OF
OSKAR
DUNKELBLICK

HATTIE HOLDEN EDMONDS

Published by RedDoor
www.reddoorpublishing.com

© 2018 Hattie Holden Edmonds

ISBN 978-1-910453-64-3

A CIP catalogue record for this book
is available from the British Library

Cover design: Clare Connie Shepherd
www.clareconnieshepherd.com

Typesetting: Westchester Publishing Services

Printed and bound in Denmark by Nørhaven

For my mum, Sarah Anne Edmonds
With love

'When you change the way you look at things, the things you look at change.'

– Max Planck
(German physicist and
Nobel Prize Winner, 1918)

Chapter 1

'Living the dream!' Oskar sniggered, whilst gazing down from the window of his new lodgings. His dark eyes swept over the scene before him, raking over the rotting timbers of the village houses, the barricaded shops and the cracked cobbled pavements. In the distance were the ruins of the twelfth-century church, now a dumping ground for old fridges, empty Schnapps bottles and a cack-brown corduroy sofa. A lone figure, hunched against the harsh October winds, staggered along by a sidewall, eyes blinking fearfully from behind a pair of thick black glasses.

Oskar withdrew from the window and did a little sock-dance to celebrate. Of course, he'd had high hopes when he read about the village of Keinefreude back home in Berlin two months before: highest levels of alcoholism per capita in Europe! Rocketing rate of heart disease! Zero birth rate! A trawl through some travel reviews had further fuelled his excitement – Oskar's favourite description being *'a truly grim little village set in the bleak shadows of the Black Forest with absolutely nothing to offer except for relief at one's exit.'*

Oskar had only been in Keinefreude for three days and already he'd seen the small acts of daily spite, the sly bickering and rampant greed rife amongst the villagers (a punch-up in the butcher's over a piece of pork was not uncommon). He'd gleefully noted their addiction to cheap daytime TV and cut-price alcohol, and to his delight he'd discovered that almost everyone's eyesight was rapidly deteriorating, due to the lack of fresh fruit and vegetables following the closure of the grocer's.

All in all, Oskar was having a whale of a time.

Inhaling a lungful of choking grey smog from the nearby gravel processing plant, Oskar picked up his sketchbook next to his bed and began a rough outline of the village. As he sketched, he thought of those painters who believed that the artist's role was to inspire humanity through visions of beauty, to offer people a glimpse of the divine, helping them to momentarily forget their horrid little lives.

Quatsch! The true artist should document life as it was, steeped in suffering. '*This hell of individual existence*' as Nietzsche had so perfectly put it, should be revealed in all its glory. Why try to rose-tint reality with pretty pastel colours when they'd only fade to reveal the grey undercoat of torment?

Oskar glanced around his new home that lay on the top floor of the tall, 400-year-old house at the end of the village's main street. Although it was only temporary – three months max before he headed back to Berlin – he rather liked the building, with its scowling wooden gargoyle that guarded the front door. It did, however, lean markedly to the left. Consequently the few sticks of furniture that came with the house were clustered on that same one side along with the stand-alone sink, the one ring gas stove, the wood burner and the wardrobe with the broken mirror. Only his iron bed, salvaged from the psychiatric wing of an old Berlin hospital, was stationed at the other end, tethered to the wall to prevent that too from joining the jamboree of household clutter.

Along the wall next to the wardrobe hung his canvases,

amongst them one painting he'd kept from his breakthrough exhibition *The Dark Side of Mother* one year ago, when he had just turned seventeen. That was the exhibition which had made the papers, securing him his first proper art gallery. Berlin's youngest outsider artist! The teenage misery merchant! Abandoned and alone on the streets since the age of thirteen! How he'd revelled in the art critics' headlines.

But now, of course, he had to follow up that success by painting something even more sensational. Twelve months was a long time in the art world and people would soon forget who he was. Hence the need to get cracking asap. So having spent those first three days scouring the village for potential subjects – now it was time for his meet and greet.

Comb in hand, Oskar considered his lanky reflection in the cracked mirror: baby-fine black hair styled into a high quiff; forehead a little too large to fit the rest of his face; deep-set cheekbones; dark leather trousers and a sweatshirt depicting Edvard Munch's *The Scream*. It was a shame that his eyes were giving him so much grief. He'd left his special prescription drops in Berlin and now they were all red and itchy from the chronic conjunctivitis. Still, a trip to the chemist's would hopefully sort that.

Fastening the metal buttons of his black trench coat, Oskar pointed at himself in the mirror with one long forefinger. Looking good, Oskar Dunkelblick. Looking good.

Ten minutes later he was down on the high street, gazing into the window of the bakery, which lay next to the abandoned florist's. Inside, the owner Frau Miesel, who Oskar had already singled out as a possible sitter, was standing by the dough-rolling table wearing a stiff white apron and a rigid grimace. Skinny as a skateboard and brittle as a biscuit, her coarse grey hair was cut in a block fringe, which ended just above her pointy black glasses.

Stepping through the door, Oskar adopted a casual smile. After four years on the streets he prided himself on his blade-sharp survival skills and his ability to adapt his language and behaviour to almost any social situation. Simple old-school flattery should nail this one.

'That's a nice outfit, Frau Miesel.'

Frau Miesel narrowed her already narrow eyes. 'It's an apron.'

'I know, but a well-starched apron.'

'What do you want?' Frau Miesel's voice sounded like steel bullets ricocheting off sheet metal.

'Hmmm...' Oskar replied, scouring the shelves as if they were heaving with all kinds of tasty treats, instead of just loaves of grey sourdough and pumpernickel. 'Let me see.'

This hesitation was a good opportunity for Oskar to gather data on this tempting specimen. As Frau Miesel turned back to the table to measure out some dry yeast, he studied her from behind: the turkey-scrag neck; the bony varicose-veined legs; the bizarre helmet hair... ooh, and a nice little skin rash peeking above her collar. Eczema? Psoriasis? Or maybe even shingles? Oskar made a mental note to consult his medical dictionary when he got home.

Oskar had been fascinated by sickness for some time. As a six-year old he'd become obsessed with Herr Hinkel, who lived in the flat opposite him and his mother in the Altona district of Hamburg. Herr Hinkel had lost a leg in a motorbike accident and now the right side of his trouser-leg ended abruptly at the knee, safety-pinned together to prevent prying eyes. One of Oskar's first life goals had been to snatch a peek at the severed limb. Consequently he'd developed a range of tactics – from peering through the keyhole to spontaneous visits with offerings of liver sausage – hoping to catch Herr Hinkel on the hop, with his trousers down.

At the age of nine, Oskar had bought his first medical dictionary and many a happy hour was spent skipping through the symptoms of renal failure or Crohn's disease. This was followed by the discovery of Dr. Sommer's problem page in the teen magazine *Bravo*, in which Dr. Sommer would advise German youth on matters of health, particularly sexual health. *Mein Penis ist krumm ... Mein Busen sind zu klein ... Ich habe Herpes ...* were all regular complaints. Once there was a whole double-page spread featuring in-depth descriptions of sexually transmitted diseases, the details of which Oskar would silently repeat whenever he found himself at a loose end.

'Made up your mind yet?' Frau Miesel was facing him once more, bony hands on hips.

Oskar stared at the barren shelves. 'Do you have any *Apfelstrudel*?'

Frau Miesel shook her head yet her metal-grey hair didn't move a millimetre.

'Poppyseed whirls?'

Frau Miesel pursed her blueish lips.

'Black Forest gateau?'

Another head shake. Was that helmet of a hair-do welded to her skull?

'This is a bakery, isn't it?'

'No, it's an abattoir,' snapped Frau Miesel. The deadpan delivery took Oskar by surprise. He glanced around quickly, just to be sure.

'Ha ha,' he replied. 'So no cakes at all?'

'No cakes at all,' said Frau Miesel, tartly.

Oskar left the bakery with a loaf of sourdough under his arm, while behind him he heard the bolt being dragged across the door. Subject Number 1: Sorted.

His next stop was the local *Bierkeller*, which was bang opposite the bakery. Inside, Oskar noted with glee the gaping cracks in the walls, the cobwebs that clung to the ceiling and the windows caked in grime. Thomas, the owner, was slumped over the bar, clutching a brandy glass while staring at the television screen in front of him. His shirt was stained a dark yellow and his matted brownish-grey beard looked more like something you'd wipe your feet on, rather than grow on your face.

'*Groossies!*' said Oskar, delighted with his customised *Grüss Gott* greeting.

From behind his grease-smeared glasses, Thomas's gaze remained fixed on the television, which was broadcasting scenes from a flood somewhere in central Germany.

'A *Dunkelbier*, please,' said Oskar.

Thomas turned towards him and glared.

Oskar hadn't seen potential Subject Number 2's eyes close up before. They really were quite marvellous. The eyeballs were threaded with little red veins like those fun joke ones with which you could scare small children and the dark iris was filled with a look of such torment that Oskar could only stare in fascination.

'Had this place long?' asked Oskar, while Thomas filled his glass from the pump.

Thomas grunted before sliding the beer towards him and retreating to the armchair to stare at the TV, which now showed an entire village submerged underwater.

Oskar sipped the flat beer and watched the screen, where an old-fashioned television set on top of a pile of splintered planks floated into view.

'Hope there's nothing good on the Goggler tonight,' he chuckled, 'or the owners of that telly will be super sour.'

Thomas said nothing.

'Just look at those two!' Oskar pointed to the woman and small boy in pyjamas, who'd clambered into a tree above the

6

torrents. 'They could have dressed for the occasion. Don't they know they're on national TV?'

Thomas eyed him menacingly.

'Wow, I'm liking this joint more and more,' said Oskar. 'Warm welcome, cool décor, great beer . . . you're onto a winner here.'

'If you don't like it, you can piss off.' Thomas's reply was spiked with such hostility that Oskar jerked backwards, noticing how the man's right fist was bunched like a hand grenade.

'You know what?' he said, quickly. 'I think I'm done here for today.' He took a final slurp of his beer, slipped off the stool and dashed towards the door as fast as his black brothel creepers would allow.

Relieved to have dodged any possible violence, Oskar continued on to the final shop in the row. Krank's the chemist occupied two premises and its shadow crept halfway up the high street. The windows were decorated with antidepressant offers of the week mounted on bright orange cut-outs shaped like smiley faces. Three packs of Dopazine for the price of two! One month's free trial of Seratox! Half price Trixilon! Of course, Oskar knew all of these brands and many more besides. One of the best presents that Franz, his former flatmate, had left behind in the Berlin apartment rented by Oskar's gallery, was a hardback book entitled *Depression. Don't Let it Get You Down*, which contained descriptions of every antidepressant known to the Western world.

As Oskar surveyed the cheery cardboard faces, he thought of Franz. Franz from Füssen, whom Oskar had hoped would catapult him and his art career to international fame following *The Dark Side of Mother* triumph. Fat lot of good Franz had turned out to be.

Feeling his mood plummet, Oskar pushed his way inside the chemist's and joined the queue. Behind the counter, the owner Krank cut a fascinating figure with his thin black hair draped around his shoulders like an oily stole, his glacial smile and pointy nose. He reminded Oskar of his favourite character from one of E T A Hoffmann's stories, *The Sandman*, who used to throw sand in the faces of little children to blind them before pulling out their eyes and feeding them to his own children who lived on the moon.

'May I help you?' Herr Krank's voice was slippery as an eel in Oskar's ear.

'I just want some eye drops.' Oskar pointed to the reddened rim of his right eye. 'Conjunctivitis.'

Krank reached behind him. 'Do you suffer from headaches as well?'

'Sometimes,' said Oskar. The headaches came mostly when he thought about his school days and what had happened in the months before he'd run away from home.

Krank nodded and gestured towards the stand displaying dozens of black spectacles. He removed a pair and twirled them between his fingers. 'Perhaps these might help?'

Oskar shook his head. 'No thanks, just the eye –'

And that's when he stopped, pulled up in his tracks by what he had spied in the stockroom. For there she was: Greta, the chemist's junior assistant hunched over a clipboard, pale blonde hair hanging down her face like bleached weeds. And what was going on with that droopy left lid? Could it be a lazy eye? Oskar suppressed a whoop.

'Have you been feeling a little down lately?' Krank was fingering a white packet of pills, when Oskar turned reluctantly back to the counter.

Oskar's eyes darted back to Greta in the stockroom. She was

perfect! Together with Frau Miesel and the barman he had his hat trick.

'Actually, Herr Krank,' he beamed, 'life's pretty peachy right now.'

Oskar was still feeling pretty peachy when he left the chemist's and headed back home. As he walked up the high street, he struck up a whistle from his favourite Wagner opera. But when he passed the empty florist's next to the bakery, he noticed that the two blinds had been drawn down over the windows and behind them was a sort of *glowing*, a luminous shimmer that appeared to make the whole front wall pulsate.

Oskar backtracked a couple of steps to get a better view. It was then that he heard a voice calling his name.

'Oskar.' The voice had a warm, velvety depth to it, which seemed to wrap itself around him, drawing him closer.

'Oskar,' the voice called again.

Was it coming from inside the shop – or inside his head? Oskar wasn't sure but he felt a melting sensation as if his body was filling with liquid honey. With it came a fluttery feeling in his heart, a light, happy feeling that he'd not had since . . .

Don't be stupid! Oskar gave himself a stern telling off. Your mind's playing tricks. You're just over-excited. Ignore it.

So he did.

And when he looked back at the shop once more, the glowing was gone and everything was deliciously dark again.

Chapter 2

Oskar was homemaking. He'd already had his breakfast – a Kinder Bueno bar and a mug of strawberry Nesquik – and now he was creating an *al fresco* larder. Since the absentee landlord seemed unwilling to replace the broken fridge, he was forced to use the outside window ledge to store his food. So far it housed the leftovers from last night's supper – a half empty tin of meatballs and a pile of mashed potato, both of which he intended to fry up for his lunch. *Yummsky*!

After admiring his initiative, Oskar's eyes drifted down the high street to the homes of his new sitters: Frau Miesel, Thomas and Greta. What a perfect trio! A holy trinity of tragedy! Now all he had to do was persuade them to sit for him – and somehow avoid getting his head kicked in by Thomas.

Some, those who knew no better, might say that Oskar should have compassion for such people, but where was the fun in that? Compassion. Ha! What a load of overrated *Schnick-Schnack*.

Oskar remembered clearly the first time he'd heard the C-word. He was ten and it was the last day of the Easter term. Returning from school on the Friday afternoon, he'd found his mother on the sofa in the sitting room, holding hands with his grandmother. Oskar had never much cared for Omi Blumental, partly because she was stingy with presents and partly because she always seemed to have some sob story on the go – the most recent of which was the stomach tumour of her husband, Oskar's grandfather.

'Come and sit down,' his mother sniffed, patting the sofa cushion next to her. 'I have some sad news.'

Oskar sat down and pulled his special Accident and Emergency sketchbook from his satchel.

'Now, you know that Grandpa hasn't been very well lately,' his mother began.

Oskar nodded.

'Well, darling,' his mother inhaled deeply. 'He died this morning.'

Oskar shrugged and started flicking through his A&E sketchbook to admire his choice of subjects, which ranged from simple accidents around the home (burning oil spilled on naked flesh, hands trapped in waste disposal units) to large-scale catastrophes involving industrial machinery.

'Did you hear what I said?'

'Yes.' Oskar peered around his mother and watched his grandmother snivelling into her hankie. 'I suppose *she's* going to be staying with us now?'

'Oskar!'

Oskar rarely saw his mother that angry. Her face was all red and her hands were shaking.

'Her husband of forty years, my father and your grandfather, has just died! Where's your compassion?'

'Compassion? Does that mean feeling sorry for someone?'

His mother nodded.

'Compassion is for losers.' Oskar stared over at his grandmother again. 'Exactly *how* long is she hoping to milk this one?'

Compassion! Thought Oskar. What a waste of space. No, the people of Keinefreude were to be observed and each detail of their sad lives was to be noted, relished and committed to canvas. In no way would he become involved. No compassion, no empathy, no kindness . . .

Oskar skidded down the sloping floor to where he kept his Wagner records and pulled out one of the composer's lesser-known works, *A Faust Overture*. He laid it on the turntable of his vintage portable record player and headed over to the window. As the opening notes of the tuba filled the room, he grabbed his imaginary conductor's baton. Ta da! He swung his arms above his head in time to the thump of the double bass while musing on the inspiration for the overture – the sixteenth-century sorcerer Doctor Faustus. Oh, how he loved the story of the alchemist's demise: starting with his ill-advised attempt to turn base metal into gold, and ending with him blowing himself and the guesthouse where he was staying to bits. BOOF!

Oskar stabbed the air in time with the kettledrums, picturing Doctor Faustus's final moments with furniture and fried food flying everywhere. But just as he was gearing up for the climax something down on the street caught his eye. He peered closer, frowning, before yanking the record off its turntable and jamming the imaginary baton back into its imaginary case.

What the hell had happened to the florist's?

Act casual, thought Oskar as he sidled past the shop front, which had a new sign written in large gold script: *Dr. Sehle's Spectacle Shop*. Beneath it the window display, once the home of wilted wreaths, brown ribbons and chipped vases, now glittered with spectacles of every design and colour from plain oval gold ones and fluorescent pink bifocals to emerald green monocles and tortoiseshell pince-nez, all dangling from invisible threads, glinting through the morning gloom.

Oskar stood for several seconds, transfixed by the sparkling colours. A small pair of round silver glasses, similar to those worn by Nietzsche, stood out and he took a step closer. Stylish and intelligent-looking, teamed with his black polo neck they'd definitely make for a crafty distraction from the conjunctivitis.

The entrance to the shop was so low that despite stooping to pass through the door, Oskar still banged the top of his head. Cursing whichever undersized architect had designed the doorway, he readjusted his quiff and closed the door behind him. A sign was pinned to the back of it:

> *'A human being is a part of a whole, although he*
> *experiences himself as something separated from the*
> *rest . . . a kind of optical delusion of his consciousness.'*
> – Albert Einstein

Oskar read the sentence a couple of times and shook his head irritatedly. Part of a whole! What a load of rubbish. He, Oskar, wasn't part of anything. He was a one-man show! But what did Einstein know? He was just a silly old scientist who couldn't tell his *Arsch* from his elbow.

The main room was unattended and lit by flickering oil lamps. In the middle, a wrought iron staircase spiralled up through the ceiling to the first floor. On the right hand wall were a series of oak cabinets crammed with optical instruments including eye test charts, china eyebaths and wooden sight-measuring sticks. In the last cabinet, laid upon tiny cushions of burgundy velvet, were dozens of blue, green and brown glass eyeballs, all of which seemed to be staring straight at Oskar.

On the opposite wall were several framed drawings. Up close, the first one by the shop door showed a turbaned man holding some kind of stone in his fingers: *'The History of the Spectacle begins in the eleventh century when the Arab scientist, Abu-Ali-Alhazen discovered that quartz stone could be used as a magnifier for reading.'*

The second picture was of a craftsman in a calf-length leather apron holding up a single glass lens. Oskar noted the man's lustrous brown locks and wondered how such thickness had been achieved when hair products were presumably a little thin on the ground. Due to his own baby-fine hair, he was always on the lookout for volumising tips. The text however did nothing to enlighten him: *'In the thirteenth-century, craftsmen in Venice made small discs of glass which could be worn in a frame . . .'*

Dull. Dull. Oskar yawned and moved onto the third drawing, which featured a man in a frock coat and a woman in a large flouncy skirt walking along a cobbled street. Both wore a pair of lenses set into pearl frames and secured with ribbons around the back of their heads.

'Following the invention of the printing press in the 1450s, people everywhere developed the desire to read. By the early 1800s lenses had become the fashion accessory for the aristocracy.'

Thud!

Oskar jumped at the sound of footsteps from the floor above. He wheeled around and saw a pair of leather walking boots at the top of the spiral staircase. Next into view came a pair of dark green trousers and a thick brown woollen jacket, and finally a woodsman's cap with fur-lined ear flaps.

'Groossies,' said Oskar, a little half-heartedly while staring at the figure of the elderly man in front of him. He looked like someone from the sixteenth-century and his skin was all puckered and leathery-looking.

'Good morning,' said the man, whose eyes were brown with

flashes of amber as though he'd spent too long gazing into a fire. A hand as wrinkled as the face was thrust towards Oskar. 'I am Dr. Sehle.'

'And I am Oskar,' said Oskar, ignoring the man's out-stretched fingers. Handshaking, along with any other form of bodily contact, was not to be encouraged. Instead he gave a brief salute.

'You are wanting to buy some spectacles?' Dr. Sehle's voice had a velvety depth to it and an old-fashioned accent that Oskar found hard to place.

'Maybe,' said Oskar.

'Then I will need to perform an eye test on you.'

'Actually, I have perfect vision,' said Oskar. 'They would be for more decorative purposes.'

'I see,' said Dr. Sehle. As he moved towards Oskar, he started coughing quite violently, before whipping out a handkerchief to deposit into it whatever had come up.

Wow! Was that *emphysema?* Or even tuberculosis?

'Tell me, Oskar, when was the last time that you felt any real joy?' Dr. Sehle took a step forward.

'Joy?' said Oskar.

'Yes, joy.'

Oskar hesitated, momentarily stumped.

Dr. Sehle moved closer.

Oskar stepped backwards, wondering if the man's puckered skin was the result of an accident and if so, whether it had been at home or in the workplace.

'Have you ever experienced love?' asked Dr. Sehle.

'Listen, old man,' said Oskar, whose back was now rammed against the wall. 'I just came in for a pair of glasses.' He pointed to the round Nietzschean spectacles hanging in the window. 'How much?'

Dr. Sehle held up his hand. 'First we need to do the eye test.'

'Like I said, 20/20 vision,' said Oskar in a sing-song voice.

Dr. Sehle raised a wrinkled forefinger and smiled. 'If you take the eye test then I will give you the glasses for free.'

'What's the catch?' said Oskar. In his world nothing came for free.

'There is no catch,' said Dr. Sehle. 'You are my first customer in the village, and I often give first customers a gratis pair of glasses. It helps to promote the product.'

'In that case,' said Oskar. 'It's a deal.'

Dr. Sehle led the way up the spiral staircase and Oskar followed several steps behind. At the end of the first floor landing was a green door leading into a small attic room, whose walls and ceiling were covered with quotations written in thick gold ink. Once inside, Oskar read the one nearest the door: *A man sees the world as he imagines it to be.* Immanuel Kant. Another, above the little window was credited to Gustave Flaubert: *There is no truth. There is only perception.* A third was looped across the ceiling: *The real voyage of discovery consists not in seeking new landscapes but in having new eyes.* Marcel Proust.

Oskar smirked at the last one, recalling Proust's many sicknesses and his subsequent three-year confinement to bed before dying of a pulmonary abscess and pneumonia.

The rest of the attic room was sparsely furnished with a red leather barber's chair and above it on the wall, an illuminated glass box for the eyesight tests. Down the middle of the box were four lines of block letters, growing smaller as they neared the bottom. Oskar read them:

KINDNESS

COMPASSION

JOY

LOVE

'So, Oskar, do you know how your eyes work?' Dr. Sehle was bent over a tattered leather doctor's bag in the far corner.

'No idea,' said Oskar, who was sitting, as instructed, in the red leather barber's chair.

Dr. Sehle pulled a small silver torch from the bag. 'Your eyes function like a camera, recording the world around you, then sending the images to your brain to be processed and interpreted.' He advanced towards Oskar, torch in hand. 'But sometimes these images can be distorted. Do you know why?'

'Nope.'

Dr. Sehle smiled. 'It all depends on the perspective of the person who is operating the camera – their life experience, their beliefs, their judgements. Whatever these may be, will determine what the eyes see.'

'If you say so.' Oskar squinted at the man's skin once more. Maybe he'd been the victim of a freak accident involving a giant flamethrower?

Dr. Sehle flicked the switch of his torch and before Oskar could protest, the man was angling the beam straight into his eyes. Seconds later, he was back burrowing in his doctor's bag from which he lifted first a small wooden box then a pair of metal eye-testing glasses with two lens-less round frames, each one the size of a satsuma, which protruded from the front like mini telescopes.

'Put these on, please,' said Dr. Sehle, walking back over to Oskar and handing him the test glasses.

Oskar tentatively put them on and stared at the mirror in front of him, which reflected the reversed letters from the illuminated box. He now saw that what he had thought were random letters on each line actually made up a word.

'And these are my most recent invention,' said Dr. Sehle, lifting the lid of the small wooden box to reveal the purple velvet lining inside, into which was slotted a variety of coloured lenses. Having selected two, he held the amber discs up towards the faint ray of light slanting through the small window.

'These lenses have the ability to absorb and retain sunlight,' he said. 'So that the wearer sees the world through a lens of pure light, which . . .' he paused, shaking his head in wonder. '. . . can completely blow one's mind.'

Dr. Sehle dropped the lenses into the two empty frames of the eye test glasses. 'Now I want you to read aloud those first three words that you see reflected in the mirror.'

Oskar hesitated. They weren't exactly words he used in everyday life but if it meant getting a pair of glasses for free, he was willing to compromise.

KINDNESS

COMPASSION

JOY

The words felt strange in his mouth but somehow they left a sweet taste on his tongue.

'Now close your eyes and repeat the fourth word in your mind over and over until you can feel it in every cell of your body,' said Dr. Sehle.

Reluctantly, Oskar did as he was asked.

LOVE

'Open your eyes, please.'

Oskar opened his eyes, staring around him at the glowing light, which filled the room. It seemed to pulse with life and intelligence as if it wished to communicate with him. He glanced down at his hands, which suddenly felt all tingly. Somehow they didn't look solid anymore. Instead the boundary between his skin and the air around it had dissolved into one swirling mass of light and colour.

'Now walk over to the window,' said Dr. Sehle.

As if in a trance Oskar walked to the window and gazed down at the scene below.

'What the f . . . ?' He shut his eyes, counted to thirteen and re-opened them.

'What do you see?' Behind him, Dr. Sehle sounded as if he was calling from the end of a long tunnel.

Oskar tried to reply but he was beyond language. In fact, he was beyond everything. He started to smile and his eyes filled with tears. Moments later his whole body was fizzing with joy, so intense and so overwhelming that he thought he might explode.

Chapter 3

Oskar was lying star-shaped on his bed. His forehead and eyes were covered with a salmon pink flannel to block out the light. Within handy reach on the bedside table lay his medical dictionary, a half empty mug of chocolate milk and a biography of Nietzsche. In the twenty four hours since his visit to Dr. Sehle's shop, he'd been trying to comfort himself by re-reading the bit about the philosopher's psychotic breakdown, resulting in his confinement in Jena's mental asylum. Usually the passage gave Oskar a great deal of pleasure, but not anymore.

The medical dictionary had also been consulted in Oskar's search for information about what he might be suffering from. He still hadn't ruled out the possibility of his own psychotic/schizophrenic breakdown, brought on by a chemical imbalance in the brain after looking through the lenses. According to the medical dictionary the symptoms of schizophrenia included hallucinations, delusions, irrational beliefs and grossly disturbed behaviour. It all sort of fitted, yet there was no mention of Oskar's other symptoms, the ones that worried him most: that deep sense of love which had brought tears to his eyes, the overwhelming joy, together with a feeling of ... it was difficult to find the word for it but if he was forced at gunpoint he would probably say ... *Wholeness*.

During those twenty four hours Oskar had tried to retrace in his memory exactly what had happened when he had peered through the lenses. The first part he could remember quite clearly; the shimmering light when he'd opened his eyes and the altered appearance of everything in that attic room. For nothing seemed to have a solid form and everything from the barber's chair and the doctor's bag to Dr. Sehle and even Oskar's own hands appeared to be just a mass of pulsating energy.

That part was strange enough, but it was the next bit where Dr. Sehle had called him over to the window, that had freaked him out big time. Staring through the lenses at the village below, the sky had lost its lead-grey colour and was now electric blue, while the trees in the forest fringing the village were vibrant green. The shops and houses, once so rundown, were freshly painted and on every windowsill bloomed pots of red and pink geraniums. At the end of the street, the rubbish tip surrounding the church had been replaced by a small park filled with rosemary bushes and lavender-lined walkways.

Pressing his face to the window as close as the eye test glasses allowed, Oskar could see Frau Miesel standing at the counter in the bakery. She was filling storage jars with plump currants, succulent dates and sticky figs while behind her, the shelves buckled under the weight of plum tarts, almond flans, cream horns and raspberry meringues. When she looked up and saw Oskar at the attic window she smiled, a broad, beaming smile that lit up her whole face.

Through the doors of the *Bierkeller* Oskar saw Thomas washing the windows. The radio was on, tuned to a Beethoven concerto and as Oskar listened to the soaring violins, it seemed that he could sense the musical notes as colours, like a Kandinsky picture he'd once seen; emerald green, sunflower yellow and a dazzling gold. The more he listened the more he could hear another melody beneath that first one, a melody so beautiful that his eyes filled with tears again. The music of the spheres, he thought to himself.

Further down the high street, Oskar noticed that Krank's windows were emptied of the usual black-rimmed glasses and antidepressant adverts. Instead, rows of wooden shelves held glass jars containing dried herbs, thick golden oils and different coloured tinctures. Standing next to them was Greta, chatting to one of the customers, her eyes shining with happiness.

Just as Oskar was trying to take all this in – Frau Miesel and her shelves of cakes, Thomas and the sublime music, Greta's shining eyes – a curious thought occurred to him, a thought so bizarre that initially he tried to ignore it. But it wouldn't go away, tugging at his mind like a persistent child at a parent's sleeve until he was forced to acknowledge it.

Everything I see is part of me. Nothing is separate.

No! said Oskar leaping from his bed and knocking over his mug which promptly spewed chocolate milk all down his pyjamas. NOTHING is a part of me. I am NOT connected to this bunch of losers or this dead-end village in any way. I am a completely detached observer who no one can ever touch and no one can ever hurt.

He skidded down to the kitchenette, repeating these words like a mantra. Snatching up a damp cloth, he sponged down his pyjama bottoms as he remembered the very first time he'd learnt that the world might not be as friendly as his mother had always said it was.

*

Oskar was seven and had been at his new school for a week. He was sitting on his own at the edge of the playground with his sketchbook after lunch. Until now he'd been at the small

23

primary school where his mum taught, so he didn't really know the rules here yet. He reckoned the best thing was to stay at the side and look busy until he got the hang of things.

The whole week had been a bit strange. Two days before, he'd begged his mum to tell him more about his dad, now that he was going to big school. All he knew was that he was called Werner and they had met in Hamburg when she was an art student. Now she told him some more; that he'd lived in Kreuzberg in Berlin and had been studying German literature at the university there; he was in Hamburg for just five days when they'd met, doing research for his first book and he had a scar down the left side of his face.

Although Werner was a bit unusual, there was something his mother liked about the dark-eyed man with the long leather coat and a copy of Goethe's *Faust* under his arm. So after he had bought her supper in a Turkish restaurant she agreed to see him again.

For the next few evenings they hung out together (Oskar's mum didn't say what they did), but on the final morning, they went for a walk where he said that he had really enjoyed being with her but that he didn't want a relationship. Instead he intended to devote his life to writing and he was returning to Berlin the next day to start on his first novel.

'Does . . . does he know that I even exist?' Oskar asked, after he had taken in all this new information.

His mother nodded. 'I tracked him down through the university. But when I told him that I was pregnant, he said that he was only twenty four and that he didn't want to be a father.'

'Maybe we could look for him again now?' said Oskar. 'He might have changed his mind.'

His mother took his hand. 'I tried to contact him once again, when you were three years old, and again when you were five, but he must have changed his surname, because I couldn't find him.'

Oskar wiped away a tear with his sleeve.

'Maybe it's better that you never knew him,' she said, squeezing his hand. 'I don't think he would have been a very good father to you.'

So now Oskar was in the playground, trying to draw a man with a scar down his left cheek and a long leather coat. He didn't know what his dad's hair would look like so he made it look like his own, cut short and with a fringe.

'What are you drawing?' Oskar jumped and looked up to see a boy from the year above standing in front of him in a black jumper and black trousers that were too short.

'It's private, if you don't mind,' said Oskar in his most polite voice.

'Let me see!' said the boy, who Oskar recognised from his second day, when he had seen him in a playground fight. Afterwards in the queue for lunch, Oskar had heard two other boys talking about the fight and how Jonas had started it. Apparently he lived in a care home and had changed schools three times in the last year.

'Show me!' Jonas pushed Oskar's shoulder.

Oskar reluctantly opened the sketchbook at the picture of his father. 'It's meant to be my dad,' he said quietly.

'Looks like a total weirdo,' Jonas laughed, hooking his thumbs inside his leather belt, whose bronze buckle glinted in the sun. 'Do you live with him?'

Oskar shook his head. 'It's just me and my mum.'

Jonas laughed. 'Am I supposed to feel sorry for you?'

'No,' said Oskar. He'd only said it because he thought it might make Jonas feel better about living in a care home without his own mum and dad.

'Good, because feeling sorry for people is for losers,' said Jonas. 'Got that?'

'Yes,' Oskar mumbled.

Jonas lowered his face in line with Oskar's.

'Why are your eyes all red?'

'Because I have conjunctivitis.' Oskar tried to make the word sound grown up and important and not the ugly, itchy, burning thing, which made other children point at him on the school bus.

'You look like a rat,' said Jonas. 'They have red eyes too.'

Oskar nodded and kept his head down. Having seen the fight earlier in the week, it was definitely not a good idea to answer back.

The boy laughed then pushed Oskar's shoulder again, this time a little harder. 'See you around, Rat Kid.'

*

So there! thought Oskar, marching over to the window from where he gave the spectacle shop a *Stinkefinger*. I'm Oskar Dunkelblick, the tough teenage artist, and no trickster optician is going to meddle with my mind and make me think otherwise.

Chapter 4

Oskar had been in the village for almost a week now and he really needed to start painting. Since the gallery was funding this project, they wanted to see results sooner rather than later. That's why he'd been studying Greta's weekly routine and he now knew that during her Monday lunch break she went to the butcher's at 12.30 p.m. before heading home for half an hour. So this was the plan. He'd set himself up in *Schlachter & Sohn* at 12.25 to await her arrival, then offer to carry her shopping. Once outside her house it would only be polite for Oskar to take the bags upstairs, where a thank-you coffee would be brewed and Oskar could then invite her to be part of his new and incredibly exciting art project.

A trip to the butcher's would also serve another purpose. Like all the best artists, Oskar often plundered his dreams to provide him with images for his work and recently they'd been decidedly boring. He'd already tried the more conventional remedies including lots of cheese and a good dose of Hoffmann's stories before bedtime but none had produced the desired effect. So it was time to road-test the remedy advocated by the painter Füssli, who ate raw liver before lights out to induce the vivid dreams from which had sprung such masterpieces as *The Night-Hag*.

Before he entered the butcher's, Oskar took a moment to admire the window display, which included a large purple ox tongue, some shrivelled kidneys and a mound of red, grey and brown meat ground together to make what was known in the village as the *Schlachter Surprise.* Each week customers were invited to guess the contents of this mystery meat combo and the winner would win a kilo to take home.

Most of the people in the butcher's that morning were familiar to Oskar: Herr Schlachter himself, whose complexion was reminiscent of five-day-old pork; Frau Trundel with the tiny feet; Frau Fettler, a big Brunhilde of a woman and Herr Kozma, the Hungarian with the sad eyes. At the counter was Frau Zwoll, whose painfully swollen purple calves were a sure-fire sign of Smoker's Leg.

Oskar watched Zwoll's eyes swivel along the row of meat behind the glass, lingering briefly at the *Schlachter Surprise,* before travelling on to the leaner cuts.

Go for the fatty ham hock, Oskar murmured under his breath as her eyes continued to sweep across the meat vista. A couple of kilos of the high cholesterol *Eisbein* and she'd be heading for the biggest coronary in Christendom. But sadly, Zwoll's pudgy finger was now pointing at a low-fat turkey roll. For a few brief but disappointing seconds, it hovered there, then just at the last moment, it did a U-turn and finally, trembling from the effort of it all, came to rest on the ham hock.

Nice one! Oskar grinned to himself and was about to congratulate Zwoll on her wise choice when the door of the butcher's opened and in walked Greta.

'Hi!' said Oskar, perhaps, with hindsight, a little too enthusiastically.

'Hello.' Greta's reply was both quiet and curt, making it difficult to work out whether she was incredibly shy or just rude. Now that she wasn't hunched over a clipboard, Oskar realised that she was really quite tall, and close up he could see the colour of her eyes (at least of her fully open right eye), which was a deep grey-green. She wore a thick blue coat and matching woollen hat under which her light blond hair hung down to her shoulders.

'So, what's cooking?' he said.

'Sorry?' said Greta.

'You know, how's tricks?'

'When you're ready, young man,' came the sound of Herr Schlachter's voice behind him.

'Alright, alright.' Frowning, Oskar twisted towards Herr Schlachter and reviewed the meat options. 'Hmmm,' he placed his finger on his chin to denote deep thought, aware that he shouldn't make too quick a decision or else he'd be finished way before Greta and would have to wait outside for her, looking stalkerish.

'A quarter of a kilo of liver, please and . . .' he twisted around to inspect the other basic groceries that the butcher stocked.

Herr Schlachter shifted impatiently from one red welly to another.

'Decisions, decisions,' said Oskar.

A collective sigh of irritation rose from the back of the queue.

'I'd like to enter this week's *Schlachter Surprise* competition,' said Oskar. 'I can feel it's my lucky day.'

Grumbling to himself, Herr Schlachter retreated to retrieve a piece of paper and a pencil, which he thrust towards Oskar before indicating that he should stand aside while the next customer was served.

Oskar stared at the mound of meat threaded with purple veins and gristly yellow tubes. 'What the hell was in it? Cow? Pig? Baby?'

'Thank you,' said the voice to Oskar's right.

So preoccupied was Oskar that it took him a few seconds to

realise that it was Greta's voice. She'd obviously been shunted to the front of the queue, perhaps due to her short lunch break. By the time he looked up, she was already turning towards the door clutching a small package.

'Pig-Baby.' Oskar scribbled hastily on the piece of paper and tossing some coins onto the counter, he grabbed his raw liver and hurried after Greta.

He caught her up just outside. 'So what did you buy?'

'Some eggs and milk,' said Greta.

'Good choice,' said Oskar. 'I bought some raw liver.' He tossed his package up in the air, catching it again to indicate a relaxed, playful nature.

Greta strode on, saying nothing.

The fact that she had bought so little in the butcher's made things a bit tricky. It would look silly to offer to carry just one carton of eggs and some milk, so instead he needed to engage her in lively conversation.

'Quite chilly, isn't it?' Oskar let out a puff of breath that clouded the air in front of them. He glanced at the sky, which was streaked with blue.

'Anything exciting happen at the chemist's this morning? A hold-up at the hairspray counter? A run on the laxatives?' Oskar chuckled but his joke was met with silence.

'So what *did* you get up to? Apart from mainlining morphine in the stockroom,' he said, grinning.

Greta stared at him.

'I was trying to be funny,' said Oskar.

'Right,' said Greta.

Oskar frowned. Was he losing his knackers? Back in Berlin he'd prided himself on his ability to coax conversation from even the shyest of creatures (if indeed Greta was shy rather than just standoffish). In the bars around Kreuzberg, armed with his fake ID, he would single out the loneliest looking girls, and approach them with a wide smile. Trademark opening lines (compiled after studying the lists for the most popular non-fiction books bought by women) would include: 'Have you ever read Peter Wohlleben's *The Spiritual Life of Animals*? What a wise man. So in tune with the natural world!' Or 'I just love Eckhart Tolle! His words really touch my *soul*.' Here Oskar would pause to show that he did indeed have a soul and adopt a sad, faraway expression to imply that same soul had already been tainted with grief. Girls seemed to love that!

Oskar toyed with the idea of asking Greta if she had ever read any Eckhart Tolle but he decided against it. Instead they walked in silence up the high street. When they passed the former florist's Oskar remembered to avert his gaze to the opposite side of the road. He was proud that he'd managed to ignore the presence of the spectacle shop since his visit there. In this way he could pretend that Dr. Sehle and his strange lenses had never existed, that the entire afternoon had been a figment of his imagination.

'This is my house,' said Greta, taking the keys from her bag.

'So soon?' Oskar feigned surprise at the crooked house with dark beams and tiny windows, although he already knew exactly where she lived from his research.

Greta slotted the key into the door.

Think, Oskar, think.

'Aaargh.' Oskar moaned and clamped his liver-free hand to his forehead before slumping against the wall.

Greta turned from the door.

Oskar moaned a bit more. 'I'm feeling quite dizzy. I'm diabetic, you see,' he murmured. 'I don't suppose you have something sweet at home. A slice of cake? A biscuit?'

Again that indecipherable expression.

'A couple of raisins?'

Although Oskar's original plan had been to accompany Greta into her home and get a glimpse of where this sad specimen with the lazy eye nested, he realised it was better to stay put. If he raced after her it would look suspicious and he didn't want to blow it so early on.

As the front door slammed behind Greta, it dawned on Oskar that it wasn't going to be quite so easy to gain her trust. Not like Franz.

Sitting down on the doorstep with his lump of liver in his lap, Oskar recalled that first delightful meeting with his former flatmate nine months before – a meeting that had promised so much.

*

Franz

The sell-out success of Oskar's *The Dark Side of Mother* exhibition meant that he now had a prestigious art gallery behind him to act as the guarantor for the two-bedroom Kreuzberg flat he'd found. So now he had the time and living space to develop the concept for his next exhibition, something both sensational and original, guaranteed to secure his position as Berlin's most daring teenage artist.

Up until that point, Oskar had focused on still-life despair, depicting static moments of individual suffering, but how exciting it would be to portray misery in motion! To follow one human's journey from mental and physical health to a full-blown psychotic breakdown. People had painted bowls of rotting fruit before, they'd photographed dead animals at different stages of decay, they'd even filmed the putrefying flesh of a human corpse. But who had captured on canvas the unfolding deterioration of a living, breathing human being before?

In the hope of attracting on-site inspiration, Oskar advertised the second bedroom of the Kreuzberg flat, although 'bedroom' was a little optimistic for what was barely bigger than a broom cupboard. There were fourteen respondents to the carefully worded ad, but none of them quite fitted the bill. There was, however, a naive Swiss exchange student who seemed keen, but then he mentioned having a girlfriend in Berlin, so that wouldn't work at all.

Oskar was just beginning to give up when, on the final Saturday of interviews, shortly before 10 p.m. Franz knocked at the door. His face was slathered in sweat from climbing the five floors and pocked with what Oskar knew from his medical dictionary to be *acne vulgaris*. His hair, which was even greasier than his face, was mouse-brown and shoulder length with a centre parting. He wore a pair of stretchy jeans, teamed with a slightly too tight denim jacket and a Sven Väth T-shirt.

Once Franz was installed on the sofa, Oskar ran through the interview questions. Friends? Franz had recently moved to Berlin so hadn't had a chance to make any. Family? All of them were back home in the small Bavarian town of Füssen. Food preferences? Mostly currywurst. Franz's music taste was a little dodgy – psy-trance and techno, but that was easily sorted. In fact the only obvious downside to Franz was an unhealthy interest in sport, but Oskar had a plan to take care of that.

Franz's reason for leaving Füssen was to rekindle his relationship with Astrid, a Swedish au pair who he'd met in his local bar and who had recently relocated to Berlin. Unfortunately she wasn't keen to rekindle, but rather than returning to boring small town life, Franz had found a job as a garage mechanic in Zehlendorf.

To Oskar, Franz fitted the bill perfectly: no nearby friends or family to keep an eye on him; recently rejected in love; little direction in life; a nervous, eager-to-please nature, all neatly topped off with *acne vulgaris*.

'It's all yours, Franz.' Oskar nodded towards the broom cupboard from his interview chair. 'I think we're going to have a blast.'

Opposite him on the sofa, Franz's face glowed with a combination of gratitude, sweat and acne. 'Thank you!'

And that was that. Franz was in and the game was on.

*

'I could only find this.' Oskar was jolted from his thoughts by a tap on the shoulder and the offer of one small oat biscuit studded with three small raisins.

'Perfect,' Oskar said brightly, looking up at Greta. 'You're very kind.' He took a bite of the biscuit and leant back against the doorframe. 'So, have you lived here for long, Greta?'

'If you don't mind, I've got things to do,' said Greta, already turning in the doorway.

Oscar popped the rest of the biscuit in his mouth and levered himself and the liver up from the step. 'One quick thing before I go. I'm doing a series of portraits of people in the village and I wondered if you'd like to sit for me.'

'Me?' Greta asked.

'Yes, you!' Oskar replied with all the zeal of a quiz show host congratulating a winning competitor.

'I'd rather not.'

Oskar smiled. 'You don't have to say yes now. Sleep on it.'

And with that, he raised one hand in what he felt was a friendly see-you-around sort of farewell. Extracting a hardened raisin that had lodged between his back teeth, Oskar turned slowly up the street with the smile fading from his face. This one, unlike Franz, was going to be tough as old turds.

Chapter 5

Oskar was waiting to be served in the *Bierkeller*. He wasn't accustomed to afternoon drinking but he needed a pick-me-up after the experience of trying to sweet-talk Greta. He also needed time and headspace to work out why his usually foolproof approach had failed.

The bar was empty, probably because it was only 1.30 in the afternoon, but from the thudding noises below Oskar's feet, he guessed that Thomas was in the cellar. On the top of the counter was a copy of *die Bild-Zeitung*, which Oskar opened, lingering briefly over a picture of 'Lisette from Karlsruhe' who had recently been picked to present some new late night game show and who was demonstrating her considerable presenting skills by posing in a red leather top and matching pants.

Having dispensed with Lisette, Oskar glanced around the bar, noting the filthy table tops and the windows spattered with dead flies.

'What do you want?' said Thomas, hauling himself and a barrel of beer out of the cellar hole. His face was ridged with lines so deep it looked as though someone had carved them with a knife and his eyes were even more bloodshot than the last time.

'A beer would be nice,' said Oskar.

Thomas let the barrel drop down so hard that the wooden floorboards shuddered. Then he stomped over to the bar where he pulled down a glass from the shelf.

'So how's life?' said Oskar.

'Never been better,' said Thomas, filling the glass and slamming it down on the bar top with such a force that half the beer splashed onto Oskar's trench coat.

Oskar brushed off the excess liquid. 'What you need is some in-house entertainment.' He tapped page 3 of *die Bild-Zeitung*. 'Like Lisette from Karlsruhe.'

Thomas didn't reply but reached up to one of the bottles and poured himself a double brandy. As he did so, it struck Oskar, not for the first time, that there was something familiar about the man.

'Or what about a quiz night? That always gets the drinkers in midweek.'

Thomas eyed Oskar before downing the brandy and turning on the TV.

Oskar stayed at the bar, sipping his beer in silence. Occasionally his eyes would stray over to Thomas as he tried to remember where he might have seen him before. It wasn't in Berlin, he was sure of that. Had he spied such a tortured face he would definitely have singled it out for a solo portrait.

But about fifteen minutes later, when the news channel announced the recent winner of the Nobel Prize for Physics, an image of a blackboard with the name Professor Thomas Kepler dropped into Oskar's head. And with it came the smell of boys' sweaty socks and stale classroom air. Suddenly Oskar was back at school, aged twelve, sketching away in one of his least favourite lessons.

*

Physics, along with sport, had never been a big hit with Oskar, mostly because it was about things you couldn't see – atoms, photons, electrons and a load of other useless nonsense. Usually he zoned out during classes, drawing pictures of pupils being involved in exciting Bunsen Burner explosions or slumping to the floor with as yet undetected heart defects. But one day, shortly after the start of the summer term, something that the physics teacher said, made Oskar stop sketching.

Herr Brugger was standing at the blackboard, pointing to the two names he had just written: Werner Heisenberg and, below it, Professor Thomas Kepler.

'Can anyone tell me who Werner Heisenberg was?' he asked, tapping the first name with his finger.

Silence.

'Come now. A world-famous Nobel Prize winning scientist and no one has even heard of him?' Herr Brugger shook his head in disappointment, something he often did during class. 'Werner Heisenberg was one of the first quantum physicists to show us that the act of observing something changes that which is being observed.'

Oskar sat up straighter in his chair. Observation was, after all, his speciality.

'As any scientist will tell you,' Herr Brugger continued, 'matter is not solid, but is made up of a mass of vibrating particles, each one affecting the next. Nothing can exist in isolation because at a subatomic level everything is interconnected.'

Oskar coughed. 'No, it's not.'

Without even turning around from the blackboard, Herr Brugger sighed. 'I think you'll find it is, Oskar.'

'Well, I'm not interconnected.'

'Perhaps you're not aware, Oskar, that every atom and every particle in your body has been circulating the earth since life began over 3.2 billion years ago.' Herr Brugger spun round to face him. 'So every part of you from your heart and your brain, even your eyes, was once part of something else – a star, a tree, another human body. I think that makes you pretty interconnected.'

'No, it doesn't,' said Oskar.

Herr Brugger turned back to the blackboard. 'If you're suddenly so interested in physics, I suggest we discuss this afterwards.' He traced his finger down to the second name. 'In the meantime I would like to introduce you to the more recent work of another scientist, Professor Thomas Kepler.'

In the school library that afternoon, while trying to cobble together enough information for his homework essay, Oskar discovered a few more facts about Professor Kepler, 'Germany's foremost expert in the science of vision.' At just nineteen he had gained a First Class M.A. in Applied Physics, before taking up a research post at Munich University. Here he delivered a series of groundbreaking lectures on the Observer Effect for which he was awarded the Max Planck Research prize, as a photograph in the science magazine *Zeit Wissen* proved. Ten years later, following a series of high-profile papers, he became part of the research team at the Carl Zeiss Institute in Jena, Europe's most prestigious optical lens specialists.

Yawn, yawn, thought Oskar checking the library clock. It was almost five and his stomach was rumbling, so he shoved the magazines and journals back on the nearest shelf and ran out of the library, just in time for tea.

*

But that photograph had somehow snagged in Oskar's brain and sitting in the *Bierkeller* he recalled the young face of Professor Kepler with a clarity that surprised him. Admittedly, the intervening years had changed the man's appearance radically what with the sunken cheeks, the scraggy beard and the haunted eyes, but it was definitely the same person.

Well, well, thought Oskar. One of Germany's brightest physicists and a 'scientific visionary' reduced to working in a filthy bar and drinking himself to death. Bet he never saw that one coming! And with that thought, Oskar took one last slug of his beer, said a swift goodbye and left.

Chapter 6

Oskar was knackered. It was probably the liver supper (fried because he couldn't stomach it raw), which had produced such a crazy and exhausting jumble of dreams the previous night. In all of them Oskar was trapped in the attic room with Dr. Sehle, who was hustling him to try on a selection of glasses. Each pair had a different effect, so for example when he looked through the lens of a large green monocle, Oskar felt his heart expand to fill his whole chest while a feeling of such intense love washed through him that he wanted to weep.

On peering through the tortoiseshell glasses that Dr. Sehle had thrust at him next, suddenly he seemed to just *know* everything about all the objects in the room from the barber's chair to the doctor's leather bag. He could name the craftsmen who had made them, the workshops where they had originated, the necessary journeys undertaken for them to arrive at the spectacle shop . . .

But the final pair of glasses were the strangest. Round with large gold frames, their pale blue lenses resembled clock faces but without minute or hour hands. When he gazed through them, he had the curious sensation that time had become *stretchy*, expanding and contracting around him. It wasn't something fixed but it was relative, just as Einstein had said. And if you travelled at the speed of light, then time stopped altogether and there was no distinction between past, present and future.

With this thought, Oskar had turned to Dr. Sehle in his dream, seeing for a moment the familiar figure in the woodman's cap. But moments later, his face morphed into that of a man with a white handlebar moustache and droopy bloodhound eyes. The man was clutching a torch whose beam pointed directly at Oskar. Before long this second image was replaced by a younger man with long, black curly hair, holding up a single spectacle lens.

Who are you? thought Oskar, but by then the curly-haired man had vanished and in front of him stood a woman wearing a nun's habit and wimple, eyes gleaming. Seconds later she too disappeared, dissolving in a blaze of light.

When Oskar finally awoke at 7 a.m, he was so shattered he felt like he'd run halfway around the globe. Stumbling out of bed, he slid down to the window, where for the first time in a week he dared to look over at the spectacle shop.

What?!

Oskar shut his eyes and shook his head as if to rejig the scene before him, but when he looked again, nothing had changed. The shop as he knew it was gone. No longer were the windows filled with glittering glasses, instead they were blacked out with blinds that had been pulled down like two closed eyelids. The sign outside had been wrenched from the wall and the little window in the attic room had been smashed. Across the door was a heavy iron chain secured with a padlock and beneath that, written in big black letters, the words **No Entry.**

Stuffing a screwdriver in the pocket of his trench coat, Oskar hurried down the stairs and out into the street. As he drew closer to the spectacle shop, he saw the eviction notice pinned beneath the **No Entry** sign: '*24 hours has been given for the vacation of these premises. Thereafter, bailiffs will remove the illegal occupant,* *if necessary with force.'* The notice ended with a scrawled signature and an official-looking stamp.

Oskar inspected the padlock. It was a big one, but living on the Berlin streets had given him plenty of practice at opening locks, usually belonging to disused warehouses and empty shops where he could sleep for the night. He took out the screwdriver and after a quick scan to ensure there were no witnesses, he twisted it into the padlock's keyhole with a sharp upward motion until he heard the familiar click.

Once inside the shop, Oskar felt his way over to one blinded window and raised the black canvas. The early morning light filtered through the room, showing the empty cabinets and the floor strewn with spectacles, their frames twisted and broken like the snapped-off legs of giant insects. The pictures of the monks, Venetian craftsmen and eighteenth-century spectacle wearers had been ripped from the walls and there was a sharp, metallic smell . . . like blood.

Oskar's heart began to pound and his palms were suddenly sticky with sweat. It was over eight years since he had last seen Jonas, but so many things still triggered the panic attacks.

*

'Have you been avoiding me, Rat Kid?' Jonas was standing by Oskar's locker in the changing rooms. He had a split bottom lip and a scab of blood crusted his chin, probably from another fight.

'No,' said Oskar, although this was obviously a lie. In fact, since their last meeting in the boys' toilets a week ago, he'd spent most of his lunch breaks hiding in empty classrooms to make sure that their paths didn't cross.

'I saw your mother dropping you off this morning,' said Jonas. 'Why didn't you get the bus like usual?'

'Didn't feel like it,' Oskar shrugged. In the three months that he had known Jonas, he'd learnt to shrug quite a lot, pretending things didn't matter when really they did. Like when Jonas grabbed his sketchbook and rammed it down the toilet. Or when he snapped Oskar's favourite paintbrush in half. So he certainly wasn't about to tell Jonas that his mother had insisted on driving him to and from school now because the bus driver had reported some kids teasing him about his red eyes.

'Your mother looks like a dirty hippy,' said Jonas.

'She's an art teacher,' said Oskar, unable to stop himself from defending his mother. 'She gets paint on her clothes sometimes.'

'And what does Rat Kid's dad do?' smirked Jonas.

'I don't know,' said Oskar. 'I've never met him.'

Jonas laughed. 'Don't blame him. If I knew I was going to father a freak like you, I wouldn't stick around.'

Oskar swallowed hard.

'Is Rat Kid going to cry?'

'No,' said Oskar.

'Oh sorry, it's the conjuncti-whatever,' said Jonas, knocking against Oskar and making him stumble sideways into the open door of his locker.

Oskar rubbed the left side of his head where it had hit the metal catch. When he took his fingers away, there was blood on them.

'It's for your own good, Rat Kid. The world's a shit hole and you'd better get used to it.'

*

Taking several deep breaths, Oskar forced his legs to move towards the spiral staircase in the centre of the room. It's OK, he repeated to himself, just keep moving forward. By the time he had reached the steps the sick feeling, which came whenever he thought about Jonas, had subsided a little.

Upstairs, the door to the attic room had been kicked in and the walls were now daubed with black paint. Someone had slashed the red leather barber's chair so that its yellow foam stuffing spilled out like aged intestines. The mirror on the opposite wall was smashed, and the once-illuminated box, from which he had read the words lay on the floor.

Oskar found himself scanning the room in search of the eye test glasses. Obviously he didn't really believe that what he had seen through those lenses was real, but he was still curious to know if they had survived.

He peered under the barber's chair then ran over to the window in case the glasses or even just the lenses had been tossed down onto the street. But no, they weren't there. It wasn't until he turned around that he noticed something amber-coloured shimmering beneath the cracked cream glass of the box.

Racing over, Oskar carefully lifted up the box and there beneath it, were the glasses. Although they were a bit bent out of shape, the two lenses were still inside, intact. He grabbed them and hurried over to the window. Now he could finally prove that his vision – or whatever you wanted to call it – had just been a trick of his imagination.

The glasses still fitted on the bridge of his nose and having already selected the forest in the distance to do the eye test, Oskar stared over at what was once just a bunch of brown trees. But now, looking through the lenses, those same trees appeared to be enveloped in a haze of light, their rich evergreen colours dazzling Oskar's eyes. As he gazed at them, he was filled with a deep sense of belonging.

Oskar had no idea how long he had been standing there, mesmerised by that warm expansive feeling, but suddenly he was jerked back to the attic room by the sound of heavy boots on the staircase.

'Who's in there?' came a loud voice from outside in the corridor.

Oskar snatched the eye test glasses from his face and hid them behind his back. Seconds later a man in a shiny black jacket and steel-capped boots was standing in the threshold.

'You're trespassing!' The man was built like a nightclub bouncer, but had a creepy falsetto voice.

'Out.' A thumb, wide as a *Weisswurst,* jerked in the direction of the door.

'Of course,' said Oskar, sidling away from the window.

'Stealing another person's property isn't a very nice thing to do, is it?' The bouncer-man was blocking the exit.

'No,' said Oskar. 'Not nice at all.'

'In which case, you'd better give me what you're hiding behind your back.'

'Here.' Oskar held out the glasses. 'Have them.' All those times with Jonas had taught him that to avoid getting hurt, he needed to do exactly what he was told. Not that it had always worked.

A pair of hefty hands snatched the test glasses from his clasp. For a second the two men stood facing each other. Then the larger of the two curled his fingers around the frames and with a powerful crushing motion, compacted the metal to a gnarled heap.

Oskar stared at the wrecked glasses. One of the lenses had been shattered, but the other, remarkably, had survived. Maybe if he asked very nicely . . .

'Excuse me,' he began, bowing to show deference. 'I don't suppose I could take that lens with me. It's quite a pretty colour and being an artist and all –'

Before he had time to finish, the man clamped a hand on Oskar's shoulder and pulled him forward so their noses were almost touching. Then his mouth twisted into a tight smile. 'Now get out, before I do the same to your head.'

Chapter 7

Oskar was feeling pretty shaky. Three days had passed since the encounter and he still couldn't keep any solids down. Instead he'd been living off Banana Nesquik and Maggi mushroom soup. But it wasn't only the bouncer and his threat that was making him feel so unsettled. It was also the memory of those lenses. Now that he'd tried them on for a second time, he couldn't stop thinking about them. That soft, merging sensation as he'd stared at the forest and that warm, secure feeling of belonging was intoxicating. And if there was even the slightest chance that he could look through that one surviving lens again, then . . .

No! thought Oskar. He needed to stop obsessing about what he had seen and crack on with his work in Keinefreude. Then he could get the hell out of this freaky village and get on with his normal life. But to do that he needed sitters and his top two weren't exactly cooperating, what with Greta acting so coolly and Thomas being a nutter. So that left Frau Miesel.

Oskar knew Frau Miesel's schedule by heart. Wednesday was the day she closed the bakery at 2.30 p.m. and scuttled over to the butcher's for her turkey slices, cartons of milk and tins of sauerkraut. After that she would hurry home where, from the drawn curtains and the muffled sound of the television, he assumed she was watching the afternoon soaps.

'Would you care for some help with those heavy bags, *gnädige Frau*?' said Oskar, having intercepted Frau Miesel's path back to her house that afternoon.

'I can manage on my own, thank you,' said Frau Miesel crisply.

'They do look *really* heavy,' said Oskar. This wasn't a lie. In fact, the strain on the plastic handles of the bags was causing them to elongate considerably.

'So,' said Oskar, figuring that it was only a matter of seconds before one of the bags' handles snapped. 'Are you keeping warm? I'm not very good with the cold myself. Three layers plus my thermal long johns . . .'

Oskar could see that Frau Miesel wasn't at all interested in how many layers he was wearing but he ploughed on, willing the handles to snap.

'Although the plus side to the cold weather is that I don't actually need a fridge; the ledge outside the window works brilliantly. Plenty of room for leftovers . . .'

At that moment the bulkier of the two bags did exactly what Oskar had been hoping and several sauerkraut tins clattered to the cobbles.

Oskar shook his head and tutted. 'Now you'll *have* to let me help you, Frau Miesel.' He grinned down at her. 'And if you're extra nice, I'll even take your shopping upstairs.'

Having stuffed the tins back into the broken bag, Oskar followed a very grumpy Frau Miesel to her front door. Then it was through the bakery, up the stairs to the top floor, another door with another lock and finally they were inside.

It was Oskar's guess that the person who came up with the saying 'the kitchen is the heart of the home' had probably not seen Frau Miesel's cooking quarters. The thin room had beige walls and metal shutters over the windows and contained just one high backed wooden chair, one small square table with very pointy corners, a tiny hob stove and a steel sink. The overall effect was more of a prison cell than a cosy kitchen.

Oskar set the bag down on the sideboard, ignoring Frau Miesel's obvious irritation.

'This is . . .' He searched for a fitting adjective to describe the kitchen. 'Functional!'

'It suits me!' snapped Frau Miesel.

Sure does, sugardoll, thought Oskar.

'If that's all . . .' Frau Miesel was standing with her arms folded tightly against her grey winter coat and her eyes trained on the door.

'I don't suppose you have any coffee?'

A pursing of Frau Miesel's lips indicated that this wasn't what she'd planned at all.

'And if you don't mind I'll have a little sit down. Those stairs are pretty steep, even for a young stag like myself!' Oskar gestured towards the corridor and the larger of two side rooms. 'Through there, I presume?'

Perfect! Oskar grinned when he clapped eyes on the sitting room. It wasn't much cheerier than the kitchen with just two small armchairs, an old television, a print of a Venetian canal and a teak-effect coffee table on which lay a magazine open at that day's TV listings.

Oskar plumped himself down in one of the chairs, causing the fake leather to squeak like a little mouse. After examining the selection of programmes ringed in red ink in the listings magazine, he listened to Frau Miesel next door as she filled the kettle. But from the lengthy silence that followed it was clear that Frau Miesel was also listening to him.

Hmmm, thought Oskar. This one was suspicious as hell, unlike Franz. He hadn't suspected a thing – like a little lamb to the slaughter.

*

Franz

'So, when are we going to get started?' Franz grinned as he sat at the kitchen table in front of the congealed remains of the previous night's takeaway currywurst.

'Soon, Franz,' said Oskar. 'Real soon.'

'Can I smoke during the sittings?'

'Smoke away, Franz.' Although invisible to the human eye, furred arteries, emphysema and potentially cancer-riddled lungs all added nicely to Franz's allure.

It had been a week since Franz's arrival and those first days were an important part of the process, allowing Oskar to study his subject in depth. Although it had to be admitted there wasn't much depth to Franz. When he wasn't working at the garage or reading sci-fi books, he liked nothing more than to sit in front of Eurosport, chain-smoking roll-ups and swigging Berliner Kindl.

The time also gave Oskar the chance to work out how the *Seven Steps to Hell* project would look. There would, obviously, be seven stages, each charting the steady decline in Franz's mental and physical well-being. The first of these would see Franz at the start of his journey, in his familiar armchair pose, cigs, beer and takeaway leftovers festering at his feet.

Some people might have seen Franz in this first stage as a one-trick pony but to Oskar he was the perfect representation of man's pointless existence. In fact, the very monotonousness of Franz's daily routine was its beauty because if you thought about it (which Oskar did quite a lot), Franz's life was no different from millions of others around the world: get up, go to work, come home, eat dinner, watch telly, go to bed.

Oskar had picked Monday morning for the start of the psychological campaign. The location was just outside the bathroom, inside which Franz was presumably applying steroid cream to his acne, something he did a lot of.

'Franz?' Oskar called from the corridor. 'Can I have a quick word?'

Franz's head appeared, eyes peeping out from a Cortisone-coated face like a startled laboratory rabbit.

'Listen mate, I don't mind you using my milk, but can you replace what you've taken?'

A short pause as this information sunk in. Franz had indeed turned out to be even thicker than Oskar could have hoped. On top of that, his daily dope habit made him wonderfully forgetful.

'B-but I didn't t-take it.' Franz's bunny-eyes widened.

'It's cool,' said Oskar with a smile. 'As long as I know.'

'I'm sure I would have remembered,' said Franz, not sounding sure at all.

Oskar let out a gentle sigh. 'But Franz, there are just the two of us here. It could only be you or me – and I'm hardly likely to steal my own milk, am I?'

Franz conceded this wasn't very likely.

'All you need to do is ask, Franz.'

Franz shook his head in puzzlement, mumbled an apology and retreated back to the bathroom to resume the hopeless battle against his pimples.

It really was amazing what could go missing in such a small flat. The items ranged from toothpaste ('I wouldn't mind Franz, but I bought it from my special dentist and it's quite expensive'),

Nesquik, flannels, socks, books, chocolate bars, towels, a watch from Oskar's Grandpa Blumental ('We were so close, Franz'), a computer keyboard and a pair of Oskar's Doctor Martens.

In fact, this first stage proved to be so amusing that Oskar was reluctant to leave it behind after the allocated three weeks and move onto Stage 2. A bit like a small child is reluctant to relinquish a treasured teddy but, as everyone knows, grown-up toys are so much more exciting.

*

'Here's your coffee!' said Frau Miesel, plonking a mug of brown murk onto the teak-effect table in front of Oskar.

'Too kind.' Oskar smiled, watching the overspill trickle to the edge of the table.

Frau Miesel remained standing, staring pointedly at the clock on the mantelpiece that was shaped like a little wooden chalet. Oskar shifted a brothel creeper to avoid the brown liquid that was now dripping onto the carpet.

Silence hummed.

'So, here we are,' said Oskar, stirring his coffee with the tea-spoon provided.

A curt nod from Frau Miesel confirmed that yes, they were indeed there.

Oskar scanned the room for inspiration. In the corner beneath a small bookshelf was a stack of records, the top one featuring a very pale middle-aged man with white hair and dark glasses.

'You like Heino? Me too!' Oskar wasn't lying – he'd always been fascinated by the albino crooner from the 1970s with a thyroid condition so chronic that he had to wear a polo neck to conceal the resulting swollen neck.

'What's your favourite song then?' Oskar started to hum

Rosamunde, a personal favourite. He arrived at the first chorus with zero reaction from Frau Miesel, so he left it there.

To fill the following awkward silence, Oskar picked up his teaspoon and examined it closely. The reflection of his elongated face and wide alien-looking forehead was really quite intriguing. In fact, he'd have liked to stare a little longer but now wasn't a good time. Save that for later when he got home. He set the spoon down against the edge of the listings mag.

'*Die Schwarzwaldklinik*!' he exclaimed as if he'd only just spotted the circled programme. 'I used to love that! All those kind doctors and nurses caring for the sick at the health clinic! It's brilliant that they're broadcasting the old episodes!'

'Are they?' Frau Miesel's feigned indifference certainly wasn't fooling Oskar.

'Oh yes,' said Oskar. 'Shame I have nothing to watch it on.' He cast a doleful look at Frau Miesel's television. 'I don't suppose –'

But he never finished his request, on account of the loud banging coming from behind the right hand wall.

'Whooaa,' said Oskar. 'What's all that about?'

Frau Miesel looked over at the shuddering wall. 'They're renovating next door.'

'The spectacle shop?'

'If you mean the old florist's, yes.'

Now it was Oskar's turn to feign indifference. 'Has someone moved in there already?'

'Herr Krank.'

'Aaah.' Oskar needed a few moments to digest this information so he picked up his teaspoon once more and twirled it around in his fingers like a baton. Thoughts tumbled into his mind. What could Krank be planning for the spectacle shop? Yet more storage space for his antidepressants? Or was he plotting something even more sinister?

'Do you know what he's going to do with it?' Oskar asked, his voice much higher than he'd intended.

'No,' said Frau Miesel. 'Herr Krank does not inform me of his every move.'

'Of course not,' said Oskar.

'Perhaps he's planning a late night cocktail bar.'

'Really?' said Oskar.

'No,' said Frau Miesel. 'Not really.'

'Aah, I see,' said Oskar. 'That's a joke, right?' He paused. 'You don't think . . .' he said, voicing the deeply worrying thought, which was just taking shape in his head, '. . . that he might be intending to open another optician's?'

Chapter 8

Oskar was in a right old stress. It was ten o'clock in the morning and he'd been thinking about his afternoon at Frau Miesel's for almost thirty-six hours. Could Krank really be planning to open another optician's, even though the previous one had been trashed? And if he was, then would he be selling his own black-rimmed spectacles? Or was he plotting a new line using the one surviving lens from the eye test glasses as the prototype?

As Oskar unwrapped his breakfast, a Kinder Surprise egg, he ran through his main concerns about Krank selling spectacles made from Dr. Sehle's lenses:

1. If those lenses had the same effect on others as they'd had on him and the news spread, then the whole village would change in a flash. There'd be no more acts of spite, no more greed or cruelty, because if people believed that nothing was separate from them, then it followed that whatever hurt someone else would also hurt themselves. Which meant everyone would start being kind to each other, doing good deeds, donating to charity . . . Big fat disaster.

2. If Krank was cunning and started up a nationwide chain, so that everyone had access to lenses like that, then Oskar's business was buggered. He wouldn't be able to sell a single

painting. Misery art would be a thing of the past. Instead people would want nature scenes – meadows and kittens and flowers and crap like that.

So this was the plan: Oskar needed to get hold of that remaining lens, stash it somewhere super safe like at the back of his sock drawer, and make sure no one else ever got to look through it. Simple but hopefully very effective.

Satisfied, Oskar took the final bite of his Kinder Surprise, before inspecting the unassembled toy that had come with it. He read through the instructions: *Attach the two wings to the main body of the plane (Diagram A). The propeller slots onto the front section of the plane (Diagram B) and the wheels fit onto the underside of the plane's fuselage (Diagram C). The stabilizer will then slot onto the rear section of the plane (Diagram D) . . .*

Oskar frowned at the unnecessarily complicated instructions. He could feel a headache coming on and he needed fresh air. Not his usual remedy for a headache but he hoped that a short walk might see the thing off.

The sky was pale blue that morning and shiny like a newly hatched thrush's egg. The first snow of November had fallen overnight, smothering the rooftops, lampposts and even the litter bins in a duvet of white feathery down. Ice clung to the windows of every house and shop, sparkling like diamonds in the morning sunshine . . .

The sky like a newly hatched thrush's egg! Ice sparkling like diamonds! Oskar's mind screeched to a halt. What the hell was he thinking? The sky didn't look like a thrush's egg and ice certainly didn't sparkle like diamonds. In fact, it was just frozen water, teeming with treacherous levels of nitric acid and sulphur dioxide.

Scowling, Oskar made his way along the icy cobbled pavement. And aah yes, there was Miesel at her dough table looking about as sorrowful as – What!! He peered closer through the bakery windows. Frau Miesel wasn't looking sorrowful at all. Instead her mouth, so often drawn in a tight grimace, seemed more relaxed and if he was not mistaken, the corners were slightly lifted as though she was about to smile.

Oskar leapt behind a wheelie bin so he could study her in more detail. Where was that turkey-scrag neck that he had so admired? Those suspicious, darting eyes? That little skin rash?

Usually when Oskar singled someone out for a portrait back in the Berlin bars, it wasn't just their air of misery and loneliness that attracted him, it was also their flaws. Like Bettina, whose left hand had been crushed in a car door as a child and now hung lifelessly at her side; Paula the pretty Spanish girl with the big inheritance, whose cleft palate Papa's fortune hadn't quite managed to fix; Sandra, whose childhood scoliosis had resulted in a heavy limp . . .

The set-up was always the same. After admiring the young women's gleaming imperfections, Oskar would open proceedings with some book chat about Peter Wohlleben or Eckhart Tolle. Once that was out of the way, he would lean forward and run his fingers over the flaw.

'You know the most beautiful thing about you,' he'd whisper, tracing the outline of say, an over-sized ganglion on the neck. 'It's this. This is what makes you so special.'

The following week he would invite them to an exhibition (more often than not, Monet, Matisse or Renoir) and halfway through, while looking at a dreary garden or chubby woman dancing in some village square, he would sigh and say quietly that one day he longed to paint *them*, to show the world *their* beauty.

For the second date Oskar would ask them to dinner at the cheap Italian restaurant on Wiener Straße, where he would confide in them that he couldn't seem to find a girlfriend, at least none with any substance. They all seemed to be cast from the same mould: perfect long blonde hair, perfect lips, perfect body, yet none of this attracted him. Even though he was only twenty (ahem! That fake ID, which they all should have clocked on the first night, was indispensable), he wanted a real woman, flaws and all. Someone he could be himself with, let down his guard, show his soft side to . . . blah blah blah.

By the fifth date (a film or a picnic in the Botanical Gardens), it was only a matter of time before the young women would broach the subject of a relationship. The usual setting was dinner at their flats or if they still lived at home, at a friend's borrowed apartment. There would be a candlelit table, calves liver or steak, which Oskar would have already mentioned as being his favourites, and a chocolate cake, if they'd been listening correctly, cooling on the sideboard. Just before pudding (this was irritating – love declarations should come *after* pudding), they would lay a hand on his.

Oskar, they'd say, I've got something to tell you.

'Yes?' Oskar would reply with an encouraging smile.

Some were more hesitant than others but they were all basically singing from the same song sheet: how he was so kind and sensitive and such a good listener; how they loved so many of the same things (yeah right!); how they'd never believed they would meet someone, who could accept them for who they really were . . .

'You're in love with *me*?' Oskar would reply with well-practised incredulity once they had finished.

'Yes,' they'd say.

'But you barely know me!'

'It's enough to know how much I care about you.'

'Are you mental?'

Here he would take a final mouthful of calves liver, chew slowly then set down his knife and fork. 'The last thing I want is a relationship. In fact, I'd rather eat my own head.'

And it was this next part that Oskar would savour for days, often weeks afterwards. That exquisite split second when the hopeful smile faded and a whole new set of facial muscles set to work. Their eyes would widen and hands would be removed from Oskar's arm as expressions of shock and confusion spread across their faces.

Some would demand that Oskar left immediately, others would ask for further explanation and a few, those precious few, would run to the bathroom, sobbing.

When they finally returned to the table, having pulled themselves together a little, Oskar would smile, rub his stomach and glance over at the cake on the sideboard.

'How about a slice of that delicious *Sachertorte*?'

*

From behind the wheelie bin, Oskar could see that Frau Miesel had disappeared into the back room so, still confused by her apparent change in appearance, he stomped off back towards his home. He was stomping so speedily that it wasn't until he almost tripped over Frau Trundel that he actually saw her. Admittedly she was pretty easy to miss, being so small, added to which she wasn't even upright but lying on the pavement like an overturned beetle with her skirt hitched up to her hips. Her little feet were scuffling against the ice, trying to get a hold, while her gloved hands waved frantically in the air.

'Here,' said Oskar, reaching out his arm. 'Take my hand.'

Frau Trundel looked up, her features frozen with fear.

'Go on or we'll be here all day.' Oskar thrust his arm a little nearer and slowly the woman's gloved fingers extended towards his coat sleeve.

'Hang on tight,' said Oskar, stepping back to gain a firmer footing while Frau Trundel, after a few moments of hesitation, brought one shaky knee up to rest on the pavement.

Oskar waited till she had recovered her breath before encouraging her to do the same with the second knee. Finally, still clutching onto his arm and whimpering, she levered herself up to a standing position.

Oskar reached down to pick up her handbag. 'Nice one, Frau T. You're good to go.'

That evening, while eating a bowl of *Birkel* macaroni at home, Oskar replayed the incident with astonishment. Usually his re-action to such a gem as a frail old woman scrabbling around on the ice would have been simple: spot the accident, step back to where he couldn't be seen and observe. He would have noted the expression of panic on Frau Trundel's face, the tiny feet whir-ring, the torn section of hosiery exposing the bruised knee . . .

But that's not what happened this time.

As he chewed on the cheesy tubes, he wondered whether his extraordinary behaviour was the start of something more worry-ing. If so, what next? He'd heard about people who couldn't help themselves doing good deeds, people who actually derived plea-sure from assisting their fellow men. In fact, he remembered once seeing a documentary that claimed doing someone a kind turn not only released certain 'feel good' chemicals in the brain but also improved the do-gooder's health. To prove this, a group of volunteers had undergone rigorous testing before and after view-ing footage of Mother Teresa tending to a sick child in a Calcutta hospital. According to the (obviously rigged) results, every single person showed a marked increase in serotonin levels and feelings of satisfaction and happiness. In addition to this, their bodies revealed a substantial reduction of the stress hormone cortisol, along with a significant boosting of their immune system.

Doing a good turn makes you happier and healthier! My skinny *Arsch*, thought Oskar. He wasn't going to fall for that crap. The incident with Trundel was definitely a one-off – a temporary behavioural glitch triggered by all the recent stress. There was really nothing to worry about. Was there?

Chapter 9

Oskar was on his way to the chemist's. In the twenty-four hours since the Trundel fiasco, he'd forgotten about Krank and his possible plans for a new spectacle shop. It was only when he'd spotted him that morning entering the old florist's with two large boxes, that he remembered his panic at the prospect of the man peddling replicas of Dr. Sehle's lenses. So now it was crucial to find out exactly what he was plotting and to set about dissuading him.

The best way to do this, Oskar had decided, was to invite Krank out for a few jars of tongue-loosening alcohol and if his fears were confirmed, then Oskar would persuade him against it. The future of glasses was not looking good what with all the corrective laser treatments these days. Why didn't Krank branch out into something else? The heady world of hair care, for example? That was big bucks nowadays.

And once Oskar had dissuaded Krank from expanding his spectacle empire, he would make casual enquiries about that one remaining lens. What did a chemist want with a piece of old glass? Why didn't he give it to Oskar – not that it was worth anything of course, but he might be able to use it for one of his art projects.

The chemist's was empty that morning except for Frau Zwoll who was dragging her trolley around the aisles as Oskar entered. He nodded hello and she gave him a painful little smile before puffing past him. Greta was obviously in the stockroom, which suited Oskar because he didn't want her knowing what he was up to. Krank was in the shop window, positioning a new cardboard cut-out of a wizened old man in swimming trunks leaping into the sea, laughing like a lunatic.

'What's he on?' said Oskar, nodding at the gurning octogenarian.

Krank smiled, stepped back from the window front and patted the cardboard cut-out's shoulder. 'Equavol – probably the most effective antidepressant on the market today.' He paused and looked at Oskar, 'so if you ever feel a little down, if life seems a bit flat ...'

'Say no more,' said Oskar, tapping the side of his nose.

Krank walked back towards the counter. 'What can I do for you?'

Trotting behind him, Oskar lowered his voice. 'I have something I need to discuss. It's of a ... personal nature.' He shot a look at Frau Zwoll, who was inspecting an asthma inhaler in a nearby aisle. 'I mean *really* personal. That's why I'd prefer to discuss it in private. Could we meet after work tonight in the *Bierkeller*?'

'Is that necessary?'

'It really is a very delicate matter,' said Oskar.

Oskar could see that Krank's curiosity had been mildly aroused. It wasn't important that he himself had no idea what this delicate matter might be. He'd think about that later.

'Shall we say around six?' Oskar smiled. 'It should be empty then. Oh, and the beers are on me.'

Only Herr Kozma was in the bar that evening, sitting at a corner table with a Schnapps. Thomas himself was propped up on

61

a stool, staring at a pile of bills. Having arrived early, Oskar ordered himself a *Weizenbier*, then retreated to the table furthest away from Herr Kozma and the bar.

As he sat there with a few minutes to spare, he studied Thomas, noting the large veiny nose, the red blotchy skin and the eyes dulled with drink. Was that really the same man he'd read about in the science magazines?

*

Oskar's physics homework hadn't been the only source of information about Professor Kepler. Four years later and now living in Berlin, he happened to pick up a copy of *Spektrum der Wissenschaft* while travelling on the S-Bahn. Flicking through, he glimpsed that same face smiling out from the pages. Having nothing better to do, Oskar began reading the accompanying article:

The Role of the Observer

In the 1920s the scientists Niels Bohr and Erwin Schrödinger both demonstrated that before the act of observation takes place, 'reality' exists as a number of different possibilities, as a wave outside of time and space. It is only when something is observed, i.e. human consciousness is activated, that this wave collapses and forms a particle at which point it can be said to exist in time and space. Thus, nothing in the world of material form exists independently of consciousness.

*Recent research has proved that **how** we choose to observe something plays an important role in what will then manifest for the observer. For as Bohr and Schrödinger showed us, many realities are possible – it is simply a matter of which 'lens' the observer is choosing to view the world through that dictates the reality he or she will experience . . .*

*

Creeak! The *Bierkeller* door was opening and there was Krank in his brown fur coat.

'*Groossies*!' Oskar leapt to his feet and gestured for Krank to sit down before pointing to the bottles behind the bar. 'What's your poison?'

'I'll have a Fanta please,' Krank replied, removing one of his black leather gloves with a sharp tug.

'You'll have something stronger than that! What about a cheeky *Jägermeister*?'

Krank pulled off the second black glove and laid it neatly on the table. 'A Fanta will suffice.'

Ten minutes in and things weren't going as smoothly as Oskar had hoped. The stilted mostly weather-based opening conversation was punctuated by several frosty silences, during which Oskar tried to figure out what sort of 'personal' matter he was going to invent. He'd spent his precious planning time thinking about Thomas and the science magazine article and had completely neglected to cook up a problem urgent enough to merit a special meeting with Krank.

If only he'd relax, thought Oskar, watching Krank take several swift sips from his Fanta, which was already half empty.

'Knock knock,' said Oskar.

'Excuse me?' said Krank.

'You're meant to say – *who's there*?'

'Why?'

'Just say it. I'll explain afterwards.'

'Who's there?'

'Doctor!'

Krank stared at him.

'Then you say *Doctor Who* . . . Oh, never mind,' sighed Oskar. 'It's an English joke I once heard. It doesn't work so well in German.'

Herr Krank glanced at the door. 'So, what did you want to discuss?'

'Discuss?' said Oskar.

'The personal problem that you couldn't talk about this morning.'

'Oh right,' said Oskar. 'That.'

An imaginary medical dictionary flipped open in front of him, each page brimming with possibility. In fact, there was so much choice it was difficult to settle on one thing. Think alphabetically, Oskar. Alopecia. Bronchitis, Cystitis, Dysentery, Endometriosis . . . To add to the confusion, a clutch of Dr. Sommer's problem pages floated before his eyes. *'Ich habe Herpes . . . Mein Busen ist zu klein . . . Mein Penis ist krumm.'*

'My penis is bent.'

'Your penis is bent?'

'Yup.'

'How bent?'

'Almost a right angle.' Oskar's head filled with an image of a heavy door slamming behind him, trapping him in a very small room with Krank and a massive right-angled penis.

'Has it always been like that?'

'Oh yes. Right from the off.' Since there was no going back, Oskar needed to role-play a bit, so he pictured himself as a little boy in his bedroom, sobbing over his bent member. It made him feel a little sad actually.

'Do you have difficulty urinating?'

'Not usually.'

'Is sexual intercourse a problem?'

'Hmmm.' said Oskar. This was becoming a whole different ballgame. Would someone with a ninety degree angle dick be able to have sex? Maybe it would correct itself when erect? Or maybe he could tie something hard and straight onto it, something skin-coloured like a lolly stick?

'I have difficulty becoming . . . aroused,' he said eventually.

Krank was clearly waiting for more details but Oskar was reluctant to expand on the matter.

'There are drugs that can help,' said Krank.

'Like what?'

Krank sighed. 'You must have heard of Viagra.'

'Yes, of course I've heard of it, but aren't I a bit young for that?'

Krank shook his head. 'Viagra has proved to be suitable for all ages.'

'What about the side effects?' Oskar was keen to show his commitment to the subject.

'It's been on the market for almost two decades with minimal side effects.' From the slow yet impatient tone of his voice, Krank could have been talking to a five-year old – although the likelihood of discussing penile erectile dysfunction and its possible remedies with a child still in Kindergarten was pretty slim.

This was going nowhere.

'There is something else,' said Oskar.

'What?' said Krank coldly.

Oskar sprang up from the table. 'But first I need to urinate.' He glanced meaningfully down at his crotch. 'I may be some time.'

Oskar walked slowly to the men's toilets. This would give him a breather, a chance to think about something really convincing that would gain Krank's confidence before he raised the subject of his plans for the spectacle shop, and equally important, that one remaining lens.

As he by-passed the urinals and entered the small cubicle, Oskar thought how he must be losing his touch. For ten years he'd been honing his wits (thanks to the combination of Jonas and four years on the Berlin streets), so this setback was very worrying.

Unzipping his flies, Oskar thought back to one of his earliest and most satisfying successes.

*

Oskar was eight and it was his first trip to the psychiatrist. He hadn't wanted to go, but his mother had bribed him with a trip to the Mövenpick ice cream parlour.

'Tell me, Oskar, how are you getting on at school?' Dr. Braun, the psychiatrist, was sitting behind his desk. He had a bald head and bushy eyebrows and he spoke very slowly.

'Fine,' said Oskar quickly.

'Are you making any friends yet?'

'A few.' Oskar glanced up and smiled at Dr. Braun. Since he had started school a year ago, he'd become pretty good at lying. Like when his mother caught him stealing money from her purse and he'd said it was for the homeless man with holes in his shoes, who he passed on the way to school.

Dr. Braun wrote something down in his white notepad.

'Are any of the other children unkind to you?'

Oskar shook his head.

Dr. Braun paused. 'Are you sure, Oskar?'

'Very sure.'

'Do you feel you could talk to the teachers if you had a problem?'

'Oh, yes,' said Oskar. Inside he laughed. The idea of going to one of the teachers and telling them what was happening was ridiculous. Jonas had already threatened to break his right hand, the one he drew with, if he said anything to anyone.

Dr. Braun leant forward on his desk. 'Your mother said that you came home with bruises on your legs last week. Is that true?'

'I got them in football,' said Oskar. 'I already told mum that.'

He looked away, desperate to change the subject. On Dr. Braun's desk next to a jug of water was a picture of a smiling woman with long dark hair.

'Is that your wife?' said Oskar.

'It is,' said Dr. Braun.

'She's very beautiful.'

Dr. Braun smiled. 'We're here to talk about you, Oskar.'

Oskar pretended not to hear. 'Do you have any children, Dr. Braun?'

'No, Oskar, we don't. Now can we please –'

Oskar could see that the psychiatrist was pressing hard on his pen and his thumb was turning white. This was his chance – so he wouldn't have to tell Dr. Braun about Jonas hitting him with his belt in the boys' toilets.

'It must be very sad for you both, not having any children,' said Oskar.

Dr. Braun placed his pen very carefully next to the vase. 'Oskar, we are not here to discuss –'

'Maybe you can go to a doctor and have an operation?'

'OSKAR!' Dr. Braun's hand smacked down on the desk, toppling the jug of water so that it spilled all over his notepad.

Oskar shook his head. 'You know, Dr. Braun, mum says it's really not healthy to bottle up your emotions. Maybe you should talk to someone about it?'

*

Exiting the men's toilets, Oskar chuckled at the memory of that early triumph. If at the tender age of eight he'd managed to crack a professional psychiatrist, then Krank should be a piece of pie.

But when he arrived back at the table, Krank already had his coat on.

'You can't leave yet,' said Oskar. 'I still want to ask you about your business plans for the old florist's.' He studied the man's expressionless face closely, checking for clues.

'You could do all sorts. A café, a hairdresser's, even an optician's.'

Krank nodded and picked up one of his shiny black leather gloves.

Oskar took a deep breath. 'Did you yourself happen to visit when Dr. Sehle was there? He had some extraordinary lenses. I believe one might have survived the . . . eviction.'

Again Krank's face registered nothing, making Oskar wonder what it would take to provoke a change in the man's expression. He pictured himself stamping on one of Krank's feet or wacking him round the face with a big fish, something massive like a marlin.

'Perhaps you know what happened to it?' said Oskar.

Krank was adjusting each glove finger with the precision of a surgeon. 'I have no idea what you are referring to.' He picked up his second glove. 'And now I really have to go.'

'There was something else,' said Oskar quickly.

'Really?' Krank's voice dripped with sarcasm.

'The thing is,' said Oskar, 'I haven't been sleeping so well lately and life, well . . . it just seems a bit flat.'

'Aaah,' said Krank, placing the second black glove back down on the table next to Oskar's glass. 'In that case, I may be able to help you.'

Chapter 10

Oskar was cross. He'd imagined that pretending to be depressed and pandering to Krank's professional expertise would soften the man a little, making him spill the beans on the plans for his new premises. But Krank had simply whipped out a notepad, prescribed him six months worth of Equavol, then bid Oskar a glacial good night.

'Are you sure this is legit?' Oskar held up his prescription as he stood opposite Krank in the chemist's the following day.

'Of course,' Krank smiled from behind the counter. 'What makes you think it wouldn't be?'

Oskar smiled back. 'And there are no side effects to Equavol?'

Krank shook his head.

Oskar glanced down at his wallet knowing he'd have to buy the antidepressants to avoid looking suspicious, although he deeply resented coughing up for something he wasn't even going to swallow.

'You're lucky I've still got some in stock,' said Krank, checking the price and ringing it into the till.

'Yes,' said Oskar, gulping at the figure. 'Really lucky.'

Back home, Oskar consulted Franz's Depression book, but there was no listing under Equavol. However, after a closer inspection of the antidepressant packets, he noticed that they all had a sticker on the front. When he tried to peel it off, the glue was so strong that he ended up ripping away most of the thin cardboard layer beneath. But piecing together the tiny scraps, he could just about make out another name – Seramax.

He quickly consulted the index of the book and found an entry under the Tricyclics group:

> *Seramax is a Grade 2 tranquiliser used to treat mid-level depression. While it has proven effective in minimising mood swings and enabling patients to function at base level, it has a wide range of side effects, which include nausea, dizziness, sweating, migraines and high blood pressure. During the initial trials it was also shown in some instances to cause irreparable damage to the optic nerves. After a lengthy court case the Medical Regulatory Authority ruled that it should be withdrawn from the market. The manufacturers, Glücksvolk GmbH are currently appealing against the decision.*

Having stashed the packets of Equavol in an old biscuit tin, Oskar thought about the repercussions of Krank prescribing an illegal drug with so many side effects. An entire village, dizzy as wizards, with blood pressure rocketing through the rafters and eyesight deteriorating by the day. Even though it would make for a great painting, was that really such a good idea?

Oskar mixed up some Knorr potato puree to go with the *Knackwürste* for his lunch. One thing was for sure though – his approach had failed and he had to find another way to uncover Krank's plans.

By the time, he'd swallowed the second sausage he had come up with a possible solution.

———————

'Well, hello there.' Oskar was leaning against the doorframe when Greta answered his knock just after midday the following Sunday.

'Hello,' Greta replied, evenly. She was wearing a pair of old jeans, thick woollen socks and a pale yellow jumper. Her hair was brushed back into a ponytail with strands falling around her ears and as usual her left eyelid was hovering at the half way mark.

'I've come for the portrait,' said Oskar, motioning towards the newly stretched canvas under his arm.

Greta frowned. 'I said I didn't want to do it.'

Oskar coughed. 'Perhaps I didn't explain the project properly. You see, it's not just *you* that I want to paint, it's the village as a *whole*. In fact, I intend to use the medium of art to *unite* the village.'

'Really?' said Greta, raising an eyebrow.

Oskar rested his head against the doorframe and adopted a dreamy expression. 'The potential of this village is staggering. It could be such a beautiful place – everyone living happily side by side, doing nice neighbourly things for each other like . . .' He paused, trying to think of what nice neighbourly things people could do. '. . . like picking someone up from the pavement.'

'Are you sure about that?' said Greta.

'Oh yes,' said Oskar, 'because I've learnt that if you can visualise it in here.' He tapped the side of his head, 'then it's more likely to become reality.' He hesitated, unsure where the words were coming from, then pressed on. 'So if I can visualise it *and* paint it, who knows what might happen!' he said, pointing his right forefinger at Greta. 'And I'll tell you another thing for free. What you focus on expands, so if you focus on the beauty of life, the goodness in people, the kindness that we're all capable of, that's what you will see more of.'

'You can honestly see this village as a *beautiful* place?' said Greta.

'Early days,' said Oskar, 'but yes.'

Whether or not it was his little speech or the fact that Greta was getting cold in the doorway that made her let him in, Oskar didn't care. The crucial thing was that he was now standing in her sitting room with his paints, easel and canvas.

Greta's sitting room bore a close resemblance to the Berlin Botanical Gardens. There were plants all over the place. Short fat spikey ones, long thin traily ones, plump succulent cacti – even the alcove above the door was sprouting something green. Where there were no plants, there were stacks of books with titles such as *Natural Healing Remedies* and *Homeopathic Pharmacy*.

'I *love* it,' said Oskar, positioning his easel next to the window. 'It's just so . . . green.'

'That's plants for you,' said Greta, who was perched on the arm of the sofa with her head cocked to one side as she studied Oskar.

There was a short, green silence.

'So,' Oskar clapped his hands together. 'Have you thought about what you might wear?'

Greta shook her head. 'No, because I didn't actually agree to sit for you yet.'

'What about that?' Oskar pointed at her uniform that was hanging from a hook on the back of the door.

'You want to paint me in my white nylon overall?'

'Why not? It'll show your role in the community. Someone helping their fellowmen, tending to the sick.'

'Can't I just wear this?' she said, plucking at her yellow jersey. 'That's if I sit for you at all.'

Oskar smiled. 'Deal.'

The setting up of the easel and canvas was achieved at breakneck speed before Greta had a chance to change her mind. Moments later she was seated on the sofa while Oskar mixed the paints on his palette.

'So, Greta, what's your favourite animal?' It was important to put the sitter at ease with some light conversation and women liked animals, didn't they?

'The minotaur,' said Greta.

'Excellent,' said Oskar. 'Minotaurs are cool.'

'I'm kidding,' said Greta. 'I don't even know what a minotaur is.'

'Yes, right, me neither,' said Oskar. 'Well, um, where were you born?'

'Twenty kilometres from here.'

Despite her obvious reluctance to talk, Oskar persevered. How had she ended up in Keinefreude? What did she do here apart from work? Favourite television programme? Life goals?

Greta answered each question with the bare minimum. She'd been born nineteen years ago in Schluchsee, a nearby village where her father was a doctor. She'd also wanted to study medicine but she hadn't got good enough grades. So Krank, who was her mother's second cousin, had offered her a job at the chemist's. Apart from work, she read a lot, looked after her plants and was just starting a course in homeopathy. As soon as she'd completed it and could earn a living without working at the chemist's, she'd move to Munich. After all, this wasn't exactly a place for young people. She didn't own a television and as for long-term goals, that was far too deep for 12.30 p.m. on a Sunday afternoon.

'Finished with the interrogation?' she said, when Oskar had finally run dry.

'For now,' Oskar smiled. 'Are you comfortable?'

'Not really.'

'You should try and relax a little.' Oskar thought for a moment. 'I know, let's pretend we're in a bar and we've just met. You're out with the girls, you're feeling good . . .' He sipped an imaginary Southern Comfort and smiled. 'So, Greta, do you come here often?'

'I live here.'

Oskar sighed. 'We're role-playing. Go with it.' He racked his brain. 'Have you ever read Peter Wohlleben? He's written a couple of books, one about animals and the other about how trees communicate.'

'You've read *The Hidden Life of Trees*!'

'Err, well . . . no.'

'Why are you talking about it then?'

'I was just trying to put you at ease. And you seem to like plants.'

'You're observant.' Greta let out a little laugh.

'Read any Eckhart Tolle, maybe?'

'I have as it happens,' said Greta. 'But don't tell me you've read any because I won't believe you.'

Oskar had given up trying to smooth-talk Greta. Instead he was layering paint onto the canvas for the first wash, trying to work out how to broach the subject of Krank. He knew he had to tread carefully, especially if she was related to the guy.

'I was just thinking the other day how Herr Krank is so versatile,' said Oskar. 'He obviously studied to become a doctor, which qualifies him to prescribe drugs and now he's a chemist. Genius!'

Greta shook her head. 'He's not a doctor, but there's a GP in the nearest village, who writes the prescriptions. They work together quite closely.'

'But Herr Krank prescribed me antidepressants,' said Oskar.

'If it was for Equavol, then that can be sold over the counter,' said Greta.

'I see,' said Oskar, trying to look as if he believed Greta. 'Anything else you know about Herr Krank? He's got such a great business model, that's why I'm so interested in him.'

'No, I can't think of anything else that you'd need for your *research*.' Greta used her two index and middle fingers to make an air quote.

Oskar looked at her, wondering where that shy, down-trodden creature from his first sighting had gone.

'You seem a little suspicious of me,' he said. 'Any reason?'

Greta shrugged. 'Do you blame me? First you barge in here, saying I had agreed to be painted when I hadn't. Then you start spouting a load of stuff about uniting the whole village, which I'm sure you don't believe. And finally you interrogate me about my boss.'

'Sorry,' said Oskar. 'Sometimes I can come across as a bit . . . insensitive. Do you want me to leave?'

'No,' Greta sighed, her expression softening a little. 'You're here now.'

Half an hour later Oskar was still there, jabbing the paint onto the canvas while trying to maintain a relaxed smile. Greta was sitting opposite him, staring out of the window at the sky. Quite why she had made him feel so awkward that he'd offered to leave, he didn't know. One thing he did know though: dealing with her was going to be a whole different kettle of *Kack* than dealing with Franz.

*

Franz

Oskar had chosen a Friday to begin *Franz Stage 2* – Friday nights being Franz's prime viewing time, kicking off with some UEFA Cup football, followed by snooker and climaxing in some late night darts. Friday was also one of Franz's days at the garage, which meant that Oskar had been able to do the prep work in peace.

Franz was back from work and crouched behind the television when Oskar arrived home from his afternoon stroll around the neighbourhood.

'You OK there, Franz?'

Franz's head poked round the side of the telly. His eyes were wide and worried.

'I can't get any reception.'

Oskar wandered over and knelt down, careful not to touch any of Franz's body parts.

'This doesn't look good,' he said, pretending to inspect the tangle of wires. 'I would get the landlord round to sort it, but I don't think he'd be too happy to see you.'

'What do you mean?' asked Franz.

'Well, I'm not supposed to sublet the small room. It's just meant to be me living here.'

'Oh,' said Franz.

Oskar shook his head. 'And it says in the contract that the landlord has to deal with all the repairs. Wouldn't want to piss him off by getting someone else in to mend this.' He patted the top of the telly. 'Oh well, it's probably for the best.'

'Why?'

'Franz, you live in the most exciting city in Europe and all you do is watch television. Think what else is out there. The fun, the clubs, the girls.' Oskar grinned. 'Tell you what! I'll get us some invites to a few gallery openings, some cool clubs. Franz, my good man, your new life has just begun.'

Eight days passed before Franz raised the matter of their new social life again. It was Saturday evening and he was sitting in the kitchen, staring at the rain trickling down the windows. His white jacket, which he'd been wearing most of the week, was mapped with beer stains and cigarette ash. On the table in front of him were the lumpy remains of his mince and boiled potato supper, the only other thing Franz could cook apart from a fry up.

'About those openings and clubs you mentioned. Anything come up yet?' he asked, pinching some Drum tobacco into the Rizla balanced on his knee.

Oskar shook his head. 'I just don't understand why it's all gone quiet.'

Franz held his lighter beneath a black nugget of dope before crumbling half of it into the Rizla. 'Oh well, looks like it's just you and me.'

Oskar shook his head. 'Sorry, Franz, I'm off out. Some of my artist mates are having a party in Friedrichshain.'

'Oh?' said Franz.

'It should be quite a night. One of them has invited some girls from the art college where he studies.' Oskar winked at Franz before picking up his keys and making for the door. 'I would ask you,' he said over his shoulder, 'but you know these creative types. Very cliquey.'

Over the next month Oskar's social diary, at least according to Franz, was non-stop. In one week alone he attended a promotion party for Bazic vodka ('You should have seen the women they used to promote it! Bummer I only had one ticket, huh?'), the opening of an art gallery in Prenzlauer Berg and the launch of a new model agency in Mitte ('Now that was Fun, Franz, with a capital F!').

Of course, Franz wasn't to know that these exciting nocturnal forays were entirely fictional and all the time Oskar was just round the corner, sitting on an overturned beer crate in Risiko's bar while observing the dark underbelly of Berlin and sketching *Franz Stage 2*.

Oskar loved this second stage almost as much as the first. What a fascinating range of facial expressions it unleashed in Franz. But one month later, after a sum total of fifteen fictitious and fun-packed evenings to which Franz had not been invited, it was time to tighten the screws.

*

'Oskar?' Greta's voice pulled him back to the sitting room where he was standing in front of the canvas, paintbrush in hand.

'Are you OK?'

'Yeah, super, smashing,' said Oskar, although he didn't feel super or smashing at all.

He frowned. In the past whenever he thought of Franz at this early stage, he'd feel a toasty glow of satisfaction; but this time that had been replaced by another feeling – a feeling he couldn't quite put his finger on. Oskar dredged his memory for clues. Could it be . . . ? No, it couldn't possibly be *that*. Oskar Dunkelblick didn't feel things like . . . *guilt*!

'Are you really alright?' said Greta, rising from the sofa.

'I feel strange,' said Oskar.

'Take a few deep breaths,' said Greta, standing next to him. 'It will pass.'

But as he turned to look at her calm face, Oskar had a sneaky feeling that whatever was happening to him, was definitely *not* going to pass.

Chapter 11

Oskar was really fretting. Fair enough, Frau Trundel could have been a one-off, and the inability to focus on the flaws of Frau Miesel could also be explained (new environment, wrong choice of subject etc) but the previous day's behaviour at Greta's was a whole new level. And what had triggered it was even more serious.

All night, thoughts had flapped around his head. What was happening to him? People didn't just start feeling *guilt* willy-nilly! That's not how it worked. No, guilt was just emotional self-sabotage, a clever device designed to control people and stop them from doing what they wanted: the really fun stuff.

But what could have caused it? Little had changed in his life, aside from the obvious move to Keinfreude. Could it be down to diet? Oskar thought about some of the meals he'd eaten over the past few weeks: *Knackwürste*, Kinder Surprise, potato puree, Maggi noodles, Bueno bars, liver and some caramel puddings. But those foods had been his staples for years.

No, the only thing he could think of, again, was Dr. Sehle.

Applying his pink flannel to his feverish forehead, Oskar ran through the afternoon in the spectacle shop yet again: the glasses glinting in the window; the painted eyeballs all staring at him; Dr. Sehle with his puckered skin and that super-strength torch;

those amber-coloured lenses . . . Oskar shook his head. Could those lenses really be responsible for his present condition?

'I need to talk to you.' Oskar was in the bar, hanging over the front cover of *die Bild-Zeitung*, which featured a photo of a famous American actress waving to the crowds at a recent Berlin film premiere. Thomas was stretched out on the bench with the newspaper covering his face.

'Please,' said Oskar. 'It's very important.'

The picture moved fractionally, causing a crinkle in the actress's cream sheath dress.

'I'm busy,' said Thomas.

'It's about your work at the Carl Zeiss Institute,' said Oskar, tapping the actress's tummy to make sure Thomas was listening. 'I know who you are because I've seen articles in science magazines. You're Professor Kepler.'

Another grunt from beneath *die Bild-Zeitung*.

'If you don't tell me, I'm just going to stay here all day and irritate you.'

Slowly Thomas's head emerged. His face was puffy and his breath stank of brandy.

'What do you want to know?'

'I want to know about optical lenses.'

'And if I tell you, you'll leave me alone?'

After Oskar had promised never to pester him again and Thomas had told him about the two boxes of research material stored in the cellar, Oskar headed down the wooden steps. The air was thick and inky and seemed to close in around him as he fumbled along the sidewall for the light.

It's OK, Oskar, you'll be out again in a few minutes, this is important. Oskar stopped to wipe the sweat from his forehead, trying to push down the memory, the one that would always lurk just beneath the surface.

*

Oskar was walking home from school in the rain. He had told his mother that the boys on the bus had stopped teasing him about his eyes, so she wouldn't insist on picking him up anymore. As he passed the fenced-off building site where the new luxury flats were going to be, he saw that the foundations had been laid and now the whole area was full of concrete blocks and big black metal pipes.

'Surprise!' said a voice behind him.

Oskar jumped and whirled around. Eighteen months of being at the same school as Jonas had made his reflexes pretty sharp.

'How you doing, Rat Kid?' said Jonas, who had a black eye, probably from yet another playground fight.

Oskar tried to smile. 'Fine.'

Jonas took a step towards a small gap in the fence and nodded at the new foundations. 'Those flats will be really expensive,' he said. 'My parents are going to live in one of them when they're finished.'

'But I thought you lived in...' Oskar stopped quickly. Something told him it wasn't a good idea to tell Jonas that he knew about the care home.

'Are you calling me a liar?'

Oskar shook his head.

'Good,' said Jonas, grabbing Oskar's shoulders and pushing him through the gap. 'You could be living here too,' he laughed and pointed to one of the larger exposed pipes sunk down into the foundations. 'In a drainpipe with the other rats.'

Oskar said nothing.

Jonas shoved Oskar towards the pipe. 'Get in then.'

'I don't want to,' said Oskar.

'If you don't, I'll tell everyone that your dad's a paedo,' said Jonas, fingering his bronze belt buckle.

Oskar bit his lip to stop himself from crying. 'Please don't.'

Jonas gave him another shove and Oskar slid down the wet mud into the hole by the pipe.

'Oskar's dad is a paedo!' Jonas chanted, standing above him on one of the concrete squares.

Oskar looked at the pipe. Maybe it wouldn't be so bad to crawl in, then he could wait for Jonas to leave and he could climb out again.

He got down on all fours and poked his head inside the pipe. It was dark and stank of filthy rainwater.

'Hurry up! I don't fancy hanging around here in the rain all afternoon,' said Jonas, climbing down behind him to give him a push with his boot.

Oskar crawled inside. The pipe was just broad enough for his shoulders, although his head scraped against the top. He couldn't turn around.

He heard Jonas laughing behind him, then came a dragging sound, and moments later, there was a loud thud, which shook the pipe. Suddenly everything was pitch black.

'Sleep well, Rat Kid.' He heard Jonas's muffled voice from the outside. 'And don't bother shouting because no one will hear you.'

Oskar lay on his stomach, taking deep breaths to stop the panicky feeling, just like his mother had once shown him, when he'd been frightened by a thunderstorm. It was difficult to know if Jonas was still there, so he waited a bit then nudged his foot against whatever was blocking the pipe. It must be pretty heavy, he thought, pushing harder with both feet. When that didn't work, he tried to shuffle backwards on his tummy, using all of his weight but it still didn't move.

Oskar's heart was racing and he felt sick. He tried some more deep breaths but it didn't help. The darkness was suffocating him, creeping down his throat and into his lungs. What if no one found him and he was left to rot? What if the rats came for him? He screamed for Jonas to let him out. Being beaten with the belt would be better than being trapped here all night. And he could always offer to steal something else for Jonas, something big and expensive to stop him from saying those horrible things about his dad.

Oskar was still screaming by the time the builders found him the next morning. When they pulled him from the pipe, shaking with fright and soaked through with rainwater, they wrapped him in a blanket and called his mother. It took two days before he could stop shivering.

*

Breathe, Oskar, breathe. Oskar was still taking deep breaths when he finally felt the light switch. He pressed it and a single bulb flickered to life. Now all he had to do was focus on the task – finding Thomas's papers – then he could get out of that cold, dark cellar as quickly as possible.

The cardboard boxes were next to the beer barrels in the far corner, just as Thomas had said. The first one was stamped with the crest of the Technische Universität München but it was the second box with the logo of the Carl Zeiss Institute that Oskar was interested in.

He ripped it open and inside were dozens of documents which included research papers, funding applications and certificates for science prizes. But beneath all that lay a wad of typed A4 bound paper, whose title immediately caught Oskar's attention. He shoved it under his arm and raced back towards the cellar steps, leaving the dark behind him.

Upstairs, Thomas was in the small kitchen to the right of the bar, so Oskar settled down at one of the nearby tables and began to read:

Perception and Perceived Reality

The average human being is capable of perceiving only a small percentage of what is happening around them at any given time. Otherwise the brain would be overloaded and unable to process all the information. Consequently, everything that the brain cannot understand or which does not fit into the belief system of the observer will automatically be edited out.

A simple example would be a pessimist and an optimist visiting the same stretch of seaside. The pessimist believes the beach to be a dirty, expensive place full of tourist cafés and hawkers who are out to take his money. He will therefore, consciously or unconsciously, be looking for evidence to validate his beliefs, selecting and editing from all the incoming data to arrive at his particular worldview. The second man, the optimist, believes the seaside to be filled with kind and generous people, eager to make his day out a happy one. Correspondingly he will select and edit until his experience shows that his belief was correct.

But what if there was a device, or even a lens, which would liberate our minds, if only temporarily, from the usual judgements, beliefs and prejudices? What sort of reality would we then see?

'Can I borrow these?' said Oskar, pointing to the A4 stack of papers, when Thomas finally emerged from the kitchen.

'If it means you'll leave me alone, then yes,' said Thomas.

Oskar nodded. 'I'll be off then.' He picked up the papers

and raised his left hand in a goodbye gesture, but just before he reached the door, he turned around.

'You had it all, Thomas,' he said, 'awards for the most outstanding young scientist, a top job on the research team at the Carl Zeiss Institute . . . What happened?'

'None of your business,' said Thomas.

'But it is,' said Oskar. 'I live in the same village and I see you almost every day, looking about as miserable as it's possible for a human to be. So I'd like to know what's wrong and if I can help in any –' Oskar stopped abruptly when he realised what he was saying.

'You know what?' he muttered. 'I think I left the gas on.' And with that he tightened his grip on the bundle of paper and bolted out into the street.

Chapter 12

Oskar was worried. The gallery had just called to say that they needed to see some work by the end of the month. They reminded him it was already mid November and that this wasn't a holiday. If he wanted his rent in Keinefreude to continue being paid, he should pull out his finger – or rather his paintbrush.

But to paint Oskar needed inspiration and therein lay the problem. The portrait that he'd done of Greta hadn't turned out at all as he'd wanted. For a start the lazy eye, which should have been the focal point, actually made her face look quite attractive in a sleepy, just-tumbled-out-of-bed way. And when Oskar had tried to make it more pronounced and hopefully less attractive, the rest of her face just looked out of proportion. As for his solo portrait of Thomas, Oskar was beginning to wonder if he'd make such a suitable subject after all. The man had done him a favour in sharing his research, was it really fair to repay him with a scars-and-all painting?

Maybe some more liver would kick start his creative juices and he could find some other subjects? Admittedly, it had only resulted in confusing and exhausting dreams the first time, but maybe that was because he'd cooked it. This time he'd raise the dose to half a kilo and consume it raw within an hour of bedtime.

Marching down the high street, Oskar raised his fist for a motivational air-punch, but at that exact moment, he spotted a crocodile skin wallet lying in the snow. He picked it up and a couple of coins fell out onto the ground, where they lay like two gleaming golden eyes. Oskar glanced up and down the street. New wallet. Nice one.

And yet when it came to popping it in his pocket, Oskar found his hands wouldn't obey the order. What was wrong *now*? In those first two years at school he'd become quite a pro at stealing stuff for Jonas – anything from Bazooka bubblegum to a new belt buckle. And later when he'd arrived in Berlin, that's how he fed and clothed himself until his first career took off, the one where he'd delivered 'packages'.

I'll just check whom it belongs to, thought Oskar. He opened the wallet and saw a small faded photograph tucked into the plastic square. The woman peering back at him had an angular face, black caterpillar eyebrows and dark plaits coiled around her ears like croissants.

'What have you got there?' A voice barked in his ear.

'Nothing,' said Oskar, instinctively hiding the wallet behind his back before looking up to see Frau Fettler in front of him.

'Well, why are you bothering to hide nothing?' Frau Fettler was trying to peek around his back.

'I wasn't,' said Oskar. 'I was just keeping it safe.' He produced the wallet to confirm this.

'Anything in it?'

'Just some small change – and a photograph,' said Oskar, opening it again so she could look.

'That's Frau Kozma.'

'Herr Kozma has a wife?'

'Dead,' said Frau Fettler. 'Six years ago. Coronary.' She thumped her heart with a meaty fist, presumably to show Oskar what a coronary was. Then her eyes darted back to the wallet.

'Were you planning to steal that?'

'Of course not.'

Frau Fettler stared at him for a further few seconds, then with a snort she turned heel towards her house. 'I'll be checking with Herr Kozma that you have returned it,' she shouted over her shoulder.

Of course, Oskar had no choice in the matter now. He'd have to give the wallet back or Frau Fettler would snitch on him. Besides, now that he had seen the picture of Herr Kozma's wife, something in him *wanted* to return it. So, shortly after six that evening he found himself standing outside the fourth floor flat of the rundown house near the chemist's where Herr Kozma lived.

'What you want?' Herr Kozma was wearing a brown-checked dressing gown over a ribbed vest and white underpants. In his right hand was a fire poker.

'I've brought your wallet back,' said Oskar.

Herr Kozma squinted from behind a pair of foggy black-framed glasses. 'Wallet?'

'Yes, wallet,' said Oskar, waving the leather pouch for clarification.

Slowly Herr Kozma's mouth curled into a smile. 'Wallet!' he whooped, letting the poker fall to the floor. '*Köszönöm.* Thank you. Thank you.' He grabbed the wallet from Oskar's hand, kissed it several times and flung open the door. 'Come in. *Kérem.* Please.'

As soon as Oskar entered Herr Kozma's small apartment he was slapped full in the face by a wall of hot, peppery steam. Immediately his eyes were streaming and he started to sneeze. Herr Kozma, seemingly oblivious, trotted down the corridor alternately kissing the wallet and thanking Oskar.

Once in the sitting room, Oskar mopped his eyes with his

sleeve and looked around. Through the steam clouds that billowed from the kitchen he saw that the walls were papered with pages ripped from magazines featuring faded scenes of wooded hillsides and green valleys.

'You very kind man,' said Herr Kozma, opening his wallet. 'I must pay back.'

'No, really,' said Oskar, wondering how quickly he could get out of the house. 'Not necessary.'

'Tssssh,' said Herr Kozma. 'You my guest now.' He pulled out the picture and held it about five centimetres from his face.

'My wife. Beautiful, no?'

'She's very . . . handsome,' said Oskar.

Herr Kozma's nose was almost touching the photo. 'The first thing I notice about her is the eyes. I am seventeen years old and we just arrive from Hungary. We are in church for Easter service. When singing starts I hear terrible noise behind me.' He clamped his left hand over his ear. 'I turn round and there she is. Her voice is horrible but her eyes . . . I just stare and stare.' Herr Kozma let out a long sigh before whipping out a handkerchief and dabbing at his eyes.

Oskar coughed. 'Maybe I should make a move.'

Herr Kozma shook his head.

'But I can see you're expecting a guest.' Oskar pointed to the second table setting.

'Guest?' repeated Herr Kozma as though hearing the word for the first time.

'Oh, that,' said Herr Kozma, following Oskar's finger. 'That is for Eva.'

'Eva?'

'My wife.'

'Okaaay,' said Oskar, eyeing the exit.

'You like *gulasch*?' asked Herr Kozma. 'I make very hot. Lots of paprika.'

Although Oskar had intended to leg it out of the flat asap, there was something about the way the old man looked at him that made him stay. So now he was sitting down to a humongous bowl of *gulasch* with Herr Kozma opposite, enthusing about how his wife was always able to track down the smokiest sausages to make her own *gulasch* and how she would be so happy that he had found a new friend.

'Is that where you were born?' asked Oskar, when a miniscule gap appeared in Herr Kozma's running monologue. He nodded to one of the oil paintings on the wall, which showed a village of orangey-brown buildings on top of a hill of sloping vineyards.

Herr Kozma sighed. 'Yes. Is called Tokaj.'

'So how come you ended up in Keinefreude?'

'My parents move here to open music shop and sell violins.' Herr Kozma let out a wistful sigh. 'Keinefreude was lovely village then. There was market every Saturday and a park for children. But now is ugly place.'

'It's got some good points,' said Oskar. 'It can look quite pretty in the snow. And the sky this morning was a beautiful blue.'

Herr Kozma laughed as he refilled their glasses from the bottle of sweet Hungarian wine. 'Sky was grey this morning.'

'No, it wasn't,' said Oskar, whose nose was now running so riotously he had to stem the tide with his cuff. 'It was blue.'

Herr Kozma began to chuckle, which soon turned into a laugh and then a heaving guffaw and finally a choking splutter.

'I think,' he said, face crimson with mirth and excess paprika, 'you need eye test!'

The *gulasch* soup was followed by a cheese aged in Gundel wine and studded with walnuts. Herr Kozma was just filling their glasses from a bottle of apricot brandy, when Oskar caught sight of a small white oblong box on top of the television.

'How long have you been taking those?' Oskar gestured towards the packet of pills, recognising the logo immediately.

'A few months,' said Herr Kozma.

'You realise that Equavol, which is actually called Seramax, can have some serious side effects? Migraines, high blood pressure, maybe even blindness.'

'*Szar*. Rubbish,' snorted Herr Kozma.

'Not rubbish,' said Oskar. 'Truth.'

'Why Herr Krank sell it then?'

'Maybe Krank has other motives beside your mental health,' said Oskar carefully.

Herr Kozma glared at Oskar like a cross owl. 'Herr Krank is good man,' he said, before pushing himself up from the table and walking over to the cabinet in the corner. 'Enough bad talk. We make music now.' He pulled out a bundle swaddled in muslin from inside the cabinet and removed the material, before holding the violin towards Oskar with a smile.

'See this wood here?' he said and tapped the varnished hourglass body. 'Is made from finest maple.' He grinned, before whipping out the bow from behind him like a magician's wand. 'And this is from hair of grey stallion.' He gave the violin a few gentle strokes with the bow then motioned towards the back wall, where there was a black and white picture of a man with a thick moustache. His hand was resting on the shoulder of the little boy standing beside him.

'My father make for me,' said Herr Kozma, tucking the violin under his chin. 'I play gypsy song for you. Is about family,' he said, smiling at the picture. 'Families are most important thing in world, yes?'

Oskar didn't reply. Instead he stared at the photograph on

the back wall, at the little boy's happy face as the hand of his father rested protectively on his shoulder.

*

After almost two years of visiting a psychiatrist (not Dr. Braun, who had declined to see Oskar a second time), Oskar's mum agreed that he didn't have to go anymore. Not that she would've known it, but things had improved massively at school anyway because Jonas had left earlier in the term. According to the rumours, he was now living with temporary foster parents fifty kilometres away, because his care home had been closed down after one of the supervisors was accused of assaulting two boys.

Now that the summer holidays had begun, Oskar was looking forward to two months of quietly drawing, snacking and reading. But during supper on the second evening of the holiday his mother announced that she had other plans.

'We're going on a little trip,' she said, spooning a helping of orange jelly into Oskar's bowl.

'Where to?' asked Oskar, pouring condensed milk over his *Wackelpudding*.

'It's a surprise,' she smiled.

'I don't really like surprises,' said Oskar. He was about to plead with his mum to cancel the trip, when he had a sudden thought. Maybe they were going to see his father.

That night, as he packed his little red suitcase for their surprise holiday, Oskar allowed himself to think about his father, something he rarely did nowadays. Originally, when his mother had shared the few facts about Werner, he'd spent hours fantasising about what he looked like (tall, dark-haired and dark-eyed – in fact, exactly like Oskar, only older), what made him laugh, what other books he read, what paintings he loved . . . So many times did he imagine his father turning up on the doorstep of their

Hamburg flat, hugging his only son to his chest and promising never to let him out of his sight again.

But however fervently Oskar fantasised about his father, birthdays passed without so much as a card, and Christmases came and went without a single phone call. Eventually he gave up hoping.

But now something had clearly changed. Werner had been found and told about his only son, whom he was desperate to meet. So Oskar was being summoned to Berlin under the pretence of a surprise summer holiday.

'Thank you!' Oskar whispered as he placed his dog-eared copy of *Faust* along with his best new paintbrushes at the top of his suitcase.

It wasn't until his mother's orange Volkswagen Beetle neared the village of Worpswede at around six o'clock the next day that Oskar realised they weren't going to Berlin after all. Instead of city suburbs and looping ring roads, he saw only meadows full of cows and dikes, and as they entered a gravel driveway he noted with alarm an abundance of teepees, swings, geese, goats and chickens. A sign in green letters read: *Worpswede Working Farm*.

'But I thought we were going to Berlin,' said Oskar quietly.

His mother laughed as she pulled up next to a battered campervan. 'Now what made you think that, darling?'

'And this is the communal dining room,' said the woman with the brown bobbly jumper, who had led them from the car into the large stone farmhouse.

Oskar stared at the long wooden table full of smiling grown-ups and scowling children. Then he looked at his mother.

'I don't feel well.' He clutched his head. 'My brain hurts and I can't move my neck. I think I have meningitis.'

His mother knelt down beside him and Oskar let out a long moan. He was just contemplating a fainting fit when he heard a deep voice behind him.

'The boy's not ill. Look at the colour in his face. Classic case of the fakes. Won't tolerate it in my own boys.'

Oskar turned to see a stocky man with a thick brown beard extending a beefy hand towards his mother. 'I'm Gunther,' he said, before shouting over to the two boys at the end of the table. 'Dieter! Detlef! Someone your own age to play with.'

If Oskar had been thinking clearly, he would have run from the room, calling for his mother to follow and, once outside, he would have begged her to drive them both home. But he was so confused that he wasn't visiting his father as he'd imagined, that all he could do was sit down at the communal table in stunned silence.

He was still sitting there when supper was served: marrows stuffed with rice and lentils, followed by baked apples and a 'sharing' session. 'Sharing', as Oskar soon discovered, basically meant each person at the table talking about how difficult and isolating it was being a single parent and how much the support group had helped them. Gunther was the second person to 'share', telling the table how he had lost his wife to leukaemia two years previously, and how he was bringing up his two boys alone while running a canoeing school in Bremerhaven. When it came to his mother's turn, Oskar had to admit that he was a little surprised.

'It's just so lonely,' she whispered, her fingers fiddling with the material of her skirt.

'I hear you,' said Gunther.

'I'd love another grown-up to talk to,' his mother continued.

'Well,' said Gunther, shunting himself down the bench towards her, 'from now on, you know where to come.'

———

Despite the full schedule, the days limped by. Activities on the farm included bed-making, washing up, digging potatoes in the vegetable garden, nature walks and den building. At lunchtime everybody made a lentil and tofu stew together and each evening after a supper, 'creative play' sessions (poetry, African drumming and guitar solos courtesy of Gunther) took place in the barn.

And then there were Gunther's twin sons, Dieter and Detlef. Big, ruddy-faced, tracksuited twelve-year olds with whom Oskar was expected not only to share a dormitory but to do the washing up, dig potatoes, nature walk and den build. Pretty quickly Oskar decided that it would be best to ignore them, and they seemed to feel the same way, although every time they passed him in the corridor, they would snigger.

'I'm not happy here, Mum,' said Oskar after the first week. 'Can we go home a bit earlier?' They were in the vegetable patch where they had been cutting spinach for supper.

'It's only another seven days, darling,' said his mother. 'It's not that bad, is it?'

''Course, it's not!' said a voice behind them. 'He's just got too used to having things his own way.' Gunther was blocking the path, laughing.

'It's my holiday too,' his mother added, putting her arm around Oskar's shoulders. 'I haven't felt so relaxed in years.'

What worried Oskar most was the change in his mother. She seemed to be in a dream world and would giggle like a little girl, especially when she and Gunther took their evening walk around the garden together. No longer was her hair scraped back in a ponytail, instead it tumbled loosely around her shoulders, freshly washed each day and threaded with a purple ribbon.

The end of the holiday couldn't have come soon enough, and as the car swung through the gates Oskar sighed.

'Can our next holiday be at home again?' he said. 'Just you and me.'

His mother leant over and ruffled Oskar's hair. 'Let's see, darling. Who knows what might happen in the future?' She smiled and brushed a lock of purple-ribbonned hair from her cheek.

*

'Pogácsa?'

Oskar stared up at Herr Kozma. He'd been so far away in his memories that he hadn't even noticed the violin playing had stopped and Herr Kozma was now standing in front of him holding a plate of little pastries.

'Take two. *Kérem.*' Oskar did as he was told, placing one of the pastries in his mouth and the second on his knee.

'You like gypsy song?'

'Yes,' said Oskar through a mouthful of flakey pastry. 'It was very nice. This is nice too,' he added, pointing to the hamster-bulge in his cheek.

'Have another.' Herr Kozma thrust the plate at him again. 'One not enough.'

'I already took two,' said Oskar, pointing to the second un-eaten pastry.

Herr Kozma squinted at Oskar's knee.

'Can you see alright with those glasses?'

'I see very well!'

'But they look all foggy to me.' Oskar held out his hand. 'Can I try them on?'

'Why?'

'Just a little experiment.'

Herr Kozma shrugged and removed his glasses, giving them to Oskar, who put them on.

'Just as I thought. You can hardly see anything,' said Oskar. 'And everything's so dull and grey.' He returned the glasses.

'Someone else tell me my glasses no good,' said Herr Kozma. 'The gentleman who came to village a few weeks ago.'

'You mean Dr. Sehle?'

Herr Kozma nodded.

'You went into his shop?'

Another nod.

Oskar shifted to the edge of his seat. 'And?'

'He gave me new pair of spectacles.' Herr Kozma pointed to the mantelpiece where, balanced on top of a brass carriage clock, was a dark green leather glasses case.

Oskar tried to steady his voice. 'Can I see them?' Before Herr Kozma could answer, he leapt over to the mantelpiece and picked up the spectacle case. Inside was a pair of plain gold-framed glasses, which Oskar carefully lifted out.

'May I try them on?'

Herr Kozma laughed. 'Please.'

Oskar closed his eyes and put on the spectacles. Taking a deep breath, he counted to three, turned towards the window and opened his eyes again. Outside in the snow-cleared court-yard below bags of rubbish were piled up next to a black bin. A rat scuttled along a nearby gutter, pausing to sniff an old broken boot.

Oskar grabbed the glasses from his face and rubbed the lenses with his cuff. 'I don't understand,' he said, before placing them back on and looking through the window once more.

'There's something wrong with the glasses.' He pulled them off for a second time. 'They're nothing like Dr. Sehle's lenses.'

The old man chuckled. 'Those lenses! I throw them away and put in old lenses. I keep frames though. Very nice.'

'You threw the lenses away!'

Herr Kozma nodded eagerly. 'Herr Krank say is no good.'

Oskar sprang towards Herr Kozma and before he knew what he was doing, his hands were clamped around the old man's neck.

'How could you be so dumb? Those lenses were priceless!' he shouted into the old man's face.

Herr Kozma stared at him goggle-eyed. It was only when he started to cough quite violently that Oskar let his hands drop. 'I'm so sorry.'

Herr Kozma took a gulp of air.

'I don't know what came over me.' Oskar stumbled backwards, watching the old man rub his throat with a liver-spotted hand. 'Can I do anything to make it better?'

Herr Kozma was knocking back a third glass of apricot brandy. He didn't seem to have sustained any serious damage from Oskar's throttling and certainly didn't appear to hold it against him.

'Did you at least have the eye test?' Oskar asked, sipping from his own glass.

'I did.' Herr Kozma lifted his chin to stare out of the window.

'With those coloured lenses?'

Herr Kozma nodded.

'What did you see?'

The old man smiled. 'Is like . . .' he shook his head and laughed softly, 'is like seeing little piece of heaven.'

Chapter 13

Oskar was sitting on his bed with a mug of chocolate Nesquik. He'd been there for the last hour, thinking about what Herr Kozma had said the previous evening. He had to admit that he was inexplicably happy someone else had experienced a similar vision with Dr. Sehle's lenses. But now matters were even more complicated. What exactly had he and Herr Kozma both seen? Was it a different version of reality where everything looked a lot rosier, and if so, how many different versions of reality were there?

Swigging back the Nesquik, Oskar tried to imagine a universe where numerous alternative realities were possible. At school Herr Brugger had briefly covered the theory of multiverses, in which there were multiple parallel universes all containing the entirety of space, time, matter and energy. Apparently even respected scientists such as the British physicist Stephen Hawking (who'd always fascinated Oskar what with the voice/wheelchair situation) actively supported this theory.

But if, as the theory stated, there were infinite other versions of this universe, would there be infinite other versions of people to inhabit those universes? And if so, did these other versions of people, which presumably would include different versions of himself, behave differently according to which universe they found themselves in? And could their behaviour in one universe affect their behaviour in another?

By the time Oskar had finished his Nesquik, his brain felt like it was going to blow up. It was also nearly two o'clock and he didn't want to be late for his afternoon in front of the telly with Frau Miesel. So he pulled on his trench coat and headed down onto the high street. He was halfway to the bakery, when he heard birdsong spilling over from the snow-tipped trees in the distance. He tilted his head to one side and listened for a few minutes, smiling, before striding on.

'Yoo hoo, it's me,' Oskar called to Frau Miesel through the slatted bakery blinds. 'It's nearly show time.'

From the other side of the window where she was wiping down the dough table, Frau Miesel gave him a hesitant smile.

'*Die Schwarzwaldklinik*,' he called.

'What about it?' Frau Miesel called back.

'It starts in ten minutes.'

Frau Miesel made an unconvincing attempt at a shrug.

Oskar grinned. 'I just thought you might be watching it since you ringed it twice in your TV listings magazine.'

Frau Miesel eyed Oskar through the slats for a few seconds. 'You don't give up, do you?' she said, before opening the door. 'You can only stay for the programme,' she added, leading the way upstairs to the sitting room.

By the time they were both seated in the armchairs, watching the adverts, conversation had already worn quite thin. So instead Oskar studied Frau Miesel out of the corner of his eye. He'd never noticed the pink glow of her skin before, nor the little dimples in her cheeks.

The final advert before the programme began showed a young blonde woman in white hot pants, dangling by a harness from a rock face while laughing cheerily into the hundred metre chasm.

'Check out that crazy lady!' Oskar chuckled, just as the

whooping anthem erupted from the telly, praising the benefits of a new ultra-absorbent sanitary towel.

Oskar coughed and fiddled with his sleeve until the ad finished and then, finally, came the theme tune to *Die Schwarzwaldklinik*.

The opening scene showed the soap's star, Klausjürgen Wussow in the lead role as Doktor Brinkmann, saying good-bye to his son, Udo, and driving from his beautiful country house in Glottertal towards the clinic. Once there, he strode into the large chalet-style building to greet his new team and meet the patients.

After checking on the health of two elderly women playing cards in the day room, he walked through the wards and stopped to talk to a young man lying in bed and staring up at the ceiling. His yellowing skin was drawn tightly over his cheeks and his hollow eyes looked so haunted that after watching for a couple of seconds, Oskar was forced to turn away.

*

Franz

Without the television or the thrilling social whirl as promised by Oskar, Franz was predictably sinking into the first stages of depression. All the telltale signs were there: the lead-weight lethargy; the neglect of personal hygiene; the deadening of the eyes . . .

One cold Saturday night, Oskar returned from Risiko's to find Franz slouched at the kitchen table sifting through a pile of junk mail brochures.

'What are you doing, Franz?'

'Nothing,' said Franz, quietly.

Oskar picked up one of the pamphlets, which showed a bikini-clad blonde frolicking in a turquoise sea: *Experience the holiday of your dreams AND win a set of luxury luggage when you book with Paradise Vacations!*

'You know what, Franz?' said Oskar, turning over the pamphlet to view the free leather-effect travel bag. 'The gallery has just sold two more paintings so I'd like to treat us both to a holiday. Where do you fancy?' The first part of this statement was true, the gallery had indeed recently sold two more pictures for a tidy total of 5,000 Euros.

'Mauritius, Morocco, the Maldives?'

Franz shrugged, chipping with his thumbnail at a lump of grey mince on the table.

'How about Vegas? Or even Bangkok?' Oskar grinned. 'We can go anywhere we want!'

Franz stopped the chipping. 'Really?'

'Really!' said Oskar. 'Franz, my good man, this'll be the holiday of a lifetime!'

Next morning, unlike the other Sunday mornings of the past two weeks, Franz was in the kitchen by nine o'clock, cooking his fry up.

'What's this for?' asked Oskar, sitting down at the table in his black silk dressing gown.

'I wanted to say thank you.' Franz handed him a plate of sausage, kidneys and some sort of fried mince scenario – cheap supermarket mince now being Franz's main food source.

'For what?' Oskar yawned.

'For offering to take me on holiday,' said Franz, sliding two fried eggs onto Oskar's plate. 'It's really generous of you.'

Oskar prodded the yellow dome of one of the eggs with his knife, releasing a stream of yoke. 'Holiday?'

'Yes,' said Franz. 'I thought that maybe Bangkok would be fun.'

Oskar forked a piece of sausage into his mouth. 'I'm sorry, Franz, but you've lost me.'

'The holiday plans?' said Franz. 'Last night, when we were sitting at the kitchen table . . .'

'Sorry, mate,' said Oskar. 'You must have misunderstood.' He bit into a piece of toast with a loud crunch and chewed for a little longer than was necessary.

'The money could pay for *me* to go on holiday, but I need the rest of it to live on.'

And there it was – that perfect moment. First the residual glimmer of excitement from the previous evening, the eager smile, the bright eyes. But seconds later, the shoulders slumped, the smile faded and the eyes dimmed. Oskar quickly finished the fry up and hurried to his room to re-create the image on canvas.

At this point, given the tragic state of Franz's life, one might have thought that he would toss in the towel and return to Füssen. But as Oskar well knew from the stories, there was nothing there to tempt him back.

'Do you ever wonder what's the point of it all?' asked Franz one Wednesday night as he slouched on the sofa, shredding pieces of Rizla into a small pile.

Oskar, who was just slipping into his smoking jacket in preparation for a fictional gallery opening, shook his head. 'I'm not sure what you mean, Franz.'

Franz pulled out another Rizla and began tearing it into strips. 'Well, I can't help thinking there should be more to life. And recently, I've been having these thoughts . . .'

Oskar brushed a piece of non-existent fluff from his lapel. 'What kind of thoughts, Franz?'

'Dark ones.'

'Oh, Franz, that's not good.'

'Don't you ever have dark thoughts?'

Oskar shook his head. 'Can't say I do.' He gave his quiff a

final adjustment and checked his watch. 'Better run, Franz. Nighty night!'

*

The sound of *Die Schwarzwaldklinik's* theme tune pulled Oskar back to the final credits. As the last shot of Doktor Brinkmann's face faded from the screen, a sigh escaped from Frau Miesel's lips.

'Do you fancy Doktor Brinkmann?' Oskar was glad for the distraction from the Franz thoughts.

Two little red circles flared on Frau Miesel's cheeks. 'Klausjürgen Wussow happens to be a very talented actor.'

'I bet you were a member of his fan club.'

'Don't be ridiculous.'

'Well, why,' said Oskar, twisting ever so slowly towards the shelf behind them, 'do you have a signed photo of Herr Wussow then?'

'Well, I may have been a member – just briefly.'

'I knew it!' said Oskar. 'Did you write letters?'

'Perhaps.'

'Did he ever reply?'

'No,' answered Frau Miesel. 'Not once.'

'Meany,' said Oskar.

'That's men for you,' said Frau Miesel.

Children's hour on the TV had begun and a collection of garishly-painted puppets were skipping jerkily around a log in a forest. Oskar quite fancied watching them but it was important not to outstay his welcome on this first telly visit.

He set down his mug and rose from the chair. 'Before I go, any more news on Herr Krank's second business?'

Frau Miesel shook her head. 'Although I did see something the other day,' she said. 'He was standing inside the shop near the window with something pressed to his right eye. It looked like a piece of coloured glass.'

'Really?' Oskar shuffled forward in his chair.

'Then again my eyesight isn't great and it was pretty far away,' said Frau Miesel.

'Well,' said Oskar, 'if you should see it happen again, let me know.' He pointed to her glasses. 'Surely those are meant to improve your eyesight?'

Frau Miesel shrugged. 'It's a losing battle.'

'Can I try them on?'

'What for?'

'I'm just doing some research,' said Oskar. 'Go on, indulge me.'

Frau Miesel passed him her glasses and Oskar put them on, peering through the lenses.

'They're exactly like Herr Kozma's,' he said. 'Everything looks so gloomy.'

Frau Miesel gave a little laugh. 'That, my dear Oskar, is called life.'

'But maybe things don't have to look like that,' said Oskar. 'Maybe there's another way to see the world,' he paused, trying to remember the details of the multiverse theory so he could test it out on Frau Miesel. But she wasn't listening anyway and was already collecting up the mugs.

'Same time next week then?' said Oskar, a little louder.

Frau Miesel picked up the two remaining teaspoons from the table. 'I may be busy next week.'

'Doing what?'

'I've just enrolled on a new lunchtime course. Bare-knuckle fighting for the over Fifties.'

'What?' Oskar spluttered.

'That was a joke,' said Frau Miesel.

Oskar grinned. 'So, that's a yes for next week?'

Frau Miesel lifted one of the teaspoons up to eye level with a look of mild curiosity. 'I believe it is,' she replied, with a flicker of a smile.

Chapter 14

Oskar was on a stake-out. Stationed behind the curtains of his sitting room window with a bird's eye view of the crime scene, he'd already started on his snacks – a bag of *Gummibärchen* and three small bars of Kinder Chocolate. It was 10.04 a.m. but there was no sign of the suspect so far. Not to worry – DI Dunkelblick could play a long game.

The plan was simple: wait by the window until Krank entered the spectacle shop, then head over there and involve him in a lengthy and confusing conversation about health matters, all the while scanning for what he was sure from Frau Miesel's report was the missing lens. As for what he would do with the lens, if he got hold of it, Oskar wasn't quite sure. To stash it at the back of his sock drawer somehow seemed a bit of a waste now.

10.13 a.m. – Aha, there he was, chief suspect Krank walking down the high street carrying a large unidentified cardboard box. Oskar popped a green *Gummibärchen* in his mouth and grabbed his coat.

By the time he had reached the shop, Herr Krank was already at the far end of the room, sitting beside a table on which there were four other cardboard boxes and two large computers. Oskar could make out several packets of pills in his left hand and in his right, a sticker machine like they used in supermarkets. He was sticking something on the front of each packet then placing it into one of the cardboard boxes, which was stamped with the Glücksvolk logo.

'Aaachoo!' Oskar hadn't felt the sneeze approaching, but now it was out, he needed to move fast.

'Herr Krank! I'm so glad I've found you!' Oskar panted as though he'd just run through the shop door. 'My tummy really hurts.'

Herr Krank jumped up from the chair then edged to his left to block from view the two computers on the table. 'Take some aspirin then.'

'I did,' Oskar groaned. 'It didn't help. And you know that other thing I was telling you about in the bar.' He winced, glancing down at his groin. 'It's much worse. White spots have appeared and there's an angry red rash all down one side.' Oskar was pleased that this time he'd prepared his fictitious problem well in advance.

'Is that all?'

'Not quite,' said Oskar. 'My lymph nodes are enlarged.'

'Have you engaged in unprotected sex during the last six months?'

'No!' said Oskar. Years of Dr. Sommer's problem pages had instilled in him a morbid fear of STDs.

'And you wash your penis regularly?'

'Of course I do!'

'You may be suffering from a yeast infection, for which I can give you a salve.'

'Excellent,' said Oskar, looking around the room again. 'You keep it pretty dark in here. Any reason for that?'

'None whatsoever,' Krank snapped. 'Now if you don't mind, I need to get on with my day.' He motioned Oskar towards the door, but Oskar didn't move. Instead he stared up at what looked like a disc of amber light that he'd just spotted shining on the ceiling above the shelves. Without a word, he lunged for the chair, dragged it over to the wall and leapt on top. And there it was – the lens. He stretched out his hand and had just folded the smooth oval disc into his palm when he felt a hard shove against his calves.

The second shove was even harder. Oskar grabbed onto the side of the shelf with his left hand, but the chair was wobbling too much and seconds later, he fell to the floor and the lens flew from his fist.

Oskar was splayed out on the shop floor and Krank was standing above him. In front of them both was the lens about arm's length from Oskar's face. He edged forward, but before he could grab it, a black, pointy shoe lifted in the air beside his left ear. Then, with a thud, it slammed down onto the ground, smashing the lens to smithereens.

Chapter 15

Oskar was *stinksauer*. He'd been trying to get a fire going in the stove for almost an hour with zero success. He could light it alright but after the brief and rather thrilling burst of flame, the wretched thing would start hissing, throw out a few subdued sparks, then die, leaving a heap of charred wood and blackened pieces of newspaper. Stupid stove! He gave it a kick and sat back for a sulk and a strategy rethink.

Things hadn't been going well since he'd visited Krank the previous week. Worst of all, of course, was the smashed lens, the splinters of which had been far too tiny to glue together – not that Krank would have let him anyway. What Oskar couldn't quite fathom, was why he felt so upset about it. It's only a lens, he kept telling himself. But somehow, he couldn't bear the thought of never looking through it again, never experiencing that extraordinary feeling of . . . *Wholeness*.

Then there was the obvious suspicion with which Krank now viewed Oskar, making any future investigations regarding Equavol even trickier. On top of all that was the rather pressing question: what was he actually still doing in this village?

For five days running now he'd stood in front of a blank canvas trying to capture at least one of Frau Miesel's imperfections. It should have been so easy: a lonely woman with a turkey-scrag neck and a crush on a fictional television character. Pure gold. Yet nothing was coming. Instead, whenever Oskar thought about Frau Miesel, he could only see that soft pink glow of her skin, her gentle smile and the way her eyes twinkled when she told one of her little jokes.

How much longer could this creative cul-de-sac continue? A week? Three months? A year? The gallery had already made it clear that if he failed to fulfil his contractual obligations, they could no longer support his artistic career. He now had until the end of December to send the paintings he had promised them. That meant he had about . . . Oskar glanced at the calendar on the wall and saw with a jolt that today was the 6th December, Saint Nikolaus Day.

Oskar sat on the edge of his bed, sucking a piece of Kinder Bueno bar as images from his childhood swirled through his head. He could see himself as a six-year old, carefully setting his shoes outside his bedroom door the night before Saint Nikolaus arrived, then waking the following morning to find them choc-full of treats; marvelling at the Pez sweet dispenser shaped like Pluto with tiny pink lozenges that popped out of the dog's yellow plastic head . . .

More memories followed and he saw himself racing down to the kitchen to show his mother what Saint Nikolaus had brought. He could smell the sweet cinnamon pancakes she was cooking and hear her laugh when he snapped open the mouth of his Pluto Pez. With a lump in his throat he watched as he and his mother walked around the cobbled square in front of St Petri church later that afternoon. The air was scented with nutmeg and cloves and they were munching on heart-shaped ginger biscuits . . .

Oskar lay down on his bed and swallowed a third piece of

Kinder Bueno bar with a painful gulp. For the first time in years he allowed himself to think back to the beginning of the end.

*

Almost nine months had passed since the holiday in Worpswede and Oskar was in his bedroom reading his favourite story from *Shockheaded Peter*. He'd just got to the juicy bit where the little Suck-A-Thumb's thumbs are snipped off by a roving tailor and his giant pair of scissors, when there was a knock at his door.

'I've got something to tell you,' said his mum, perching next to him on the bed. 'It might come as a bit of a surprise but Gunther has asked us both to live with him.'

Oskar stared at her. 'Why?'

His mother smiled. 'Because we've grown very fond of each other.'

'But you hardly know him,' said Oskar.

'That's not true, darling. We speak almost every night on the phone and he came down for those three weekends.'

Oskar had tried to forget about those weekends, when Gunther made them both go walking and insisted that they all play Pictionary together in the evenings. Still, at least he'd left the boys behind with their grandmother.

'But Gunther doesn't like me,' said Oskar.

'You're still getting used to each other,' said his mother. 'These things take time.'

Oskar needed to think of something fast. He raised his right hand to his chest and took a shallow breath. 'I can't possibly live in Bremerhaven because I can't be near water. It'll trigger my tuberculosis.'

'But you don't have tuberculosis, darling.'

'I might do. It's very common in boys my age.'

111

Over the next few months Oskar pulled out all the stops in his attempt to prevent the move to Bremerhaven. Almost every illness in his medical dictionary was used as ammunition. But his mother, boosted by the daily telephone conversations with Gunther, remained adamant.

'This is your room,' announced Dieter and Detlef, opening the door to what could only be described as a rabbit hutch lit by a single bare bulb with one cot bed and a ridiculously small window. Oskar turned to his mother, who was standing behind them and who at least had the good grace to look surprised at the size of the 'bedroom'.

'I can't stay here,' said Oskar. 'I suffer from claustrophobia.'

'Don't worry about that,' laughed Gunther, placing a chunky arm around his mother's shoulders. 'You won't be spending much time in here. You'll be outside all day, won't he, boys?'

Oskar's new life was very, very different from his old one. The day began with morning chores, which included emptying the rubbish bins, sweeping the backyard and washing Gunther's car. After that came seven hours of school (trying to skive classes wasn't a good idea and the one time Oskar had tried it, Gunther had slapped him). Late afternoons were taken up with sport – football, ice hockey and of course, canoeing, while the evenings were devoted to homework, supper and Gunther's educational talks. The end of the day was rounded off with relaxation time, which basically meant everyone sitting on the living room floor playing Pictionary.

Just like on the working farm holiday, it was impossible to talk to his mother because Gunther always seemed to be nearby. And when Oskar did manage to catch her on her own and tell her how unhappy he was, she just said to give it more time.

'But you keep saying that, Mum. And Gunther's still not very nice to me,' said Oskar. 'He threw a bucket of water at me the other day when I forgot to wash his car wheels.'

'Are you sure you're not exaggerating, darling?' said his mum. 'You know how you're not very good at telling the truth.'

Oskar bit his lip. His mum was right. During those two years that Jonas had been at school he had learnt to lie a lot: like why his legs and arms were bruised so often; why he had stolen money from his mother's purse; how he had come to be trapped in a drainpipe overnight.

'Please, Mum. I don't like it here.'

His mum put her arm around his shoulders. 'OK, darling. Let me talk to Gunther.'

But when his mother did speak to Gunther, he started shouting at her and slammed the sitting room door so hard that the coat rack in the corridor outside fell off the wall.

And then there was Dieter and Detlef. During the day they ignored Oskar, but at night when the rest of the household slept he would hear their hot breath through the keyhole of his rabbit hutch: 'Go away, Oskar, nobody wants you.' Things went missing from his room: his special Choco-Milch mug; his blue jacket with the velvet collar; and worst of all, his copy of *Faust* which he later found with the cover picture of Faust's face scrawled with the words: *Oskar ist ein Wixer*. Oskar is a wanker.

Since the night before the Worpswede holiday, when he'd been so stupid as to believe that his mother might be taking him to Berlin, Oskar had tried hard not to think about his father. But now that figure, about whom he knew frustratingly little, became his refuge. He began a journal, filling the pages with different scenarios in which his father, having hired a private detective to track down his son, would storm the house at midnight, snatching Oskar from his cot bed and carrying him off to a new life in Berlin.

So often did Oskar imagine these scenarios, that in his mind it was only a matter of time. Therefore it was wise to do all he could to bridge that gap of twelve lost years. With very few facts to go on, Oskar did know one thing: that Werner liked books and wanted to write a novel himself. So naturally, Oskar should familiarise himself with other great writers.

Each night after he had written in his journal, Oskar curled up under his bed covers to read the works of Böll, Goethe, Grass, Kafka and Mann. Admittedly, some of them were a little advanced for him, but that only gave him more reason to note down questions for future discussion with his father: Do you think that events in *The Trial* are symbolic of Franz Kafka's relationship with his own tyrannical father? (Here Oskar would have a chance to describe the *Drecksack* Gunther.) Are the tuberculosis-riddled patients at the sanatorium in Thomas Mann's *The Magic Mountain* simply a metaphor for the sickness of society? Did Oskar Matzerath from *The Tin Drum* refuse to grow up to emphasise his alienation from the rest of the world?

Oskar also needed to have a back-up plan, just in case his dad wasn't able to find him. For that he would need money to go to Berlin. So he began stealing from his mum's purse again, this time for himself, rather than Jonas. After five months, he already had eighty-three Euros.

Meanwhile winter turned to spring, then summer, which meant two weeks hiking in the French Pyrenees. It was on the last day of this holiday, on the peak of Mont Perdu, that Gunther and his mother announced their wedding plans. That night as Oskar lay on the thin hostel bunkbed, staring up at the ceiling, he honestly thought things couldn't get any worse.

*

Oskar was still lying on his bed, staring at the empty Kinder Bueno wrapper beside him. Outside, dusk had fallen and the

114

street lamps were flickering to life, spotlighting the snowflakes that swirled silently through the air. Inside, in Oskar's head, images from his childhood were still playing, and as he watched them he felt something wet trickle down his cheek. He tilted his head towards the ceiling, wondering if there was a leak in the roof. Or maybe it was blood from a small shaving nick? Raising a forefinger to his cheek, Oskar wiped it away and realised with astonishment that he was crying.

Chapter 16

Trriiing! The shrill sound of the doorbell made Oskar leap from the bed and stub his left big toe on the side table. Who the hell was that? Better hide and hope the caller would go away.

Trriiiiing! There it was again, louder and longer this time. Oskar quickly rubbed the wetness from his eyes and hopped over to the window to peek around the curtain. Down on the street beneath one of the lamps, he could see a figure wearing a red woollen coat and a matching knitted hat. He ducked below the windowsill.

'Too late, I've seen you,' Greta called.

Oskar poked his nose up over the sill. 'What do you want?'

'To check you're alright.'

'Why wouldn't I be?'

'Well,' called Greta, 'I know that Herr Krank prescribed you a course of . . .' she paused and glanced around her. 'Do you really want the whole village to hear this?'

Greta was standing in the kitchenette, pulling off her hat and shaking it. She'd unbuttoned her coat, but had kept it on over her white work uniform.

'So you came here to make sure I'm not planning to top myself,' said Oskar, 'now I'm on the perky pills.'

Greta shook her head. 'I came to check you weren't suffering from any side effects. Some patients report headaches and nausea after taking Equavol.'

'And what does Krank have to say about that?'

'To be honest, he doesn't really encourage my home visits.' Greta looked around her, eyes lingering on *The Dark Side of Mother* canvas and the discarded black socks littering the floor like roadkill.

'You can't stay long,' said Oskar. 'I'm extremely busy.'

'Doing what?' There was a new tone to Greta's voice, more authoritative, which Oskar put down to the fact that she was in work mode. 'Are you sure you're OK?' Greta was staring directly at him.

'Yes,' said Oskar, impatiently. 'Everything's just brilliant.'

'Why are your eyes red then?'

'Conjunctivitis,' said Oskar. 'I'm still waiting for my special eye drops to arrive from Berlin.'

'Remind me to give you some fresh aloe vera next time I see you. Just as good as eye drops,' said Greta, rubbing her hands together and blowing on her fingers. 'Maybe we could have some coffee?'

'I don't drink coffee at home.'

'Tea?'

'Nope.'

'Anything hot?'

'You can have Ovomaltine.' Oskar was low on Nesquik supplies and didn't feel like sharing.

Greta smiled. 'Ovomaltine it is then.'

Oskar and Greta were sitting at the table, sipping Ovomaltine from Frankfurter tins because all the mugs were dirty.

'So you haven't had any side effects from the Equavol?' she asked.

Oskar shook his head, wondering if he should risk telling her about what he'd discovered in Franz's Depression book.

'You're sure about that?'

Perhaps it was the concerned look on her face, or the fact that she'd asked the question twice that made him feel she genuinely cared about his health. He also wondered if Krank had told her about his little problem *down there*. If so, how much did she know?

'And all the other symptoms seem to have cleared up too,' said Oskar. 'Just like that.'

'Other symptoms?'

'All gone,' said Oskar in a sing-song voice. 'Aaaanyway,' he continued quickly, deciding to take the risk, 'there's something you should probably know.' He stood up and walked over to his bedside table to get the Depression book. Flipping it open at the by now well-thumbed page, he handed it to Greta.

'Krank has been selling that drug Seramax to the villagers, but labelling it as Equavol,' he said. 'It's dangerous stuff.'

Greta bent her head to read and when she'd finished, she placed the book down on the table with a worried look. 'High blood pressure? Damage to the optic nerves? Blindness?' She glanced up at Oskar. 'Are you sure it's the same drug?'

Oskar nodded. 'I caught him re-labelling the packets last week. Needless to say, I've not been taking my prescription.'

Greta frowned. 'No wonder he keeps the antidepressants locked away.' She shook her head. 'I can't believe he's doing that.'

Confident from her expression, Oskar pressed on. 'It makes sense. Krank sells glasses that distort people's vision – I know that because I tried on Herr Kozma's and Frau Miesel's. So he offers them a handy solution with his happy pills.' He shook his head. 'After all, it's not the first time that someone working in the pharmaceutical industry has created a problem and then miraculously found – and patented – the remedy. And there's obviously a backhander for Krank from the manufactures,' he added. 'I've already spotted two expensive new computers from Glücksvolk.'

Greta was still at Oskar's. They'd been discussing what to do for the last half hour and she'd promised to keep a close eye on all the patients she knew to be taking Equavol. She would also make a note of any new equipment that arrived, in case it was from Glücksvolk.

Munching on some chocolate *Leibniz-Keks*, they moved on to Herr Kozma. Greta told Oskar how thrilled he was to be re-united with the picture of his wife. Apparently he and Eva had only spent three days apart during their forty-year marriage.

'When she died, he didn't speak for almost eight weeks,' said Greta with a shake of her head.

A short silence followed, while Oskar pictured Herr Kozma sitting down for supper with the empty place opposite him. 'Poor old boy,' he said quietly.

'And Frau Trundel told me how you picked her up from the pavement a while back,' said Greta.

Oskar shrugged. 'It was nothing.'

'It was kind,' said Greta. 'She's had a hard enough time as it is. Adalbert, her husband, hasn't left the house for years, because of his agoraphobia,' she paused. 'I think I may have misjudged you, Oskar.'

Oskar smiled and felt himself blushing. To cover it up, he quickly pointed to his bookshelves. 'You like to read too, don't you?'

'I do, Oskar.' Greta grinned and rose from her chair, walking over to the shelf where he kept his philosophy books. 'Nietzsche, Schopenhauer, Kierkegaard . . . you sure like the fun ones.' She selected a slim volume by Schopenhauer and leafed through it.

'You probably don't want to read that,' said Oskar.

'Women are . . . childish, silly and short-sighted; a kind of intermediate stage between the child and the man, who is the actual human being.' Greta shook her head as she read, then burst out laughing, before continuing. *'Only a male intellect clouded by the sexual drive could call the stunted, narrow-shouldered, broad-hipped and short-legged sex the fair sex.'*

'Just because the book happens to be on my shelf, that doesn't mean I agree with it.' Oskar strode over to take the book from Greta's hands.

'No,' said Greta with a mock serious expression. 'Of course not.' She shivered and glanced at the stove in the corner.

'Ever wondered what that might be for?'

Oskar scowled. 'It's broken.'

'Looks fine to me,' said Greta, kneeling in front of the stove. She pulled out a handful of blackened wood then took a few sheets of newspaper, scrunching them into balls. After placing some twigs on top, she laid two logs in the centre. When she had finished, she lit the newspaper with a match.

'Didn't your father – or your mother – ever teach you how to make a fire?' she said, levering herself up from her knees.

'No,' said Oskar. 'They didn't.'

*

Even though Oskar was living in the house from hell, and Gunther and his mother were married, he still didn't allow it to spoil his hopes for his thirteenth birthday. At least for one day he could forget the *Scheisskiste* that was his life – and maybe, just maybe, his father would choose this birthday to finally turn up and take him away.

Dieter and Detlef were already at the house when he arrived home after school.

'Come and look at your cake,' whispered Dieter, nodding towards the kitchen.

Oskar studied his expression, trying to guess what trick he and his twin were about to play. But having followed them into the kitchen, he saw that all of his favourite treats were laid out on the sideboard including a plate of chocolate and hazelnut *Hanuta* squares, three packets of Bonitos and some cream puffs.

'And look at this.' Detlef whipped off a cloth to reveal the most magnificent birthday cake Oskar had ever seen. Large, square and covered in white icing, it resembled a blank canvas with a paintbrush made from hardened blue sugar across the middle. Below it, in swooping letters – 'Happy Birthday, dear Oskar.'

Oskar gazed in delight, remembering how his mother had given Dieter and Detlef a shop-bought cake on their birthday. He wondered briefly if it was guilt that had made her go to such an effort.

Detlef handed Oskar a book-shaped package. 'We hope you like it,' he said with a smile.

Still unable to believe what was happening, Oskar opened it. Inside was an illustrated edition of Kafka's *Metamorphosis*.

'There's another surprise for you.' Dieter put a finger to his lips and pointed upstairs.

In the boys' bedroom Dieter pulled out a parcel the size of a shoebox from beneath the bunk bed. Next to him, Detlef clasped his hands excitedly.

'A man came while you were still in school this afternoon. He brought this with him.' Dieter held out the parcel towards Oskar.

'Did he say his name?' Oskar's voice was so quivery that he had to repeat the question.

'Now what was it?' Dieter said, turning to Detlef.

'I think his name began with W,' said Detlef.

'Willy. No, Walfred, perhaps?' said Dieter.

Detlef shook his head. 'Wasn't it Werner?'

Oskar stared at them both, unable to speak.

'He wanted to know all about you so we told him how much you loved reading grown-up books and writing in your journal,' said Dieter.

Oskar wanted to throw his arms around them.

'Aren't you going to open it?' Dieter nodded towards the box in Oskar's hands.

There were several layers of wrapping paper and by the time the final sheet fell to the floor, Oskar felt dizzy with anticipation. The lid of the white box was sellotaped down, so Dieter fetched the kitchen scissors to cut it.

Inside was a froth of tissue paper into which Oskar plunged his hand.

'It must be very small.' He looked up at the two boys who were studying the box intently.

Oskar pulled out each layer of the tissue paper, trying not to rip them. Finally, when it was all gone, he stared in confusion at the empty box.

The sniggering started slowly, but within seconds Dieter and Detlef were hysterical with laughter. It was only then that Oskar noticed Detlef was holding his journal, open on a page containing one of the many fantasy scenes in which Werner came to rescue him.

With a howl of rage, Oskar threw himself at Detlef, clawing his face as the two boys scrabbled on the bedroom carpet.

'WHAT ON EARTH IS GOING ON?' The roar of Gunther's voice shook the whole room and Oskar felt his arm being wrenched from its socket as he was dragged up from the floor.

'I won't tolerate this anymore!' Gunther was shaking Oskar so hard that he thought his teeth would fall out.

'Oskar attacked me,' said Detlef, rubbing his face. 'I didn't do anything.'

'You're a spoilt little thug,' shouted Gunther into Oskar's

face, slamming him against the bedroom wall. 'And I've had enough of it.'

Twenty minutes later Oskar was curled up on his bed in his room, where he had been ordered by Gunther to remain for the next two hours. His head throbbed from where it had hit the bedroom wall. Downstairs he could hear voices and the clatter of cutlery. The alarm clock next to his night light said it was half past four.

At five-thirty he heard the sound of his mother's footsteps on the stairs outside.

'Gunther says you can come downstairs now, Oskar,' she said, through the door.

Oskar felt his lower lip tremble. 'Can't we have tea up here? Just you and me?'

From the other side of the door he heard his mother sigh. 'You know we can't do that. Gunther won't allow it.'

A second voice bellowed from the bottom of the stairs.

'Leave him there. If he's going to act like a hooligan, he should be treated like one.'

A short discussion followed, dominated by Gunther's booming voice. Moments later Oskar could hear him and his sons laughing.

'Isn't there someone missing?' Detlef asked loudly.

Dieter laughed even harder. 'No, it's just us. Exactly as it should be.'

Oskar suddenly understood the birthday present that the boys had given him. They'd planned his death just like the death of Gregor Samsa in *Metamorphosis*. He would end up like that poor beetle, locked in his room and starved to a skeleton then swept out with the household dust, while his mother stood by, too cowardly to do anything about it.

Oskar started packing immediately. He wouldn't need much, just some clothes, his favourite pencils and paintbrushes, a sketchbook and the two hundred Euros that he'd managed to squirrel away for the back-up plan. Then he waited until 1 a.m. to creep down the stairs and out of the house, never once looking back.

*

Oskar and Greta had been sitting in front of the fire for some time now, each submerged in their own thoughts. The sweet smell of applewood from the stove drifted around the room, while outside the December winds whistled at the window-panes. Once in a while, Oskar glanced over at Greta, whose knees were drawn up to her chin. The light from the flames made her eyes seem greener than ever. Somehow that lazy left lid, which he'd tried and failed to paint, now seemed such a part of her face that he wouldn't want to imagine her without it.

'You remember asking me about Dr. Sehle when you first came to my house?' said Greta.

Oskar nodded.

'Well, I never told you about a conversation I had with him.' She edged closer to the stove and added another log. 'The day before he disappeared, he came into the chemist's while Krank was out. I asked what I could do for him, something for his skin perhaps?

"This?" he said and raised a finger to his cheek. "This doesn't bother me anymore. It happened lifetimes ago. No, it's my feet that need attention."

'I sat him down and removed his boots. His feet were in a terrible state, covered in calluses and blisters.

"You must have walked halfway round the world to get them in this condition," I said, wiping his feet clean with tea tree oil to prevent infection. I removed the worst of the dead skin before rubbing in some arnica and applying plasters around the heel and toes. I told him to walk as little as possible over the next few weeks.

"That, I'm afraid, is out of the question," he laughed. "I am leaving the village tomorrow."

"But you've only been here one week," I said.

He stared out of the window up the high street. "I have found someone else to continue my work."'

Greta shrugged, then twisted round from the fire to face Oskar. 'He was looking directly at your house, when he said it. Any idea what he was talking about?'

Oskar shook his head, but he couldn't suppress a shiver as a bead of sweat slid down the back of his neck.

Chapter 17

Oskar was in the butcher's, studying Frau Fettler's hair. It really was remarkable, the way it cascaded down her back in shanks of coarse brown mane. What made it grow *that* thick? Was she taking a special food supplement, rich in iron and other nourishing minerals? Or maybe she was getting vigorous scalp massages to stimulate the arteries and increase the blood supply? Oskar frowned, wondering if the pricey hair-thickening mousse he'd brought from Berlin might be a bit of a rip-off.

Herr Kozma, Frau Zwoll and Frau Trundel were also in the queue ahead of Oskar, each clearly set on getting some of the *Wiener Schnitzel* that had been delivered fresh that morning. Since there were only five pieces left, someone at the back of the queue would have to go without. So everyone was trying to act all casual, with Frau Fettler staring at a tin of red cabbage, while Frau Zwoll kept a close eye on the clock and Frau Trundel watched a large bluebottle poke its proboscis into a pile of old pork cuts.

Oskar noted the time and looked out of the window to see if he could spot Greta leaving for her lunch break. In the two days since she had visited Oskar at his home, he'd wanted to talk more about her conversation with Dr. Sehle, but he didn't dare set foot in the chemist's because of Krank and to call on Greta at her house, suddenly seemed . . . well, a bit intrusive.

'I'll have two *Wiener Schnitzels*,' said Herr Kozma, now at the front of the queue.

Two? Why does he need two? He lives alone and clearly doesn't have any friends.

But then Oskar remembered the place set for Eva, Herr Kozma's dead wife, and how the old man's eyes had sparkled when he'd talked about her. Let the poor soul have his delusions, if they helped him keep the loneliness at bay.

The others in the queue were obviously not quite so relaxed about Herr Kozma snaffling two *Schnitzels*. Frau Zwoll, who was next in line and would at least get one, pursed her lips but Frau Trundel tutted loudly, tapping her feet on the tiled floor. Frau Fettler tossed her mane and let out a long sigh, which circled the butcher's like a Siberian wind.

Frau Zwoll placed her order and as predicted, it was the breaded veal. So Oskar scanned the other options for his tea, which included some sausages, a few kidneys and a glistening mound of cheap mince, exactly the sort of combination that Franz used to cook for his trademark fry up.

*

Franz

Although Oskar, had mapped out the *Seven Steps to Hell* pretty precisely, it was Franz himself who supplied an unexpected but extremely amusing little detour.

'Franz. Look at you!' said Oskar, early one Saturday evening when he spotted his flatmate in front of the sitting room mirror, tugging on his white jacket. Franz had showered and combed his hair for the first time in five days.

'One of the guys from the garage is having some birthday

drinks.' Franz rubbed half-heartedly at some cigarette ash on his black jeans. 'I'm not really in the mood, but I don't want to let him down. Reckon I look OK?'

'You look splendid, Franz.'

'Do you think a girl might . . . might want to talk to me?'

Oskar surveyed Franz's acne-pocked face, his limp centre-parted hair and his shirt hooped with sweat stains.

'Hell, yes!'

Just after 2 a.m., when Oskar was sprawled in the armchair, drinking Southern Comfort and listening to Wagner's *Götter-dämmerung,* the door opened and there was Franz holding hands with a small, smiling and not un-pretty woman.

'Oskar, this is Petra. Petra, this is Oskar,' grinned Franz.

Petra had a round, freckled face, blue eyes and long reddish hair. Granted she was a little wide of hip and the chin lacked definition, but she really wasn't bad looking at all.

'Petra's a student nurse,' said Franz proudly as the two of them sat down on the sofa.

'A drunk student nurse,' Petra hiccupped, 'who needs to lie down.'

Franz smoothed a strand of hair from her forehead. 'I can walk you home if you want.'

'I'd rather stay here,' she said, letting her head fall against the back of the sofa.

Oskar watched Franz plump up one of the cushions and place it behind Petra's head. Seconds later, she was gently snoring.

'She's so pretty, isn't she?' whispered Franz.

Oskar nodded, dumbstruck, seeing months of careful planning blown apart in seconds.

'I think she likes me,' said Franz. 'She asked me to go to the flea market with her tomorrow.' He smiled to himself then patted his top pocket.

One pat, two pats, then a third slightly more urgent pat.

'Shit.' Franz prodded his empty jeans pockets back and front. Then he rushed over to the ashtray and snatched up a crumpled packet of Drum. Having peered inside, he looked at the sleeping Petra then over at Oskar.

'Would you be able to go to the mini market for me? I don't want to leave –'

Oskar held up a hand before Franz could finish. 'You know I'd do anything for you, Franz,' he said, patting his left leg and wincing. 'But I slipped in the shower this evening and dislocated my knee.' He looked over at Petra. 'Don't worry. I'll keep an eye on her.'

By the time Oskar heard Franz's footsteps on the outside stairs again, he was lying on the sofa, listening to the final act of *Götterdämmerung*. He'd just got to his favourite part where Hagen stabs Siegfried in the back with his spear, when Franz burst through the door.

'Where's Petra?' he panted, staring at the empty space beside Oskar on the sofa.

Oskar drained the last of his Southern Comfort. 'She woke up and was feeling so unwell that she asked me to ring for a taxi.'

'Oh.' Franz's mouth was a perfect goldfish O. 'But she left her number?'

Oskar shook his head.

'A note?'

'Nix,' said Oskar.

'I can't believe it,' Franz stammered. 'She seemed so nice.' He sunk down into the armchair, staring at his newly purchased packet of Drum.

'Bummer, huh?' Oskar yawned loudly and checked his watch. 'Is that the time? Better get my head down.'

Of course, it hadn't happened exactly like that, but near enough – Petra had just needed a little nudging.

'Where's Franz?' she murmured sleepily, when Oskar had woken her shortly after Franz left for the mini market.

'He's gone,' said Oskar.

'Where?'

'To his girlfriend's round the corner.'

Petra sat up and rubbed her eyes.

Oskar shook his head and sighed. 'He thinks he's doing me a favour, bringing me pretty girls but to be honest, it's getting a little embarrassing.'

'Why would he want to bring you girls?'

Oskar looked towards the window. 'I lost my childhood sweetheart in a tragic household accident last year and since then I just haven't felt like being with anyone else. But Franz, kind soul that he is, thinks he can change that.'

Petra was standing now. 'Are you serious?' She pulled her coat from the back of the sofa. 'And what about the women? Do they have a say in this?'

'Don't hold it against him. He means well.'

'Of course he does.' She snatched her bag from the table and marched towards the front door.

'See you around!' called Oskar as she wrenched at the handle.

'I doubt it,' said Petra and disappeared into the dark hallway.

The Petra incident was never mentioned again and during the weeks that followed, Franz sank to an all-time low. He was sleeping for fifteen-hour stretches and when awake would barely eat or talk. He'd given up his job at the garage and personal hygiene was a thing of the past. The fact that he hadn't paid his rent or bills in over a month and Oskar was forced to subsidise his minimal weekly outgoings, was a small price to pay. Four stages in and Oskar was deeply satisfied with how smoothly things were progressing and how good the resulting pictures were. Although he had to admit that the next step was definitely the riskiest.

*

Oskar dragged his eyes away from the mincemeat, trying to push from his mind the memory of Franz's final few weeks. Frau Fettler was now at the front of the queue, her gaze fixed upon the two pieces of veal glinting under the glass.

'I think I'll treat myself to those last two *Wiener Schnitzels*,' she smiled at Herr Schlachter.

Herr Schlachter reached for the roll of greaseproof paper.

'Aren't I a lucky –?'

But the rest of her sentence was lost in a howl of fury as Frau Trundel elbowed her way to the meat counter.

'Those . . .' she pointed a bony finger at the breaded veal. '. . . are mine.'

'Oh?' said Frau Fettler with one raised eyebrow. 'And how did you work that out?'

Frau Trundel glowered from behind her glasses. 'You had the final *Wiener Schnitzel* last week.'

'Did I?' smirked Frau Fettler.

'Which means these ones belong to me and my husband.' Frau Trundel gave Frau Fettler a shove, causing the latter to lurch sideways into a stack of Sauerkraut tins.

'Ladies, ladies!' shouted Herr Schlachter, clearly relishing the level of passion his products were unleashing.

Frau Trundel swivelled towards Herr Schlachter. 'If you could just wrap the veal for *me*.'

But Frau Fettler was having none of it. Springing back from the Sauerkraut stack, she leapt towards Frau Trundel, landing a nifty right hook on the woman's nose and sending her spinning into the counter.

It took Frau Trundel a couple of breaths to recover but seconds later she was running at Frau Fettler and grabbing a hunk of her hair. 'Fat, greedy Frau Fettler!'

'And you,' spat Frau Fettler, face lowered in line with Frau Trundel's on account of the hair pulling, 'are a rude and nasty old hag.'

'Rude and nasty?' shouted Frau Trundel, whose face now resembled a bright red *Blutwurst*. 'That's rich coming from you!'

And then it happened.

'Stop it!' The voice was so loud that Oskar immediately rubber-necked, curious to see who else had joined the queue. But aside from Frau Fettler, Frau Trundel and Herr Schlachter, the butcher's was empty.

'Listen to yourselves!' the voice continued. 'Why do you always have to see the bad in each other? Why can't you just focus on the good for a change?'

The voice was definitely a man's, so that ruled out Frau Fettler and Frau Trundel. Oskar glanced back at Herr Schlachter but the butcher's mouth hadn't moved, so it couldn't have been him. It was only when he saw three pairs of eyes staring straight in his direction, that he realised who the voice belonged to.

Chapter 18

'Hellooo? Anyone home?' Oskar peered down through the trap-door into the cellar where, aside from the piles of empty bottles and beer barrels, he could see very little. He could smell quite a lot though, mostly stale alcohol and vomit.

'Thomas?' he called, holding his breath as he waited for a reply.

Silence.

He poked his head even further into the darkness and frowned. He'd come to the bar for information and now the only person who could help him, wasn't here.

His outburst in the butcher's the day before had freaked him out big style. He could cope with a few small acts of behind-the-scenes kindness such as returning Herr Kozma's wallet or picking Frau Trundel up from the pavement, but to make such a public spectacle of himself was going way too far.

'Thomas!' Oskar hollered, giving it one last go. This time he heard a faint moan from below.

Trying not to brush against the cobwebby wall, Oskar stepped down onto the cellar's soft floor. He couldn't find the light this time so he forced himself forward through the clammy darkness towards what at first had looked like a pile of old cushions.

'Is that you, Thomas?' He tapped what he hoped was Thomas's shoulder.

A hand, along with a bottle, emerged from the pile and Oskar watched the neck of the bottle rise to what was presumably Thomas's mouth.

'Don't you think you've had enough?' Oskar leant forward to take it from Thomas's fingers.

'Leave me alone,' Thomas growled.

'Sorry, Thomas,' said Oskar, setting the bottle down on the ground. 'That's not an option.'

It took several minutes for Oskar to manoeuvre Thomas into a sitting position and then to help him stand so he could be guided towards the stairs. He was surprisingly thin beneath the padding of clothes and could barely walk, mumbling to himself through a haze of brandy fumes.

Upstairs in the light again, Oskar settled Thomas into the armchair by the fireplace.

His nose was pulped to a dark red mass and there was a gouge in his right temple with blood streaking down his cheek and onto his already filthy shirt.

'We should clean you up a bit,' said Oskar, rummaging under the bar for a drying up cloth. He walked back over to the armchair.

'Go away!' said Thomas.

Oskar shook his head. He spat on the end of the cloth and gently dabbed at Thomas's bloody cheek, making sure to avoid the cut.

'Please!' Thomas's voice was razored with such raw pain that Oskar stopped for a moment.

'I'm not leaving you like this,' said Oskar. 'We still need to wash off some of that vomit on your shirt.' He returned to the bar and found a glass, which he was just filling when he saw

Thomas topple forwards, cracking his head on the fireguard before crashing to the floor.

Oskar crouched beside Thomas. 'You're going to kill yourself at this rate.' He took the cushion from the armchair and placed it under Thomas's head. Then he removed his own coat, laying it over his body. Seconds later, Thomas was asleep.

Oskar leant against the end of the bar, watching the jerky rise and fall of Thomas's chest, unsure of what to do next. He didn't want to leave him alone. What if he was sick again and choked on his own vomit? Or had an alcohol-induced fit?

With the cellar door wide open so that he could hear if Thomas woke and to give himself some light, Oskar tiptoed down the stairs once more and headed for the far corner. He opened the Carl Zeiss box and sifted through the research papers until he found two files with promising-looking titles. Then he hurried back upstairs again and sat down in the armchair. Thomas was still snoring on the floor when he opened the first file:

Consciousness and Matter

Since the early twentieth-century scientists have known that everything in the universe is made up of energy. This energy vibrates at different levels according to the density of the matter, so a rock, for example, will have a much lower vibration or frequency than light or electricity. Recent developments in the study of consciousness have revealed that thoughts are also a form of energy with their own frequency. Negative thoughts vibrate at a lower rate, while positive thoughts vibrate at a higher one. Since everything is interconnected at a subatomic level, it therefore follows that thoughts, like any other energy form, have the ability to affect their environment.

Having read about the work of a Japanese scientist, who specialises in researching how thoughts and consciousness can affect water, my research team and I set up a similar, highly controlled experiment. Using water taken from one source, we poured it into eight separate bottles, labelling each one with a different word. The first four were labelled with positive words (love, gratitude, forgiveness and empathy) and the second four were given negative labels (fear, hate, despair, greed). Laboratory assistants were then instructed to take one bottle each, observe it closely for ten minutes while thinking about the word on its label. This was repeated every day for one week. Afterwards the water from each bottle was frozen so that the liquid molecules crystallised and could be photographed. In the bottles that were marked with positive words, the crystals showed a natural symmetry and sharp, clear colours. The bottles of water labelled with negative words produced distorted, asymmetrical crystals with clouded colours.

This experiment was repeated eighteen times over the next year and each time the outcome was the same. Scientists from several institutions in Germany and America were invited to witness and document every stage of the process and their findings can be read at the end of this report.

If a simple thought is powerful enough to change the molecular structure of water, it raises some profound questions about the connection between mind and matter. For it should not be forgotten that the human body, and indeed our planet, is made up of 70% water . . .

'What are you doing here?' Thomas had woken and his voice was slurred with alcohol.

'I'm keeping you under observation,' said Oskar.

Thomas struggled to sit up. 'Well, you can go now.'

'No way,' said Oskar. 'You need food.' Without giving Thomas time to protest, he hopped up out of the armchair and scooted into the kitchen.

Still thinking about what he had just read, Oskar inspected

the contents of the fridge for something to cook. He pulled out a carton of eggs and some butter and on the sideboard he found a loaf of bread. While the eggs were scrambling, he dropped four slices into the toaster and as he did so, a snapshot of a childhood fantasy flashed into his mind. In it, he was standing in a kitchen next to his father who was making eggy bread for their breakfast. The two of them were chatting about their plans for that day's visit to Berlin's National Gallery.

*

The hitch hike from Bremerhaven to Berlin took around seven hours, mainly because Oskar was forced to change cars after the first driver who'd picked him up, tried to grope him. He arrived at 8 a.m., cold and exhausted. The city seemed vast in comparison with Hamburg and Bremerhaven, with huge grey buildings looming above him, blocking out the light and throwing shadows across the wide streets.

His head was still aching from where Gunther had thrown him against the wall, and his arm felt like it had been dislocated. But he didn't have time to rest. So after asking for directions, he took the U-Bahn to Kreuzberg, his father's old neighbourhood, where he desperately hoped his dad still lived. But when he arrived, it was nothing like he'd imagined. Instead of cafés and restaurants with writers and painters discussing books and art, all Oskar could see was a few doner kebab shops, some rundown bars and a lot of junkies and drunks.

He wandered around for most of the day, allowing himself just one portion of chips so that he didn't eat into his savings. Eventually at around 10 p.m. he found somewhere he thought might be safe enough for him to sleep – behind a pillar at Kottbusser Tor station.

That first night, Oskar's thoughts kept him awake until dawn. Over and over he asked the same questions. Why hadn't his mother listened to him when he told her that he was un-happy? How could she have let Gunther hurt him like that? Why did she choose that brute over her own son?

Jonas was right. The world was a shit hole.

It was dark in his little corner behind the pillar and Oskar wished he could have brought his night light, a dome-shaped painted pottery house with its family of little rabbits snuggled inside. Lying awake, he imagined crawling in with them and sit-ting at Father Rabbit's slippered feet.

The station was very noisy. There were lots of people with cans of beer and bottles of vodka, and lots of arguments. When Oskar crept out around midnight to try and find some news-papers to keep himself warm, a man stopped him and asked him if he wanted to buy some 'H'.

The next morning Oskar started his search in a café at Heinrich-Heine-Platz.

'I'm looking for my father,' he said to the guy who was wiping down the counter. 'He's called Werner and he's got a scar down the left side of his cheek. I think he's a writer.'

'Ah, I see.' The guy nodded and for a split second Oskar thought that he saw a flicker of recognition in his eyes. But then the man started to chuckle.

'Good luck,' he said, tossing the dirty cloth into the sink. 'There are probably about a hundred so-called writers called Werner in Kreuzberg, all deeply scarred in one way or another.'

That first day Oskar went into around twenty different cafés and restaurants, but no one knew his dad. In the evening he went back to Kottbusser Tor and this time he found some newspapers and cardboard by the kiosk, which he used to create a makeshift bed for himself behind the pillar.

In those first few days he tried not to think about his mother any more. He needed to concentrate on his future now, most importantly how to get hold of some more money because his two hundred Euros would be soon gone.

On the sixth night, just as Oskar was unpacking his cardboard bed, a man with a long grey ponytail approached him.

'Would you like to earn some extra cash?' he asked.

'What would I have to do?' said Oskar. According to Jonas, there was a catch to everything in this world.

'Just deliver a small package to an address near here,' said the man with a smile. 'The easiest thirty Euros you'll ever earn.'

Oskar agreed, more because he didn't have much choice at this point and he needed money, wherever it came from. But he wasn't so naive to think it was just a package. It would definitely have something dodgy inside.

They went to a nearby flat and picked up the brown, envelope-sized package. The man, whose name was Rolf, gave Oskar the address of the apartment where it was to be delivered, and told him how to get there. Ten minutes later Oskar was standing in a hallway, handing the package to a woman in a dressing gown. Within half an hour he was back at the station.

'Would you like to do that for me again?' said Rolf.

'Yes, please,' said Oskar.

*

By the time Oskar had finished making the scrambled eggs, he wasn't hungry. Instead he watched Thomas take a few mouthfuls then push the food around the plate. As he studied his swollen face and bloody nose, he realised that he had absolutely no desire to paint Thomas in such a state. If he was going to paint him at all, then it would have to wait until he had recovered.

'Why are you doing this for me?' Thomas had put down his fork and was looking at Oskar.

'Because I want to,' said Oskar. That morning he'd intended

to ask Thomas more about his work at Carl Zeiss and what he knew about the effects of optical lenses, but now that could wait.

'Why did you give up your career?' asked Oskar.

There was a short pause while Thomas downed the last of his coffee. 'I didn't have a choice.'

Oskar waited for him to continue, but Thomas was already standing, grabbing clumsily at the plates.

'Something must have happened,' said Oskar. 'What was it?'

Thomas stacked the plates on top of each other, squishing the uneaten scrambled eggs. But his hands were shaking so much that the top two plates slipped and smashed on the floor below. He sat down again, head bowed. 'You really want to know?' he asked quietly.

'I do,' said Oskar.

Thomas raised his head and looked Oskar dead in the eye. 'I killed two people.'

Chapter 19

Oskar was at home snacking on a Dr. Oetker vanilla pudding. He'd sprinkled some chocolate buttons on top, one of which was slowly dissolving on his tongue as he stared out of his window. Behind him, a fire crackled in the stove. After Greta's lesson, he'd pretty much nailed fire-building and now he had one burning most days. That morning he'd even made one for Thomas.

During the month since Oskar had helped Thomas up from the cellar, he had taken to dropping into the bar about three times a week. Sometimes he and Thomas would just sit in silence while Oskar sipped his lemonade and Thomas stared at the television. Other times Oskar would whip up a little snack for them both. Although Oskar had tried to get Thomas to talk more about what had happened, Thomas made it clear that the subject was a no-go zone.

But that didn't stop Oskar wondering. Had Thomas killed the two people by accident? Did he know them? How long ago was it? He really couldn't imagine that Thomas could have done such a thing on purpose, in which case what a terrible thing to happen. No wonder he looked so tormented all the time.

Christmas was spent alone and although Oskar didn't feel

like celebrating, he did treat himself to four Kinder Surprise. Assembling the toys was the highlight of Christmas Day, especially the red sailboat, which he perched proudly on top of his medical dictionary. But the ridiculously complicated blue tractor had been tossed out of the window in frustration. It was only as the evening lengthened that Oskar allowed himself to think about the Christmases of his childhood: helping his mother stir the candied fruits into her special *Stollen*; hanging chocolate bells on the yule tree together; waiting with her excitedly in the hallway for the arrival of the *Christkind* bringing presents for all the children in the apartment block.

*

Oskar finished his final mouthful of vanilla pudding and glanced at his alarm clock. He'd set it for 2 p.m. because he didn't want to be late for his regular Wednesday afternoon appointment with Frau Miesel. So having washed his face and given his quiff a boosting backcomb, he set off.

Frau Miesel had already made the coffee by the time he arrived, so Oskar laid out on a plate the four white doughy pastries that Herr Kozma had given him after their supper two nights before to celebrate New Year. Then they both took up position in the leatherette armchairs.

'Herr Kozma is quite a baker,' said Oskar, tucking into the first *pogácsa*.

Frau Miesel looked down at the plate. 'Shop-bought, no doubt.'

Oskar shook his head. 'Home-baked,' he sighed. 'Just imagine if the village bakery made such things!'

Frau Miesel made a humphing sound and stared at the telly where an advert showed three people dressed as giant toothbrushes dancing around a massive white molar. As the human toothbrushes grew more frenzied in their movements, Oskar began to giggle and soon Frau Miesel joined in. They were still giggling when the opening credits to *Die Schwarzwaldklinik* appeared.

It was an exciting week, mainly because Doktor Brinkmann had fallen for Christa, one of the new nurses. Repeated corridor encounters had led to an invitation from the doctor to a canteen lunch on the pretext of discussing a patient.

'He's not responding,' said Doktor Brinkmann, sitting down opposite Christa with his beef and dumpling stew.

Christa nodded and toyed with her bread roll while staring straight into the doctor's eyes. Seconds later, the camera cut to the patient, the same young man who had been diagnosed with acute depression and whose sunken eyes and skeletal frame made Oskar shift uncomfortably in his seat.

*

Franz

Franz was now about as depressed as it was possible for a living human to be. He rarely came out of his bedroom and when he did, he would slump on the sofa, staring at the walls. His skin was a mass of pustules and he'd lost so much weight that his jeans were hanging off his hips. It had been almost ten weeks since his arrival, and the project was pretty much bang on schedule.

'This is Heike,' said Oskar, standing in the sitting room doorway and gesturing towards the petite young woman with long chestnut brown hair beside him.

'Hi,' said Heike, who was dressed in jeans, boots and a clean white T-shirt.

'She's the daughter of a friend from Hamburg. You don't mind if she crashes on the sofa for a few days?'

'S'fine,' said Franz from the sofa.

'She's new in Berlin so she might need some looking after.' Oskar smiled over at Heike, then back at Franz. 'I thought I'd make dinner tonight if you fancy joining us.'

That night Oskar cooked one of his favourite dishes – *Bratwurst* with gravy, red cabbage and potatoes. Just as he was dishing it up, Franz appeared from his bedroom, book in hand and silently sat down at the table.

'What are you reading, Franz?' asked Heike.

'Jus' some sci-fi.' Franz's mumbling was getting worse. Soon he'd need an interpreter.

'What's it about?' Heike's voice was so childlike, it was hard to believe that she was twenty-three.

Franz shrugged. 'It's about a schizophrenic man who falls in love with a centaur that lives inside a giant cyborg in orbit around Saturn.' This was the longest sentence that Oskar had heard from Franz's mouth in three weeks.

'Groovy,' said Heike.

'I hope I haven't over-cooked the *Bratwurst*.' Oskar set a plate in front of Franz and one in front of Heike.

'Right,' he said, placing a hand on both Franz and Heike's shoulders. 'I'm off out to a friend's exhibition. You two will be OK, won't you?'

The first evening set the routine for the next fortnight. Oskar would prepare supper, serve it, then hotfoot it out of the flat, leaving Franz and Heike alone with two bottles of wine and a large stash of spliff.

Given that Heike was a professional, it took a little longer than expected for Franz to crack, but two weeks later on a balmy Wednesday night, when Oskar arrived back from Risiko's in the early hours, the sitting room was empty. From inside Franz's bedroom came the sound of Heike's giggle.

The next morning Franz had shaved and was wearing a fresh T-shirt and a shy smile. By the end of the week, a new tube of Hydrocortisone had appeared in the bathroom cabinet, Franz's Sunday fry up was once again on the menu and he'd even rung the garage to see if he could get back his job there.

'She's amazing.' Franz shook his head in wonder as he and Oskar sat in the kitchen over a late Sunday breakfast while Heike was in the bathroom, doing what she did every day under the pretence of taking a shower.

'I've never felt like this before.'

Oskar selected the crunchiest piece of toast from the rack. 'Good for you, Franz.'

Franz grinned. 'And she actually likes me.'

Oskar spread a thick layer of butter on the toast, before reaching for the family-sized jar of Nutella.

'It's thanks to you, Oskar.' Franz gazed out of the window as a pigeon landed on the sill, quietly cooing to itself.

Oskar unscrewed the lid on the Nutella and plunged his knife inside. 'Just being a friend, Franz.'

*

Oskar stared blankly at the television. Christa and Doktor Brinkmann had finished their lunch and were standing outside his office. Christa's hand was resting lightly on Doktor Brinkmann's arm. But Oskar couldn't concentrate because his head was still churning.

'More coffee, Frau M?' he said, desperate for a diversion.

Frau Miesel clucked impatiently without looking away from the screen. Oskar went into the kitchen and poured himself a glass of water. Thinking about Franz and what he had done to him was making him feel sick.

He filled the kettle and found the coffee in the cupboard

above the sink. Next to it was a row of cookbooks and one homemade recipe book. When he pulled the latter out, a little puff of flour clouded the air.

Inside, the pages were filled with recipes for everything a bakery could possibly sell – *Apfelstrudel*, blackcurrant cheesecake, plum tart, cherry flan, Viennese Whirls ... Oskar closed the book and placed it back in the cupboard, knocking a white oblong packet out onto the sideboard. He grabbed it and marched back into the sitting room.

'Why are you taking these?' Oskar brandished the pills in front of Frau Miesel.

Frau Miesel squinted up at the packet. 'Herr Krank prescribed them.'

'Have you any idea what Equavol can do to you?' Oskar thrust the packet closer to Frau Miesel's face. 'Nausea? Dizziness? Distorted vision? Ring any bells?'

Frau Miesel shrugged. 'Well, as you know my eyesight isn't great. And everyone gets a little nauseous now and again.' She stared at Oskar. 'Why are you so concerned?'

Oskar sat down, still clutching the pills. 'Well, it just so happens that I don't want to see you get sick because I really ...' he coughed and fiddled with the packet. '... care about you.'

Frau Miesel's eyes widened in surprise before her face softened into a smile.

Oskar coughed again. 'In a mother-son way, of course.'

Two hours later Oskar was striding up and down Greta's sitting room, having hurried there as soon as he knew she'd be back from the chemist's. Since leaving Frau Miesel's his head had been spinning with all sorts of scary scenarios. Maybe Frau Miesel's poor eyesight would cause her to trip down those steep stairs. Perhaps a fit of Equavol-induced dizziness would overcome her, say in the kitchen while she was cooking supper and she'd slump to the floor, leaving a frying pan to catch fire and engulf her in flames. Or maybe she already *had* high blood pressure in which case the pills would act like a torch to a funeral pyre, triggering who knew what? An aneurism? A stroke? Cardiac arrest?

'Calm down.' Greta sat in the armchair, watching Oskar pace. She'd changed out of her uniform and was wearing a pair of jeans and a pale grey jumper.

'Calm down?' Oskar shouted as he reached the yucca plant in the alcove for the fifth time. 'Krank's playing with people's lives!'

Greta was quiet for a moment. 'I agree we should do something and I'll definitely talk to his patients again about reducing their dosage, but Krank's away right now.'

Oskar did a U-turn and started the journey back to the pot of sage on the windowsill. 'Another business trip funded by Glücksvolk?'

Greta nodded.

'Can you get evidence of that?'

'I already have.'

'Then surely, with proof of all the bribes and backhanders and some statements from his patients, we can build up a case to take to the Medical Authorities.'

Greta looked dubious. 'Krank's a clever man.'

'*Was* a clever man,' said Oskar, shaking a fist. 'But who's the smart boy now!'

Greta invited Oskar to stay for supper but had turned down his offer of help to make it. So while she grated potatoes for the *Rösti*, he lit a fire in the hearth then wandered over to her bookcase, bottle of beer in hand. Aside from her homeopathic course books, she had many of the classics, and almost every one of them brought back memories of those hours he'd spent reading in preparation to meet his dad. Glancing through them, he could still feel his fascination with Oskar Matzerath in Günther Grass's *Tin Drum;* his shivery dread at the fate of Joseph K in Kafka's *The Trial;* his sniggery delight at the tuberculosis-riddled 'Half-a-lung club' of Thomas Mann's *The Magic Mountain*. He could even list all those questions about the books that he was planning to ask his father when they finally met.

*

Within a month, Oskar was earning over two hundred Euros a week from his 'deliveries'. Of course, he now knew that it was heroin in the packages, but how else was he going to earn such good money at his age? As Jonas had told him so many times – you had to look after yourself in this world, because no one else was going to.

Rolf had offered to rent him a small room, but Oskar hadn't taken it. He wanted to save as much cash as he could. But he wasn't sleeping behind the pillar at Kottbusser Tor anymore, instead he had found an empty shop nearby, whose side window he was able to open. Wriggling through the small space, he'd silently thanked Jonas yet again, this time for showing off his ability to gain access to any school building he wanted. No padlock, window or even tightly-screwed grate was too much for Jonas. Oskar was going to need that sort of skill in his new life.

For the next five months, Oskar spent his free time visiting every café and bar he came across, not just in Kreuzberg but further afield in Neukölln, Moabit and Wedding. By late September he had accepted that he'd probably never find his father, so he forced himself to forget all the childhood fantasies. He would focus on other things instead, like becoming a proper artist and creating his own identity through his paintings – an identity that nothing and no one could take from him.

It was now that he decided to change his surname. Not only to stop his mother from finding him, but also to advance his career. Like any successful artist, he'd need to invent a brand for himself, something that summed up his mission to focus on the darkness and misery of the world. So what better name than *Dunkelblick*?

With this new name came a whole new look: a second-hand black leather coat (much too big but at least it kept him warm at night); black jeans and a black polo neck. To compliment the outfit (and make sure that not even the police could identify him from photos), he ditched the schoolboy fringe, dyed his hair black and gave himself a quiff.

The inspiration for Oskar's first series of pictures came from the drunks of Kottbusser Tor, with their bloated red faces, tangled hair and industrial-sized bottles of vodka. Having painted eight of the series, Oskar showed them to a small outsider gallery in Kreuzberg, who agreed to take him on, partly, the owner admitted, because of the novelty of his age.

Seven months later, shortly after his fourteenth birthday Oskar had his first exhibition: *Hauptsache Bewusstlos!* (with the English subtitle *Let's Get Trolleyed!* for any potential English clients). It was held in a disused brewery in Pfuelstraße and although most of the guests were from the neighbourhood, there was a journalist from the art magazine *Spike*, who later wrote a one-page article on Berlin's darkest *enfant terrible* artist.

Over the next eighteen months, which saw a successful second exhibition entitled *The Sorrows of Young Oskar*, his work sold steadily. Not for huge amounts, but enough to keep him fed, clothed and able to buy good quality canvases and oil paints.

Yet Oskar never lost his fascination for the drunks. At least once a week he would slip back to sketch the faces of those lost souls. It was on one of these visits, on a freezing February afternoon almost three years after his move to Berlin, that he noticed a tall, dark-haired man slumped against the railings outside the train station. There was something about the man's face that drew Oskar near enough to spot the scar.

'Excuse me,' said Oskar, his heart thundering in his chest. 'Is your name Werner?'

The man glanced at him then took a swig from his can of Pils. 'Why do you want to know?'

'Because I think you might be my . . .' After years of rehearsing for this exact moment, the words jammed in Oskar's throat.

'Oi, Werner!' A woman with plastic bags on her feet stumbled out from behind a nearby wheelie bin. 'Who's your new friend?'

The man in front of Oskar shrugged then began to laugh, but the laugh turned into a cough and he spat a large glob of reddish phlegm onto the pavement by Oskar's foot.

Oskar quickly swiped away the tear that was sliding down his cheek. 'I'd actually like . . . to paint you.' Of course, this wasn't what he wanted, but to say what he did want was impossible.

'How much are you paying?' The man dragged his coat sleeve across his mouth, leaving a slimy red smear.

'What about thirty-five Euros an hour?' said Oskar, trying to stop the shake in his voice. That should be enough to make sure his father came back.

'*Knete!*' A hand with blackened nails was thrust towards Oskar, who pulled thirty-five Euros from his pocket.

'See you tomorrow then?' said Oskar, hoping that Werner hadn't noticed his wet eyes.

'Sure,' said Werner, his dad, already turning away while cramming the money into his trouser pocket.

*

'Oskar?' Greta's voice echoed through the tunnels of Oskar's mind.

150

She was standing behind him, holding the crockery. 'You can lay the table now.'

'Oh, yep, sure.' Oskar stuffed the memories back below the surface as he'd learnt to do and took the knives and forks from Greta. As their hands met, he felt a pulse of electricity pass between them.

Setting the table, he watched Greta from behind as she chopped the vegetables: the smooth curve of her neck; the wisps of blonde hair escaping from her pony tail; the two wings of her shoulder blades beneath her jumper . . .

Task completed, Oskar was back at the shelves. He pulled out a philosophy book, the cover of which featured a man with long, black curly hair, whose face he somehow recognised.

'Who's this guy?' He held up the slim volume for Greta to see.

'Baruch Spinoza,' said Greta, walking over to stand beside Oskar. 'He was a seventeenth-century philosopher and professional lens grinder.' Greta took a sip of her beer. 'He died prematurely from tuberculosis after inhaling too much dust from optical lenses.'

Oskar read from the back cover: '*Spinoza was an early advocate of the theory that a single unified substance beneath the universe's fragmented surface connects everything within our universe . . .*' he paused. 'I think Einstein said something like that as well,' he said, turning the book over. 'That a human being is part of a whole, not separated, as people often believe.'

Greta chinked her beer against his. 'I'll drink to that.'

Oskar smiled and nodded, then bent his head to study the drawing of the philosopher with the black, curly hair. Now he remembered where he had seen him before – in that liver-fuelled dream almost four months ago. Goosebumps prickled his arms and neck, but he wasn't sure if it was because Greta was standing so close to him or if it was because of the picture.

The cabbage dish topped with crispy potato and grated cheese had been eaten and Greta was drying up. Oskar stood next to her, trying to look useful by occasionally repositioning a stray piece of cutlery.

'I like your jumper,' he said, fiddling with the cheese grater. 'It's pretty.' He fiddled a bit more, staring at the tilt of her nose.

'You look very different from the day I first saw you,' he added. He couldn't really say *why* – it wasn't as if she'd chopped all her hair off or suddenly started wearing a crop top. 'Can I ask you a question, Greta?'

Greta hung the drying-up cloth against the stove and tucked a strand of hair behind her ear. 'As long as it's not what my favourite animal is or whether I've read Eckhart Tolle – we've covered those already.'

'Have you ever . . . been with . . . a man?' Oskar coughed and pretended to be fascinated by a meat fork.

'You mean have I had a boyfriend?' Greta laughed. 'Yes, Oskar, I have.'

'And when did you break up . . . assuming that you have broken up?'

'Just before I moved here – about eight months ago.'

'No one since?' Oskar's voice lifted a little.

Greta shook her head. 'Sadly Herr Kozma turned me down.'

'Ha ha,' said Oskar. 'So . . . would you ever think about . . . I mean, do you think you could . . . ?' He nudged a serving spoon a few centimetres along the sideboard, trying to find the courage to say what he wanted. But because his eyes were on Greta and he'd forgotten about the meat fork and the cheese grater, all three of them collided and clattered to the kitchen floor.

It was past midnight and the fire had burnt down to a few glowing embers, wrapping Greta's sitting room in a soft orange light.

Through the window, suspended in the dark velvet sky, the moon glowed like a fat pearly eye. In the distance the soft hoot of an owl threaded its way from the forest.

Oskar and Greta's chairs were pulled up close to the fire, side by side. On Oskar's lap was a book of poetry that Greta had just been reading from.

'So where *are* all the paintings that you're supposed to be sending to the gallery?' asked Greta.

Oskar shook his head. 'Nowhere. I had a deadline for the end of December and that's long gone. In fact, I was meant to be back in Berlin by now, but I'm not sure what I would do there.'

'How are you going to live, if you're not earning anything?'

Oskar shrugged. 'I've still got a few savings left, but that won't last me beyond March, now that I'm paying my own rent. After that, who knows?'

'Why *are* you still here?' asked Greta

'Not sure,' said Oskar. 'Maybe it's because I like the poetry,' he laughed, pointing to the collection of Goethe's poems in his lap. The page was still open at the one Greta had recited by heart earlier in the evening – *Epirrhema*.

One sentence seemed to stand out for Oskar, and he read it aloud again.

'Nothing is inside and nothing is outside,
For what is within is without.'

'I love those two lines,' said Greta. 'That the world we see outside is just a reflection of what's inside us.' She shifted around to face Oskar. 'Don't you think they're beautiful?'

'Yes,' said Oskar, unable to stop himself from falling into the grey-green oceans of her eyes. 'They are.'

Chapter 20

Oskar was lying on his bed, doing some deep breathing. It was four in the afternoon and he hadn't left the house since returning from Greta's the night before. As he took another lungful of air, he let their final moments together glide through his mind: the silken brush of Greta's warm skin as she reached up to say goodbye; the soft swell of her lips; the murmur of her breath on his cheek.

Replaying these images frame by frame, Oskar wondered yet again why he hadn't kissed her. But part of him already knew the answer – and it lay in those shadowy figures that drifted through his dreams with increasing regularity.

First there was Bettina, the film student, who he'd met in a bar on Oranienstraße when he was seventeen. She was two years older and her heart was still broken from her previous boyfriend. Winning her over wasn't easy, but when Oskar did, some nine weeks later, it took just two minutes to break it all over again. Next was Paula, the homesick eighteen-year old Spanish girl, who was so distraught when Oskar ended their short liaison that she took to wandering the cold Berlin streets in just a T-shirt. Then came Sandra, the trainee veterinary nurse also recovering from a bruised heart, who gave up her studies and hacked off her waist-length hair . . .

Even now, Oskar could recall each young woman in the greatest of detail – Bettina's tentative smile, Paula's onyx eyes, Sandra's auburn hair. The longer he thought about them, the more he could feel his cheeks burn. A wave of shame washed through him, layered with sadness and regret at what he had done to those vulnerable young women.

Oskar was still lying on his bed when he heard a loud thump outside. He jumped up and skidded down to the window so he could poke his head out. Only Herr Schlachter was visible down on the street, hosing his wellies by the butcher's.

Oskar thrust his head even further out of the window. And there, just by his front door lay a crumpled heap of winter coat from which protruded two swollen legs encased in a pair of beige support stockings.

'Are you alright?' Oskar gave Frau Zwoll's arm a little rub. Her teeth were chattering and behind her heavy black glasses, her eyes were half shut.

'Frau Zwoll?'

A shudder passed through the woman's body. 'Home,' she wheezed, in a gust of alcohol fumes.

'Home it is,' said Oskar, although he had no idea how he was going to move Frau Zwoll, given her size.

He took her left arm and placed it around his shoulders, then he scrambled up onto one knee, hefting Frau Zwoll with him.

'Up we go,' he said, in a strained voice as the first of Frau Zwoll's swollen legs jerked forward and found its footing on the snow-packed pavement. A minute later, having recovered from the effort, Frau Zwoll repeated the action with the second leg. Then with a gargantuan heave from Oskar, she was finally upright.

The ten minute stagger back to Frau Zwoll's house was

155

followed by the long climb up her front stairs to the sitting room. While Oskar pushed from behind, Frau Zwoll winched herself up by the banisters although she needed to stop every few seconds to catch her breath. So slow was their progress that Oskar imagined the seasons passing outside, winter turning to spring, mountain snow melting and meadows blooming with yellow and white alpine flowers.

When they'd finally made it to the summit, Oskar slumped to the floor, back against the wall, able only to give an exhausted whoop. Frau Zwoll flopped forward against the landing's banisters, groaning like an ancient sea monster surfacing from a long spell underwater.

Oskar had regained his breath and was standing with his back to the sitting room window, while Frau Zwoll was beached on her mauve sofa. She was breathing heavily and the stretchy support stockings had slithered down her legs, flopping around her ankles.

Oskar glanced around him, taking in the pile of Schnapps bottles by the door, the huge TV and beneath it, the basket filled with balls of wool and wooden knitting needles.

'My granny used to knit,' he said, 'mostly yellow tank tops for my grandpa.' Oskar paused, remembering with an unexpected tug of sadness how he never again heard the click of her wooden needles after the death of Opi Blumental.

'Oskar?' Frau Zwoll's swollen hand was stretching out from the sofa and her face was a worrying shade of blue. 'Inhaler,' she puffed. 'Bathroom.'

Racing next door, Oskar rifled in the bathroom cabinet amongst the aspirin bottles, arthritis bangles and support bandages. Eventually he spotted the inhaler beside a bottle of beta-blockers and six packets of Equavol. He grabbed the inhaler, ran back into the sitting room and handed it to Frau Zwoll, who jammed the plastic grey tube into her mouth and sucked noisily. Slowly her breath steadied and the wheezing subsided.

'Thought you were a goner just now,' Oskar laughed nervously.

Frau Zwoll smiled. 'It'll take a lot more than an asthma attack to finish me off!' She waved her hand in the direction of the kitchen behind her. 'How about a little Schnapps to celebrate my survival?'

Out in the kitchen, Oskar by-passed the bottles of Schnapps by the bread bin, taking a carton of orange juice from the fridge instead. All around him on the sideboard were half-eaten packets of crisps, open jars of gherkins and bowls of what looked like mouldy pork scratchings. There was also a massive cookie tin and next to it, a family-sized jar of Nutella, which Oskar found himself staring at.

*

Franz

Oskar could never have guessed what a perfect boyfriend his flatmate would make. Within a week Franz was buying Heike boxes of her favourite *Mozartkugeln* chocolates, organising surprise picnics in Viktoriapark, giving her massages when she said her limbs ached.

As for Heike, Oskar had to admit she was one of the best actresses around. But then he'd known that from the second he'd spotted her, standing on that grey stretch of road in Neukölln.

It was her fresh face that had set her apart from the other women stationed beneath the nearby lampposts. But that childlike appearance was all part of the act. As soon as Oskar heard her speak, he knew she was sharp as a newly sterilised needle.

The deal between Oskar and Heike had been worked out there and then. Food and lodging, plus enough cash to cover her twice daily fix. The initial trial period of one month would stretch to six weeks if things took longer than expected. After that, there'd be a lump sum of two thousand Euros and a cheery wave goodbye.

It was a rainy Thursday evening, four weeks into Heike's stay and she and Franz were curled up on the sitting room sofa together. Franz was rolling another spliff.

'Want something a bit stronger?' Heike pulled a small paper wrap from her jeans pocket.

'Huh?' Franz was already pretty stoned.

Heike kissed him fleetingly on the lips and took the half-rolled joint from his fingers. 'Let me make it and see what you think.'

She turned away slightly and tapped some of the wrap's brown powder into the open Rizla. Then she re-rolled it, lit it and inhaled deeply before passing the joint to Franz.

Franz took a long drag, exhaling slowly. 'What is it?'

Heike smiled and ruffled his hair. 'It's got some complicated name I can never remember. My uncle's a chemist and he makes it in Hamburg.'

Franz inhaled another lungful, before offering the joint to Oskar.

'No, thanks,' said Oskar, patting his chest. 'It might bring on my bronchitis.'

Heike took the joint once more and inhaled hard, handing it back to Franz who did the same. Within fifteen minutes he was leaning his head back against the sofa, staring up at the light fitting. A wide almost beatific smile garlanded his face.

'That's good gear,' he murmured sleepily. '*Really* good gear.'

Oskar and Heike exchanged a brief glance. The hardest part was over.

*

When Oskar returned to the sitting room, Frau Zwoll was half asleep, covered by a baby blue crocheted blanket. Her eyes opened as he set down the tray with two glasses of orange juice and a plateful of chocolate cookies.

'Where's my Schnapps?'

'I thought juice might be better,' said Oskar. 'It's not a great idea to mix alcohol with antidepressants.'

'What are you, some kind of underage doctor?'

'No,' said Oskar. 'I just don't want to see –.'

'Just give me some bloody biscuits then.' Frau Zwoll snatched two cookies from the plate. The first she crammed whole into her mouth and the second she tossed onto the small side table, next to a cork coaster.

'Do you know what happened out there on the street?' asked Oskar, taking a cookie for himself although he wasn't really hungry.

Frau Zwoll chewed and swallowed. 'I just felt a bit dizzy.'

'I noticed a bottle of beta-blockers and some Equavol in the bathroom cabinet,' said Oskar. 'Is Herr Krank treating you for high blood pressure as well as depression?'

Frau Zwoll nodded, flicking the crumbs from her chest.

'You realise that Equavol can *cause* high blood pressure.'

Frau Zwoll laughed. 'I doubt Herr Krank would give it to me if that was the case.'

'No, really!' said Oskar. 'I read about it in my book.'

'Then it must be true.' Frau Zwoll laughed. 'Dr. Dunkelblick!'

'I'm just worried about you.'

'Don't bother,' said Frau Zwoll and stretched for the second biscuit – or at least what she must have assumed was the second biscuit. Before Oskar could say anything it was in her mouth and she was chewing determinedly.

'I think you're eating the coaster,' said Oskar.

Frau Zwoll frowned, poked one pudgy index finger and

159

thumb into her mouth and extracted the soggy piece of half-masticated cork. After inspecting it, she dropped it back on the side table.

'I assume you bought your glasses from Herr Krank,' said Oskar. 'Do they actually make your eyesight better?'

'Of course,' Frau Zwoll snorted.

'But eating coasters isn't exactly *normal*.' Oskar nodded at her glasses. 'Would you let me try them on? I'm wondering if I need glasses too.'

It was the best excuse Oskar could come up with and Frau Zwoll seemed to swallow it, because she handed them over.

'Just as I thought,' said Oskar, staring through the lenses at the grey room around him. 'When did you last go to a proper optician's?' He passed the glasses back to Frau Zwoll.

'Can't remember. No wait,' Frau Zwoll laughed. 'I had an eye test here in the village last October.'

'You went to Dr. Sehle!' said Oskar. 'What did you see?'

'Oh, all sorts. Colours, music, lights. A regular little magic show.' Frau Zwoll let out a peal of laughter, then picked up the remaining biscuit from the side table and took a bite.

'Maybe it wasn't a magic show,' said Oskar.

Frau Zwoll looked over at him, forehead folded into a deep frown.

'Maybe it was . . .' Oskar paused, searching for the right words, '. . . another possible reality.'

Frau Zwoll chuckled, but that soon turned into a guffaw then moved onto a nasty choke. Her cheeks turned the colour of an aubergine and her eyes bulged like a bullfrog.

Oskar leapt up and gave her a thwack on the back and the biscuit flew out and landed on the blue crocheted blanket.

'Has anything strange happened to you since you had the test?' Oskar asked a little later when she had recovered.

'What do you mean?'

Oskar wandered over to the window, through which he could see the pink rays of the setting sun in the distance.

'Well, do things look different?'

'No.'

Oskar continued to gaze at the pink glow spreading across the snowy mountain peaks. He let out a little sigh.

'It's a sunset,' said Frau Zwoll behind him. 'Get over it.'

'Frau Zwoll?' said Oskar. 'Have you ever come across the idea that the outer world reflects the inner?' He looked back at the sun, which had almost disappeared except for a soft brushstroke of orange on the horizon. 'Or that if you cannot see the beauty inside of you, then you won't see it outside?'

He looked around to see if the silence meant that Frau Zwoll agreed with him, but she was fast asleep, her face oddly beautiful despite resembling a collapsed blancmange.

Chapter 21

Oskar was psyching himself up for the showdown. After witnessing Frau Zwoll's collapse, too many lives were at stake for him to turn a blind eye now. He really needed to confront Krank because if he waited any longer, someone was going to snuff it.

Having selected his outfit, he backcombed his quiff to maximum density, puffed up his chest and ran through his speech once more. Twenty minutes later he was standing in the chemist's. Greta was nowhere to be seen and Krank was serving Frau Trottel. The two were discussing her headaches and Krank was suggesting a new brand of aspirin, recommended by a doctor friend of his.

It was the first time Oskar had seen Frau Trottel face to face since the butcher's shop incident. He gave her a cautious wave and she responded with a smile before continuing her conversation with Krank. Oskar decided to settle his nerves with a stroll around the aisles. First he headed to the hair products where he inspected the thickening mousses. After that, he lightly fingered a scrunchie, then a web of black hair nets, both of which made him feel a bit queasy. Next he found himself scanning the shelves of the dermatological section, mesmerised by the number of lotions and creams that humans seemed to need to keep their skin in half decent nick: toning gel for cellulite; moisturiser for extra dry hands; solutions for skin rashes; hydrocortisone cream for acute acne . . . Oskar backed away.

*

Franz

Within a fortnight Franz was smoking Heike's uncle's 'special gear' every day. Gone were the walks to Viktoriapark, the little picnics and the chocolates. All he and Heike wanted to do was doss around the flat in an opiated daze. With the two of them parked permanently on the sofa or in Franz's bedroom, Oskar was beginning to lose patience. The washing up was stinking out the kitchen, cigarette ash clung to the furniture and the smell of stale sweat hung in the air like rancid onion.

But it was only temporary. He just needed to wait until Franz's habit had got a hard enough hold to merit a portrait. By the end of the month, he'd got what he wanted and after adding his signature to the new painting, he put down his brush and sauntered into the sitting room. Franz was just leaving the flat for his bi-weekly afternoon trip to the supermarket and Heike was stretched out on the sofa.

'Don't forget the Snickers bars,' called Oskar, as Franz shut the door behind him. Then he grinned over at Heike. 'Right. Let's do it.'

'Where's Heike?' said Franz, unpacking the bread, milk, Curry Kings and Snickers bars onto the kitchen table.

Oskar looked up from the new sketch he was working on. Throughout Franz's stay he'd done numerous and very flattering mock sketches of his flatmate, so Franz wouldn't need to see the real paintings.

'She left,' said Oskar.

'Left?'

'Vamoosh. Gone back to Hamburg.'

Franz sat down. 'When?'

'About twenty minutes ago. She said that lying around here all day was doing her head in.' Oskar rolled his eyes. 'Women, huh?'

'When's she coming back?'

Oskar shrugged. 'I don't think it'll be anytime soon.'

In fact, as Oskar well knew, Heike was never coming back. That was part of the deal. In a few weeks, when all the money was gone, she'd be turning tricks in Neukölln again.

'Did she leave me a note?'

Oskar shook his head. 'And there's no point calling her, because she left her phone here.' He leant over the kitchen table and picked up one of the Snickers bars. 'Franz, this is what women do. They leave you when they get a better offer.'

'But I thought she loved me.' Franz wiped a cuff across his eyes.

'I'm sure she did,' said Oskar. 'But she's obviously decided to move on.'

It took about sixty seconds for the other repercussions of Heike's departure to sink in. Franz was just shakily rolling a cigarette when he asked the million Euro question.

'Did she leave any of that stuff her uncle makes?'

Oskar took a bite of the Snickers bar, letting the peanutty chocolate melt on his tongue. 'Have a look.'

After frantically ransacking his bedroom, then the bathroom, Franz returned to the kitchen to check the drawers and cupboards. After that he searched the sitting room, overturning every cushion and scanning beneath the armchair and sofa and even behind the curtains.

'Nevermind, eh?' said Oskar. 'It's probably a good thing. You don't want to get hooked on heroin.'

Franz's eyes widened. 'Heroin?'

'Yip,' said Oskar, lobbing the Snickers wrapper into the bin with satisfying precision. 'Silly old Franz.'

*

Craaash! Oskar had been so caught up in his thoughts that he hadn't even seen the pyramid-shaped stack of facial cleaning products behind him, most of which now lay strewn across the chemist's floor. He bent down to pick them up, taking a few moments to balance the final one on top. By the time he was finished, he saw that Frau Trottel was walking towards the exit. He sidled over to the till.

'Could I have a word, Herr Krank?' he smiled. 'In private.' The smile wasn't easy – it was the first time that he had spoken to Krank since that morning when he'd pushed him off the chair and crushed the lens.

'The shop's empty,' Krank replied curtly. 'We have enough privacy here.'

Oskar lowered his voice to a whisper. 'It's about Equavol – or should I say Seramax. We wouldn't want someone to walk in and hear what you've been up to, would we?'

Having shown Oskar into his small office, Krank sat down behind the rectangular desk while Oskar took up position by the window, which faced out onto the high street. He was looking forward to debuting his impression of the bumbling cult TV detective, which he had modelled closely on *Columbo*, one of Omi Blumental's favourite programmes.

'Great view you've gaaht here,' said Oskar, in his best LA/Italian immigrant accent. 'I can even see that old flaahrist's, you moved into. Business is boomin', huh?' Oskar was pretty chuffed with his impersonation, wondering why he hadn't used it before.

'But I'm a liddle confoozed because I taut them antidepressants you bin sellin' had bin banned by the Medical Authorities.' He span around from the window and pointed an index finger at Krank. 'So what's the deal?'

From behind the desk Krank readjusted the calendar by his right elbow, which showed a woman doing a cartwheel in a cornfield. 'I have absolutely no idea what you are talking about.'

Oskar sighed and began again, this time slower. 'I'm a liddle confoozed because I taut them antidepressants you bin sellin'...'

Krank waved his hand irritatedly. 'Yes, yes, I understand what you're saying, but it makes no sense.'

'Oh, no?' Oskar rummaged in his pocket and pulled out the list he'd written that morning. '*Wiener Schnitzel, Weisswürste,* gherkins... No, that can't be right.' He rustled in his pocket again, fishing out the second list that he'd copied from the medical dictionary. He began reading:

> '*Seramax has a wide range of...*' the effort of keeping up the LA/ Italian accent while reading was too tiring. Best quit while he was ahead. '... *side effects, which include nausea, dizziness, sweating, migraines and high blood pressure. During the initial trials it was also shown in some instances to cause irreparable damage to the optic nerves. After a lengthy court case the Medical Regulatory Authority ruled that it should be withdrawn from the market. The manufacturers, Glücksvolk GmbH are currently appealing against the decision.*'

Oskar re-folded the piece of paper with a flourish. There was a short silence filled with the ticking of the clock above Krank's desk, which featured a round yellow face with the Glücksvolk logo forming the wide smile. Krank's own face featured his usual glacial expression as he twirled a biro between his fingers.

'So that's why I'm confused,' said Oskar, 'because you're selling Seramax, or rather Equavol, knowing it's both illegal and dangerous. And yesterday Frau Zwoll, who as you will know has very high blood pressure, almost died because of it.'

Herr Krank arched one eyebrow.

'And Herr Kozma's eyesight is so buggered from taking the drug that he can barely see beyond his nose,' said Oskar. 'Not forgetting Frau Miesel and her migraines. Shall I continue?'

'I don't think that's necessary,' said Herr Krank.

'I wonder,' said Oskar, drumming his fingers on his chin, 'what the Medical Authorities will have to say.'

Krank jabbed the tip of the biro onto his prescription notepad. 'I think the Medical Authorities have better things to do than listen to you.'

'Oh, yes? And what happens when they hear about you accepting bribes as well? All-expense-paid trips to conferences, free computers, smiley clocks, calendars etc.' Oskar pointed to the woman cart-wheeling in the cornfield. 'Add that to the attempted manslaughter of Frau Zwoll and I think they'd be pretty interested.'

Krank made an elaborate gesture of wiping away a tear of laughter.

'My dear Herr Dunkelblick,' he said. 'Who do you think they're going to believe? A young and mentally unstable so-called artist or a respected member of the medical community?'

'What do you mean "mentally unstable"?'

'Well, first of all you yourself admitted to suffering from depression, acute enough to purchase antidepressants from me. Then you break into my premises and attempt to steal my possessions. After that, you vandalise my shop and talk in a bizarre

Italian/American accent. Finally you accuse me of trying to poison you and most of the village . . . Doesn't look good, does it?' Herr Krank had drawn a smiley face on the prescription pad.

'I didn't vandalise your shop,' said Oskar, 'I knocked over a few facial cleaning products.'

Krank tutted. 'All in all, I would say your behaviour displays classic symptoms of a very unbalanced personality, bordering on schizophrenia.' He looked up from the pad. 'You see, that's the fascinating thing about personality disorders – those who suffer from them often have absolutely no idea, which is precisely what makes them so unpredictable, and in many cases worthy of sectioning.'

'Sectioning?' gulped Oskar.

Herr Krank leant forward and lowered his voice to a whisper. 'So if you want to see springtime in the Black Forest rather than the four walls of a psychiatric ward, I suggest you stop spreading these libellous rumours. Do you understand?'

Chapter 22

'You can come out now.' Greta peered through the *Bierkeller* window towards the chemist's. 'Krank's gone.'

'You sure?' said Oskar, who'd been crouching behind the bar for the last twenty minutes. 'What if he comes back? He might see me in here and have me carted off.'

'Don't be ridiculous,' said Greta. 'He's just trying to scare you. Herr Krank will probably be a little scared himself after what you've just said to him. He's just good at hiding it.'

Oskar straightened up behind the bar before taking a hurried gulp of his beer.

'Krank said I had a personality disorder. I don't, do I?'

Greta smiled. 'Let's just say you've made a lot of progress.'

'And if I *did* get locked up, would you visit me?'

'Oh, Oskar!' Greta laughed. 'No one's going to lock you up. Now can you give it a rest?'

By the time Oskar had finished his first beer, he and Greta had been joined by Thomas and the three of them were now sitting at the table by the fire. They were discussing Krank and Greta had suggested they let things rest for a while. It was her guess that Oskar's accusation along with Frau Zwoll's collapse would make Krank wary of taking any more risks. In the meantime, she would subtly advise those patients taking Equavol to change their brand of antidepressant to one approved by the Medical Authorities.

'But what if he finds out you're helping me?' asked Oskar.

'Then I'll leave,' said Greta. 'I'd rather not work with him anymore, given everything we know. I can always get work at my friend's market stall in Staufen. It's only six kilometres away.'

Creeak! Oskar spun round at the sound of the door to see a lone figure standing on the threshold, wearing a burgundy embroidered waistcoat and a thick wool jacket.

'Herr Kozma!' Oskar beamed with delight. 'Come and join us.'

Herr Kozma broke into a grin, shuffled over and pumped Oskar's hand.

'Let me buy you a drink,' said Oskar, dragging another chair towards the fire. 'In fact, let me buy you all a drink.'

'Are you sure about that?' Thomas smiled.

Oskar nodded and grinned.

'That's a first,' said Greta.

The drinks had been bought and the little gathering was sat at the table. Herr Kozma was telling them how Oskar had brought him some liver sausage the previous week.

'It was only leftovers,' said Oskar.

'No,' said Herr Kozma. 'It was fresh from butcher shop.'

'And he helped me carry my shopping two days ago.' The second voice came from the *Bierkeller* doorway where Frau Trundel was now standing.

'Look who it is.' Oskar leapt up from his chair and gestured to the free seat next to Greta. 'Take a pew.'

Frau Trundel sat down with a smile, warming her hands on

the fire. 'I just felt like a beer,' she said. 'Today is my birthday but Adalbert wasn't in the mood to celebrate with me.'

'Then *we* will celebrate with you instead!' said Oskar. 'Another round of drinks on me!' To hell with the money, he thought as he strode over to the bar. Frau Trundel deserved a few birthday drinks after everything she had to put up with.

After toasting Frau Trundel several times and hearing about Herr Kozma's new recipe for Hungarian chicken paprikash soup, things turned serious again. Oskar held up Frau Trundel's glasses.

'See,' he said, '*everything* looks bleak through them. So Krank advises you to buy his antidepressants, which promise to make things look better. It's a neat little business scheme.' He turned to Frau Trundel and Herr Kozma. 'But if you have high blood pressure, it's *really* not a good idea.'

'You should all get an independent eye test,' said Greta. 'And if you can quietly spread the word about what Oskar's just said, that would help.'

'But what about Herr Krank?' said Herr Kozma.

Greta laid her hand on his arm. 'As Oskar just explained, Herr Krank can look after himself quite well. He's just not very good at looking after others.' She reached for her coat. 'Right, I've got some studying to do.'

'Can't it wait?' said Oskar. 'You still haven't seen my *Columbo* impression.'

Greta laughed and leant over to kiss him on the cheek. 'Let's keep it for a rainy day.'

It was nine o'clock and everybody else had gone home for supper. Oskar had made omelettes for himself and Thomas and after they'd eaten, they sat by the fire with mugs of hot chocolate. Settled into the armchair Thomas was reading a biography of Günther Grass and opposite him, Oskar was midway through the book of Goethe's poems that Greta had lent him. But every so often he would glance over at Thomas, studying the sharp lines etched into his face like scars.

*

The following day the rain was lashing down when Oskar turned up with his sketchbook. Neither Werner nor his friends were near the station. Walking away, Oskar considered the plan that he'd been working on all night. Now that the Kreuzberg gallery were selling even more of his paintings, he would ask them to act as a guarantor for a small bedsit for him. Then, once he had gained his father's trust by drawing and talking to him every day, he would tell him that he was his son. With a bit more time, Oskar would suggest that his dad came to live with him. Once that happened, he could help him stop drinking and get healthy again – and start writing a new novel.

The rain continued for three days but by the fourth, the winter sun had finally edged around the clouds, lighting up the station with technicolour freshness. The usual crowd were gathered and although Oskar couldn't spot Werner, he still hurried over.

'Excuse me.' He tapped the shoulder of the woman with plastic bags on her feet instead of shoes. 'I had an arrangement to meet Werner.'

The woman stared at him with blank, bloodshot eyes.

'Werner,' Oskar repeated and nodded down at his sketchbook. 'I'm going to draw him.'

The woman pointed to a man smoking a roll-up by the shopping trolleys. 'Hal. He wants to see Werner.'

The guy squinted over at Oskar, then gestured to the dark red building behind him. 'Sorry mate, he's over there now.'

Oskar had never been inside Kreuzberg hospital before, let alone in the intensive care unit. Still shaking with the news, he approached the reception desk, where a young nurse with a pale thin face was reading through some papers.

'I'm looking for a man called Werner,' he said, trying to steady the tremble in his voice. 'He came in around 9.30 last night.' Hal had been surprisingly helpful, telling him about Werner's collapse the previous evening and how he and a friend had carried him to the hospital.

'What's his surname?' asked the nurse.

'I don't know,' said Oskar quietly. 'He changed it because he didn't want people to find him.'

The nurse read her notes again. 'We had two Werners admitted yesterday evening. Do you have any other details?'

'He had a scar down his left cheek.'

'Are you family?'

Oskar nodded. 'He is my . . . dad.'

The nurse scanned the papers once more. A minute later she set her pen down and her eyes met Oskar's. 'I'm so sorry. He died this morning.'

'But . . . but he can't have,' said Oskar.

The nurse reached out a hand over the reception desk and laid it on Oskar's arm. He felt his eyes fill with tears.

'Can . . . can I see him?'

The mortuary was down in the basement, behind two white swing doors. Before Oskar entered, the man in a green plastic apron who'd collected him from the reception desk, asked him if he was sure that he wanted to see 'the deceased'. Oskar nodded. He'd lied and said that he was eighteen, so now he needed to act like a grown-up.

Inside the mortuary, the walls on the right side of the room were lined with steel doors, each with a handle on. The chemical stench of disinfectant stung Oskar's eyes and he shivered from the freezing temperature. In the far corner were four large metal sinks with hosepipes snaking out of them.

The man with the plastic apron put on two see-through rubber gloves, then went over to one of the steel doors and released the handle. He pulled out the long steel drawer inside to its full length. On top of it was something about two metres long, covered in a white plastic sheet.

'You don't have to look if you don't want to,' said the man, but Oskar stepped forward. Beneath the white sheet, he could make out the shape of a body, the outline of a face.

Please don't let it be Dad.

The man lifted the corner of the sheet and Oskar stared down at the bloated face beneath him. The eyes were closed and the mouth gaped open. There was a strange waxy sheen to the skin, which was mottled with red and purple blotches. Half way down the left cheek was a scar.

'Oskar?' Oskar could hear the voice of the man standing next to him, but he didn't react. Instead he reached out his hand towards his father's face, wanting to touch him, just once. But before his fingers could make contact, a see-through gloved hand gently guided his own hand away.

Oskar couldn't remember leaving the mortuary, nor could he recall stepping back into the lift. But once up on the ground floor, he didn't get out. Instead he waited as a young family jostled their way in, a mother carrying a baby and by her side, the father, holding a carrycot in one hand. Oskar watched their reflection in the lift's mirror: the mother clasping the bundle of blankets to her chest and the father leaning over to softly stroke the forehead of his newborn child.

Oskar was still in the lift an hour later. He had no idea how many times he had gone up and down, watching the doors open and close to let in families, young couples, children and elderly grandparents. It was only when a group of nurses entered and asked him which floor he wanted, that he shook his head and brushed past them, running from the lift into the ground floor foyer, through the automatic glass doors of the hospital exit and out into the night.

*

'You're staring at me again.' Thomas was looking up from his book, smiling at Oskar.

'Am I?' said Oskar, whose thoughts were still down in the mortuary. He tried to swallow the lump in his throat. He so rarely allowed himself to think about that day.

'Thomas?' he said. 'Can we do this every week? Have supper together and read?'

'Don't see why not,' said Thomas, 'although maybe not next week. I'm thinking about going to Jena.'

'Oh?' said Oskar, feeling a flutter of panic in his stomach. 'But you're coming back, aren't you?'

Thomas nodded. 'I just need to see an old work colleague and . . .' He left the sentence unfinished. 'It's a big trip and I'm not sure if I'm ready for it yet.'

'I could come with you,' said Oskar. 'I've been wanting to go to Jena for a while. See what goes on at the Carl Zeiss HQ, check out those pancakes the city's so famous for . . .'

Thomas smiled. 'That's a kind offer, Oskar. I'll think about it.' He coughed and shook his head. 'You'd think it would get easier,' he said, in barely more than a whisper. 'It's twenty years since the accident and I still don't know how to let them go.'

'Let who go?'

Thomas fumbled for his wallet, then pulled out a crumpled photograph of a woman with pale blue eyes, gold blonde hair and freckles. She was wearing a green flowery dress and sitting in a wicker chair, with her arms wrapped around the little boy on her knee.

'That was the last picture I took of them,' said Thomas.

'Can you talk about what happened?' said Oskar, leaning forward towards Thomas.

Thomas placed the photograph on his knee and continued to stare down at it. 'We were driving home from holiday in the Czech Republic. I had just received a phone call from a colleague saying that we had lost the funding for the project we were working on. Anja, my wife, asked if I could deal with it when we got home rather than in the car. I shouted at her. Didn't she understand? This was the most important project of my career. My son, Florian, who'd been sleeping in the back seat, started to cry. Anja unbuckled her seatbelt so she could comfort him...' Thomas was shaking his head from side to side.

'I didn't see the other car until it was right in front of us so I didn't even have the time to brake. It hit us head on.' Thomas took a deep breath. 'I must have been unconscious for only a few seconds but when I opened my eyes, Anja was no longer in the passenger's seat. She'd been thrown through the windscreen and was lying on the car bonnet. By the time the ambulance arrived, she was dead.'

'And your little boy?' asked Oskar.

Thomas stared down at the picture on his knee. 'His neck was broken. He died two days later in hospital. He was only seven.'

Chapter 23

Oskar was in bed at home, shivering. He'd cocooned himself in a blanket and was wearing his hat, gloves and scarf but he was still cold. He'd barely slept, unable to forget the sight of Thomas's face the previous evening.

He could picture the crash as vividly as if he'd been driving the car himself: the shattered windscreen; Thomas's wife lying on the bonnet; the broken neck of his seven-year old son... Over and over again, the details flashed across his mind. How would you ever recover from losing your wife? How could you live with yourself after causing the death of your little boy?

It was with this final thought that another memory surged up from the depths, punching the breath from Oskar's lungs with its intensity.

*

Franz

Franz was still huddled in the armchair. His nose was running and sweat was beading on his face. He lit his roll-up with trembling fingers.

'Heroin?'

'That's the one,' Oskar replied, pulling out the Bauer yoghurt he'd stashed in the fridge earlier.

'But it can't be. Heike told me that it was just something her uncle made.'

'Hmmm,' said Oskar. 'And we now know what a clever liar Heike is, don't we?'

There was a pause while Franz absorbed this information, his expression a mixture of panic, shock and disbelief.

'Do you . . . know where I can buy some more?' Franz asked eventually in a shaky voice. 'Just a bit to take the edge off things.'

Oskar peeled back the lid of the yoghurt pot and licked the underside. Only recently had he rediscovered the hazelnut variety. *Yummsky*!

'I do,' said Oskar, 'but how are you going to pay for it, Franz? You already owe me over five hundred Euros.'

'I just need one last hit,' said Franz.

Oskar shook his head. 'It doesn't work like that. You can never have *just one* hit. You will always want another.' The idea of living full time with a heroin addict wasn't part of the plan at all. Heike had been discreet, and therefore bearable for the short term. Franz wouldn't be.

'I think you should go back to Füssen,' said Oskar. 'Stay with your parents for a while and get back on your feet.'

'I can't,' Franz mumbled. 'Not like this.'

'But you haven't got much choice,' said Oskar. 'Besides I'm probably moving out soon so where would you live without any money for rent?' This last part about moving out was a lie, but Oskar hoped it might convince Franz that Füssen was indeed the only option. Now that Oskar had all but one of the paintings in the bag, the sooner Franz moved away, the better.

That afternoon Franz said he needed to go for a walk to think about things. While he was out, Oskar sketched ideas for the last painting. But at seven o'clock that evening, he received a call from the local police station. Franz had been arrested for stealing a mobile phone from one of the *Phone Tastisch* shops.

Most inconveniently, it seemed that Oskar was expected to go to the police station. Franz had already given details of his flatmate and where they both lived, and since the shop weren't prosecuting, someone needed to pay the one hundred Euro fine. Oskar thought he'd better do as he was told. After all, he didn't want Franz blabbing any more than he already had.

When Oskar arrived at the police station, the officer on duty showed him to a room where he was subjected to half an hour of questioning. Did he know where his flatmate bought his heroin from? How long had Franz been an addict? Did Oskar himself use Class A drugs?

By the time Oskar was led into the small cell where Franz was hunched on the edge of the metal bed, he was furious.

'Now I am going to *have* to ring your parents, Franz.'

Franz scratched at a scab on his arm. 'Please, don't.'

'Who else is going to cough up for the hundred Euro fine then? If it isn't paid, you'll have to stay here.'

Franz just shook his head and stared at the floor.

In the end Franz gave Oskar his parents number and he called them. The mother answered, so after hastily introducing himself Oskar handed the phone over to her son. As they spoke he studied his former flatmate, slumped on the metal prison bed, face sweating with fear, eyes wide with panic. Now *that* would make a great image for the final painting.

'So your parents are driving from Füssen and are happy to pay the fine?' said Oskar, when the conversation had finished.

Franz nodded.

'They'll be here in . . . what . . . seven hours?'

Another nod from Franz.

'In which case, I need to push off. Parties to go to, people to meet.' Oskar gave Franz a quick pat on the shoulder. 'I guess this is goodbye.'

Franz stood up, grabbing Oskar and pulling him into a clammy hug.

'Will you visit me in Füssen?'

'Hmm,' said Oskar, extricating his upper body from the hug. 'Let's play it by ear.' He held out his right hand for a formal shake. 'It's been a blast, hasn't it?'

Franz took his hand limply. 'Thanks for everything,' he mumbled.

'You take care of yourself now,' said Oskar. Then with a hasty salute, he marched towards the door, down the corridor, through the main entrance and out into the Kreuzberg streets, just as the sun was setting.

It was only later that evening as Oskar was prepping the canvas for the last picture, that the problem dawned on him. If he was to exhibit the *Seven Steps to Hell* paintings and they received the widespread press coverage that he wanted, then things might get a little sticky with the police. Oskar had said he knew nothing about his flatmate's heroin habit, but the pictures would give the game away completely.

Oskar realised he hadn't really thought this end part through. He'd sort of assumed that Franz would conveniently disappear in the junkie underworld, leaving Oskar free to portray just another anonymous addict, one of the thousands that drift like ghosts through towns and cities across the world. But this one would have a face, a name, an address and a record at the local police station for thieving. Not good.

So that night, much to his disappointment and indeed fury, Oskar decided to shelve his plans for the exhibition, at least for the moment. A few weeks later, after a period of intense artist's block, he stumbled across the article about Keinefreude.

*

Oskar lay in bed as that final image of Franz in the prison cell swam before his eyes. What baffled him most was how he, Oskar, could have deliberately set out to cause a fellow human being so much suffering? And it wasn't only Franz that had suffered – it was his parents, whose son's life he could well have ruined.

Staring up at the ceiling, Oskar swallowed hard and in a voice hoarse with emotion, he whispered, 'I'm so sorry, Franz.'

Chapter 24

Oskar and Thomas were standing in Jena's busy market square, squinting up at the town hall's golden clock with its carved wooden figure of Schnapphans. Thomas had only decided at the last minute to come to Jena, encouraged by Oskar, who'd packed them both a picnic for the overnight train with a Kinder Surprise each.

During the journey there, which consisted of several train changes and the odd snatched half hour of sleep, Oskar had spent most of the time thinking about Franz and how he could begin to make amends for what he had done. By the time they pulled into Jena's main station the next morning, he had decided that when he was back in Keinefreude, he would ring Franz to tell him how deeply ashamed he was and to offer his former flatmate whatever help he needed to rebuild his life.

Thirty minutes later Oskar was sitting in a student café in Krautgasse with a plate of pancakes doused in cream and cherry sauce in front of him. But he wasn't that hungry so instead he read through Thomas's list of suggestions for places to visit until the two of them met again that afternoon at the Carl Zeiss building. Outside the café windows, the February carnival celebrations were in full swing. *Fasching* fools danced in their bell-trimmed boots while satin-caped magicians conjured brightly coloured handkerchiefs from behind children's ears, and black-coated plague doctors strode solemnly through the crowds with their tall peaked hats and cloth-covered mouths. Everyone was wearing their homemade red noses, shouting *Helau Helau* to each other while church bells rang through the city.

First on Thomas's list was the Friedrich-Schiller-University, which was pretty much deserted when Oskar arrived, since *Fasching* was a national holiday. So he wandered alone beneath the ancient bricked archways and across the grassy quadrangles, passing the statues of famous former students. He immediately recognised Schiller, the poet who had kept a drawer full of rotten apples in his workroom because he needed their decaying scent in order to write. He also spotted Fichte, recalling with embarrassment his former admiration for the philosopher who advocated that women should be treated as second-class citizens. But it was the statue in the fourth quadrangle that Oskar found himself staring at, before making his way over to read the plaque:

'Hermann von Helmholtz (1821–1924) was a physician, physicist and inventor of the ophthalmoscope, the instrument used to examine the inside of the eye. He was the first scientist to recognise the importance of the mind in determining what the viewer sees.'

Why do you look so familiar, thought Oskar, trying to place the man's handlebar moustache and droopy eyes. Of course! It was that guy from his dream the night before he'd gone into the trashed spectacle shop. But how could he have dreamt about someone he didn't even know existed?

Oskar was still trying to work this out, when he entered the Botanical Gardens just before noon. To be honest, the gardens hadn't been top of his wish list, but Greta had wanted him to see them because Goethe had lived there in the Inspector's House. And in fact, he rather enjoyed ambling around the giant glass-houses with their majestic ten metre tall palms. He even took the time to track down the ancient ginkgo biloba tree, that according to Greta, Goethe would lie beneath at sunrise, composing his poems.

Next on the schedule was a lunchtime snack, but as Oskar was exiting the gardens, he noticed a wooden sign nailed to the gate with the words: *House of Optics*. On the pointy arrow bit was painted the symbol of an eye. The same symbol was painted on the lamppost at the end of the street, then on a wall around the next corner. Following the arrows, which appeared every twenty metres or so, Oskar made his way around the outskirts of the town.

Having arrived at his destination – a round watchtower set into the city wall, Oskar tugged at the bell hanging from a rope. A spy hole shaped like an eye opened in the middle of the thick oak door and a small telescope protruded, moving up and down as if examining Oskar. That was replaced by a single eye, which belonged, as Oskar soon discovered, to a very grumpy curator with mayonnaise in his beard.

'It's a national holiday,' said the red-haired curator, standing in the half-open door. 'And I'm having my lunch.'

'I'm deeply sorry,' said Oskar, adopting his most formal *Hochdeutsch*. 'But I've travelled all the way from the Black Forest to gather information on important optical heritage sites, and I believe your establishment is one of them.' He pulled out his wallet and waved a twenty Euro note.

'Would this be enough to gain access?'

Slightly begrudging the twenty Euros, which he couldn't really afford, Oskar stood inside the main room of the exhibition, clutching the brochure that the curator had shoved into his hand. In front of him were two long glass cabinets, filled with spectacles dating from the fourteenth century. But Oskar didn't linger, since the curator had allowed him only thirty minutes. So after pausing by a third cabinet for a swift stare-out with an ice-blue eyeball preserved in a glass jar of brandy, he moved on.

He'd spied the peep box at the far end of the room as soon as he'd entered. It was about twice the size of Frau Miesel's telly and made from rosewood, reminding him of the peep box at the Hamburg Christmas market. That one had housed a perfect miniature replica of the Altona Theatre's interior, complete with little people in the red velvet seats, watching a performance of Grimm's *Hansel and Gretel*.

Placing his eye against this one's peephole, Oskar stared at the scaled-down room inside, noting with astonishment the red leather barber's chair and on the wall above, the illuminated glass box printed with four lines of black letters. He quickly read the words, reflected in the mirror opposite:

185

His hands were shaking as he flicked through the brochure, eventually finding the corresponding entry on page 7:

> 'The peep box on the ground floor is a reproduction of a nineteenth-century travelling eye clinic, used by opticians who would often take their trade on the road. This particular eye clinic with its unique reading chart was constructed according to written reports from villagers living in the Black Forest area during that time. Their descriptions have been typed up and can be read in the bound Optics Book volume 4 stored in the small library of this museum . . .'

'You've got fifteen minutes left,' a voice called out from the foyer. 'Then I'm closing.'

'But I need more time,' shouted Oskar. 'I haven't seen upstairs yet and I definitely have to check out the Optics Book in the library.'

'Tough,' shouted the curator. 'I've already done you a favour and opened up on a national holiday. If you outstay the allocated time, you'll be locked in, on your own, in the dark.'

Oskar gulped. 'I'll be ten minutes, tops,' he shouted and dashed out of the room and up the stairs to the second floor, which according to the brochure was entirely devoted to *The World's Greatest Visionaries.*

Wow! Oskar stood just inside the main upstairs room, gazing at the waxwork figures. There were about thirty of them, men and women, dressed in every manner of costume. He recognised Gandhi immediately, mainly due to his round glasses and the white cloth draped over his bare shoulder. He was holding a placard on which was written a quote: *An eye for an eye will make the whole world blind.* To his right stood Helen Keller, also carrying a quote: *The best and most beautiful things in the world cannot be seen or even touched, they must be felt with the heart.* Other waxworks included Leonardo da Vinci, Marie Curie, Meister Eckhart and Martin Luther King, as well as a woman wearing a nun's habit and a wimple.

'Who are you?' said Oskar, staring into the woman's dark brown eyes. After a few seconds his own eyes began to burn and he quickly consulted the brochure.

'Hildegard von Bingen (1098–1179) was a German Benedictine nun, writer, visionary, mystic and composer. From the age of three she experienced visions, which she described as 'reflections of the living light'. Her theological, scientific and prophetic writings are still studied to this day, as are her views on botany, medicine and natural healing. Despite founding a monastery, she was critical of the Catholic Church for its corruption . . .'

'Brave girl.' Oskar patted the nun's hessian shoulder and pointed to the other figures around them. 'Not much time. Must mingle.' He did a couple of swivels, before marching over to a man with black shoulder length curly hair, who was holding up a lens towards the light.

'Spinoza! Enchanté!' Oskar did a little bow in front of the philosopher and from this slightly lower position he noticed the symbol of an eye with an amber-coloured iris sewn onto the cuff of the man's left sleeve. A separate footnote in the brochure read:

> *'The symbol of the amber eye belongs to a lineage, which dates back to the eleventh century. Since then, it has been worn by philosophers, artists, writers, mystics and visionaries, who possess the ability to show others new ways of seeing the world.'*

Oskar smiled and gave Spinoza a slightly clumsy high five. He was just making his way to the exit, when he caught sight of another figure, dressed in a brown woollen jacket and leather walking boots. Granted, the woodsman's cap lacked the earflaps and the skin colour was a little too pink, but otherwise the resemblance was spot on.

'Dr. Sehle, I knew I'd see you again!' Oskar rushed over and flung his arms around the waxwork, nearly knocking it over in his eagerness. He stared into the old man's glassy brown eyes, which glinted with orange and gold. Then he read the brochure's entry:

> 'Dr. Sehle (or Seele, as it is sometimes spelt) became famous throughout Germany during the mid-nineteenth century. He was the last known travelling optician, moving from village to village where he would set up his temporary eye clinic (see Peep Box entry on page 3). Few facts are known about him due to his peripatetic lifestyle – leading some to claim he is simply a myth. But those whom he treated, appear to be irrevocably altered by the experience (see entries in Optics Book vol. 4). He is believed to have died during a fire in the town of Gengenbach, although his body was never found.'

'Time's up!' The curator was standing in the doorway of the waxwork room, jangling his keys.

'So soon?' Oskar quickly scanned Dr. Sehle's woollen jacket, then his woodsman's hat, searching for the symbol of the amber eye. In the waxwork's top jacket pocket was a cream handkerchief. He reached forward.

'Do not touch the exhibits!' shouted the curator, running over to Oskar.

'Relax,' said Oskar. 'You're taking your job way too seriously.'

'Move away!' The curator's face was really quite red.

'Fire!' shouted Oskar, hoping to throw him off track. But before his fingers could even touch the hankie, the curator had lunged at him and grappled him to the floor. Moments later he was being marched towards the main exit.

Back outside the *House of Optics*, Oskar stomped along the cobbled street. He'd tried to reason with the curator, to blag a few more minutes, but the man just threatened to call the police. Spotting a donut stall on the corner, Oskar figured that a sugar hit would calm his nerves so he bought two *Krapfen* to munch on during the short walk to the Carl Zeiss building.

Thomas was already in the foyer when he arrived and after a quick hello, they both stepped into the lift. As they ascended, Oskar wondered if he should mention the morning's events, but where would he start? The *House of Optics* . . . the peep box . . . the waxwork figure of Dr. Sehle? It all sounded so improbable and to be honest, a little bonkers. Besides, Thomas seemed happier to stay silent.

The lift opened at the eighth floor and Thomas led the way down a long corridor. Laboratory assistants kept appearing and disappearing in and out of the doors on either side and as each one passed, Thomas glanced at their faces. Halfway down, a middle-aged man with a shaved head and sandals stopped in front of them. He was wearing what appeared to be an orange dress beneath his white lab coat.

'Thomas!' The man held out his arms.

'Kensho!'

Oskar had seldom seen two men hug so warmly, and it was a good thirty seconds before Thomas pulled back and introduced his former colleague to Oskar. After that, Kensho led them to his laboratory, a room at the end of the corridor, whose walls were hung with racks of lenses of all shapes and colours. Down the middle of the room was a long steel-surfaced table covered with lens-grinding equipment.

While Kensho made green tea in the laboratory's small open kitchen, Thomas stood at the nearby window overlooking the Observatory opposite. Perched on one of the stools, Oskar watched him, wondering why he was being so quiet.

'Why now?' said Kensho, arranging cups on a tray.

Thomas shrugged. 'Twenty years seemed like enough time.'

'I was worried about you,' said Kensho.

The long silence that followed was weighted with sadness.

'Well, I'm still here,' said Thomas. 'So that's a start.'

The tea had been brewed and Oskar and Kensho were sitting at the lab table, while Thomas gazed out at the telescopes on the Observatory roof. Kensho was answering another of Oskar's questions.

'Light has one of the highest frequencies known to man, with the ability to transmute energies from a lower to a higher vibration.' Kensho pushed the sugar bowl towards Oskar. 'As far back as Egyptian times it was used to heal people. And today light therapy is used to treat conditions ranging from diabetes, cancer and arthritis to seasonal depression and visual disorders.'

Oskar dropped two sugar lumps into his tea.

'Thomas and I believed that we could use the properties of light to raise the vibration of an individual's thoughts, and therefore change their perception.' Kensho smiled as Oskar went in for a third sugar lump.

'As a practising Buddhist back in Japan, I was familiar with the idea that consciousness affects matter,' Kensho continued. 'But I'd never considered using it in my work until I moved here and met *him*,' he smiled over at Thomas.

'Together we travelled to the Institute of Light Studies in Svalbard, Norway, where we learnt how to construct a light box, similar to the one used to treat people with Seasonal Affective

Disorder. The intention was to create a light as close as possible to natural sunlight.'

Oskar nodded and took a sip of his sweet tea.

'Our first experiment was on some cuttings from a spider plant. We instructed one of the laboratory assistants to sit in front of the light box for fifteen minutes, focusing her mind on the thought of *love*. Then we removed the light box and asked her to hold the spider plant, still focusing on the thought of *love*. The second assistant was simply asked to hold and observe a second spider plant, while focusing on the thought of *fear*.'

Kensho glanced over at Thomas. 'Within six days the first plant was twice the height of the second and had grown four new green shoots. We repeated the experiment several times, sometimes with the light box and sometimes without. But each time, the plant held by the light box-treated assistant focusing on *love* was the one that thrived most markedly. The one held by the assistant focusing on the thought of *fear* barely grew at all, wilting by the day until its leaves turned brown with decay.'

Thomas turned from the window, listening.

'Next we photographed the results with a Kirlian camera, which showed that when the assistant directed the thought of *love* at the plant, its energy field lit up in blues, greens and golds. The assistant also reported seeing a light coming from *within* the plant, a light, she said, that she could somehow sense inside her own body.'

Oskar nodded again, trying to absorb everything, while his mind skimmed back and forth to what he'd read in Thomas's research papers.

'Our experiments were viewed by most people in the department as fairly unorthodox and it wasn't easy to secure the necessary funding for the research. But we managed and over the next twelve months, we experimented with different lenses to simulate the light from our light box. We tried everything from in-built prisms and holographic devices to light absorbers and luminous optic glass.' Kensho shook his head. 'With another six months we might have developed a lens capable of showing people the effect of their thoughts on the world around them, but our funding was cut.'

'What happened to all the equipment?' asked Thomas.

'The head of the department asked me to dispose of it,' Kensho replied. 'He was the one most opposed to our research, saying it was unscientific and that it would damage the reputation of the Institute.'

'Was he mad?' said Oskar, a little too loudly.

Kensho shrugged. 'You can't blame him for being sceptical, all of this work is still very much on the edge of science.'

'Have you ever heard of someone called Dr. Sehle?' said Oskar. 'He came to our village last October and opened up an optician's. His lenses were . . .' he hesitated, trying to find the right word, 'mind-blowing.'

Kensho smiled. 'No, but I am hearing such stories increasingly often. It seems that many people around the world are working towards the same goal. Sooner or later we will have the breakthrough that we need to convince the scientists.' He walked over and stood next to Thomas at the window. 'And I am still hoping that somehow Thomas and I will be able to contribute to that breakthrough.'

Oskar and Thomas had been talking with Kensho for over three hours, and around them the afternoon light was softening. Oskar had told them more about his afternoon with Dr. Sehle and what he had seen through the lenses but even now, five months after the event, he found it impossible to accurately describe their effect on him.

When it was time to leave, Oskar watched the two men as

they said goodbye, embracing each other tightly. He wondered what it must feel like to have such a close friend.

Down at street level once again, the bars were filling up and long trestle tables had been erected in the market square. Spotting a crowd of carnival goers with half litre glasses of beer and rotisserie chicken legs, Oskar suggested that he and Thomas stop for a snack but Thomas shook his head and kept walking. Without asking, Oskar sensed that wherever they were heading, Thomas shouldn't be alone.

The sky was darkening as they approached the cemetery and the clouds were tinged with mauve. At the gates a woman was packing away bunches of cream-coloured roses into a small van. Thomas bought two.

The grave was in the Nordfriedhof beneath a row of cedar trees. Thomas stopped by the stone and laid one hand on the dark green marble. Then, without a word, he knelt down, pulling at the tangle of ivy and bindweed until the two names on the grave were visible.

Anja Kepler (geb. Liebermann)
Florian Kepler

Stillness filled the cemetery, broken only by the sound of rain pattering on the ground beneath them. The light was fading yet the two roses, which Thomas had placed at the base of the stone, seemed to shine out into the dusk.

When Thomas finally stood up, his cheeks were wet with tears. As Oskar gazed at his face, he felt his own throat tighten and tears gather behind his eyes. Moving to stand beside Thomas, he raised one arm and placed it gently around his friend's shoulder.

Chapter 25

Oskar and Frau Miesel were settled in front of the telly, wearing their new *Schwarzwaldklinik* T-shirts, which Frau Miesel had bought from the fan club. She'd also baked some cinnamon buns. It was, after all, a big day at the clinic.

A month had passed since Oskar's visit to Jena and March had been unusually warm. Purple and white crocuses were pushing up through the cracks in the pavement, while the fir trees in the nearby forest had grown fresh green needles. In the roof above Oskar's makeshift larder a family of swallows were nesting, which he fed with crumbled *Leibniz-Keks* every morning.

During that month Oskar dropped in on Thomas almost every afternoon. The two would play chess or listen to music and sometimes Greta would join them at the end of her shift. Despite Oskar's encouragement, Thomas spoke neither of his wife and son, nor of their shared afternoon in the cemetery.

Twice in those four weeks Oskar had gone to dinner at Herr Kozma's, where he'd been serenaded with folk songs and glasses of apricot brandy. The second time they had both got so smashed that they'd ended up dancing on the sofa, belting out the chorus to the Hungarian national anthem *Oh God bless the Hungarian with Joy and Bounty!* while conducting themselves with soup ladles.

Most surprising of all was the invitation from Frau Trundel for Oskar to join her and Adalbert along with Frau Fettler and Herr Kozma for a weekly *Skat* session, a card game he remembered his grandparents playing and which he had to admit, was actually quite fun even if it was for old people.

In fact, there were the only two clouds on the horizon. The first was Oskar's career, or rather the lack of it. During a heated phone call the previous week, when Oskar finally admitted that he had no paintings to send them, the gallery had made it clear that they no longer wished to represent him. They had also demanded that he repay the money they'd spent on him. With little desire to paint anyway, at least not in his old style, Oskar had no idea how he was going to support himself when his savings ran out at the end of the month.

The other equally troubling cloud was Krank. The morning after his return from Jena, Oskar had received a Cease and Desist order, containing a lengthy legal description of what would happen if he continued to spread the slanderous rumours about Herr Krank and his business. In short, he was looking at a cripplingly expensive court case and a possible twelve-month prison sentence.

'Have you ever thought of getting married?' Oskar asked as he and Frau Miesel waited for the wedding ceremony of Doktor Brinkmann and Christa to begin. It was a relief to think about something other than the Cease and Desist letter and his lack of career.

Frau Miesel snorted. 'Marriage! Don't be ridiculous.'

'Come on, there must have been someone. A kind, good-looking woman like yourself!'

Frau Miesel grimaced. 'Flattery, my dear Oskar, is entirely wasted on me.'

'It's so not,' said Oskar. 'You're blushing.'

A short silence followed, during which Frau Miesel bit into her cinnamon bun and chewed loudly.

'There was someone,' she said, after a few seconds. 'But I try not to think about him.'

'Do you want to talk about it?' said Oskar.

Frau Miesel nodded. 'If you don't mind listening.' She put her bun down. 'I was twenty-nine and already running the bakery, which I had inherited from my parents. One day in spring a man came in and we started chatting. He said he was on a two-day walking holiday from Karlsruhe and he intended to stay the night in the guestroom above the bar. He'd noticed that there were only old people in the village and he wondered why a young woman like myself was living here. I told him that I wouldn't be staying much longer as the bakery had recently been sold. In fact, the money had come through earlier that week and now I was able to go to Munich and study as a pastry chef, which was always my dream.' Frau Miesel glanced out of the window where rain clouds were gathering.

We talked some more about the area and where he intended to walk. Then he said he hoped that I had stored the money from the bakery sale safely. I nodded and smiled, telling him that since I didn't believe banks could be trusted, I had found a much better place to keep it.

The next afternoon he came into the bakery and asked me to accompany him on his final walk. So I shut the shop early and we headed over to the forest. When we reached one of the little cabins there, he took my hand and told me how lonely he had been since his wife had left him. It must get lonely for you too, he said, a single woman in such a small village.

Frau Miesel paused to pour herself some more coffee. 'That evening he turned up on my doorstep and offered to make supper for me with the few ingredients he'd bought that morning. He'd also brought a bottle of red wine and a dessert wine.

Although I wasn't used to drinking, it was so delicious that I had three glasses with dinner. As I watched him on the opposite side of the table, telling me stories of his home in Karlsruhe, I began to dream. A silly dream of a woman who hadn't known much love in her life.' Frau Miesel let out a little laugh, which sounded more like a hiccup.

'With pudding he opened the Muscat and he told me how pretty I was and how he wished we could have more time together. Suddenly the room was spinning and he was at my side, suggesting I should lie down . . .'

Frau Miesel looked over at Oskar. 'I won't go into details but I didn't spend the night alone. When I woke the next morning, there was a note on the pillow, saying he'd gone to buy breakfast. I lay in bed fantasising about our future together . . . the house we would buy in Karlsruhe after I had done my pastry course, the bakery I would open there, the children we would have. Stupid naive fantasies based on nothing. An hour or so passed before it occurred to me that if he'd wanted breakfast, everything was downstairs. Bread rolls, jam, coffee . . . Only then did I remember telling him that I'd hidden the money from the sale of the bakery in the basement, in the small tunnel beneath the stairs, where villagers had once hidden stolen goods.

I ran down into the basement and over to the tunnel's entrance, which was covered by a grate. I pulled it away and felt inside for the metal box. Of course, it was gone.' Frau Miesel turned to Oskar with a shake of her head. 'He took everything. How are you going to trust anyone after that?'

'What a bastard arsehole!' said Oskar a few seconds later, still picturing Frau Miesel standing in her basement, empty-handed.

'Oskar!' Frau Miesel flapped her napkin in his direction as if flapping the words from the air.

'Sorry Frau M, but what else are you going to call him?'

Frau Miesel shrugged. 'A cad?'

'You're so last century.'

'Trickster?'

Oskar sighed and shook his head.

Frau Miesel's mouth twitched slightly and curved up at the edges. 'Thieving wanker?'

'That's a good start,' said Oskar and they both sat there, grinning at each other.

The programme had started and Christa was walking up the aisle towards Doktor Brinkmann. Frau Miesel craned forward in her chair.

'So who's here?' she whispered. 'I can see Schwester Elke already.'

'There's Dr. Schübel and Frau Gessner,' said Oskar.

'Oh, and look at Dr. Brinkmann's son, Udo,' said Frau Miesel. 'What a handsome lad!' She nibbled her second cinnamon bun. 'Do you think Christa will make a good stepmother to him? I know he's almost grown-up but a boy still needs a mother, whatever age he is.'

Oskar, who'd been about to start on his own second bun, swallowed hard and stared straight ahead at the television. It wasn't Frau Miesel's words, but the kindness within them that caught him completely off guard.

*

Oskar wasn't surprised that his mother hadn't found him. How could she have, given that he had changed his appearance and surname and now lived unregistered in a city of over three million people? If she was prepared to choose a man like Gunther over him, then Oskar no longer wanted to be her son.

But at night his mother would slip into his dreams: making him warm malted milk just like she used to before bedtime;

198

applying drops of her homemade honey remedy to soothe his itchy eyes; telling him stories about the stars on the nights he couldn't sleep. And the next morning Oskar would awaken and have to banish her from his thoughts again, reminding himself over and over how she had put her own happiness above his.

Oskar was still dreaming of his mother three years later, when he came up with *The Dark Side of Mother* idea. By painting her in the worst possible light, as a drunk, a junkie and a prostitute, he hoped to finally exorcise her memory. It was these pictures that the prestigious König's Gallery chose to exhibit at the end of the year. Before the show their PR department went into overdrive with articles about Oskar appearing in the regional and national press, along with a fifteen-minute TV documentary about Germany's youngest 'misery artist'.

Over four hundred people including press, critics and other artists, attended the opening night. By eight o'clock, when almost every painting was sold, Oskar was talking to the raven-haired arts correspondent from the *Berliner Zeitung*.

'Excuse me.' Oskar heard the voice of the gallery assistant beside him. 'There's a woman here claiming to be your mother.'

'I doubt that.' Oskar laughed and turned back to continue his conversation. But he cast his eyes around the gallery and near the entrance he spotted a woman in a blue raincoat, with a woollen floral headscarf despite the warm evening. A sharp pain knifed through his chest.

His mother was much thinner than he remembered and her skin was grey and pasty. But it was definitely his mother.

Oskar turned to the assistant. 'Never seen her before. Ask her to leave.' Excusing himself from the arts correspondent, he walked quickly toward the men's toilets, not looking back. Was his mother completely deluded? What did she imagine was going to happen? That he would run over and hug her? Forgive her at the snap of a finger?

When he returned, she was gone.

*

'Isn't that lovely!' Frau Miesel was still on the edge of her seat, hands clasped.

Oskar nodded, although his mind was still on his mother. How could he have known what would happen six weeks after that exhibition?

'You're missing the best bit.' Frau Miesel nudged him with her elbow and pointed to the screen where Doktor Brinkmann and Christa were emerging from the church, amidst a crowd of clapping guests.

'Sorry,' said Oskar. 'I'm just not really in the mood.'

Frau Miesel leant towards him, studying his face. Then she placed her hand against his forehead. 'Are you unwell?'

Oskar looked back at Frau Miesel's concerned expression as she waited for his reply, her warm palm still pressed to his forehead. He wondered if he would ever be able to talk about his mother. Maybe one day. And when that day came, Frau Miesel would be a good person to listen.

Chapter 26

Later that evening Oskar was standing at his window, staring up at the dim stars. The rain was lashing down and in the distance he could hear the wind slashing through the forest. He shivered, remembering the storms of his childhood that hurtled off the North Sea, howling at his bedroom window like a pack of rabid dogs. It was on these nights that his mother would make him warm Ovomaltine and tell him about the Greek myths surrounding the three bright blue stars of Orion's Belt. Soothed by her voice and snuggled into her arms, he'd be filled with a warm, happy feeling as he slipped back into sleep.

Other memories rolled through Oskar's head: his mother reading him his favourite stories from *Struwwelpeter*; helping him mix paint with his very first set of brushes; taking him to see *The Wanderer Above the Sea of Fog* in the Hamburg Kunsthalle.

*

During the following days, Oskar couldn't stop thinking about that thin figure in the woollen scarf at his exhibition. Two weeks later a letter arrived at the gallery. When the manager handed it to Oskar, he recognised the writing immediately. Inside, the Hamburg address was the same flat that had been his childhood home for twelve years. In the letter, his mother wrote how she should never have allowed Gunther into their lives and how she could not forgive herself for failing to protect her son against him. Her greatest regret was letting Oskar run away and if she had known where to find him before, she would have.

It was the last paragraph that Oskar read twice. His mother had been diagnosed with pancreatic cancer, which, as he might remember from Opi Blumental, ran in the family. Following two unsuccessful courses of chemotherapy, she had decided not to continue the treatment.

Oskar's immediate reaction was to rip up the letter. Surely this was just emotional blackmail, a pathetic last ditch cry for pity and forgiveness. But over the next few weeks his dreams grew increasingly intense. In almost every one his mother was sitting at the end of his bed, begging him to come home and see her before she died.

On a rainy Saturday morning, one month after opening the letter, Oskar stepped off the train at Hamburg's main station and headed towards the Altona district. The old block of flats, once his home, looked shabby in contrast to the newly renovated buildings that surrounded it. Inside, the hallway walls were daubed with graffiti and someone had left a pram to rust beneath the letterboxes.

Climbing up to the third floor, images fluttered in the air around him: Oskar and his mother racing each other up the stairs; stamping the snow off their boots outside their front door; his mother laying her head against its shiny dark wood and sighing 'Home again, Oskar.'

By the time Oskar reached the door of flat Number 9, he felt a strange quivering in his chest. He held his breath and knocked.

When no one answered, he knocked again then placed his ear against the wood.

'Is that you, Oskar?' said a voice behind him on the landing.

Oskar wheeled around to see an elderly man standing outside the door of Number 6. His right leg ended at the knee.

'Herr Hinkel!' He felt a burst of happiness at the familiar face and he held out both arms, momentarily forgetting his 'no touching' rule.

Herr Hinkel invited Oskar into his flat, where the two of them were now sitting on the sofa in the small living room. It still smelt of potato dumplings in browned butter sauce, and Herr Hinkel's beloved Dr. Oetker cookery magazines, whose recipes he would share with Oskar's mother, were still stacked beneath the television.

'Why have you come now?' Herr Hinkel squinted over at Oskar.

'I came back to see my mother,' Oskar said quietly.

'Did you not know?' Herr Hinkel shook his head. 'She died. Just five days ago.'

Oskar opened his mouth to say something but it felt like someone had stuffed his throat with barbed wire, so he just sat there, staring at his hands.

Oskar stayed for another hour, while Herr Hinkel explained how his mother had turned up on his doorstep one spring afternoon eighteen months before. She had finally found the courage to leave Gunther after he had put her in hospital yet again, this time with two broken ribs and a cracked jaw. She was staying with a friend until her old flat opposite him came up for rent again and she'd even been offered her old job back, teaching art at the nearby Steiner school.

'She did everything to find you, Oskar,' said Herr Hinkel. 'Even when she was so sick, she never gave up.'

Oskar swallowed hard.

'She was very different after she came back. That monster Gunther had broken her spirit.' Herr Hinkel stared over at Oskar. 'But it was losing you that broke her heart.'

When Oskar finally left Herr Hinkel's, dusk was falling. His head was so tangled with conflicting emotions that he could barely see straight. How could that bastard Gunther have hurt her like that? Why did she stay with him for so long? Why hadn't she tried even harder to find him after he ran away? Why didn't she push past the assistant at his exhibition and tell him that she was dying?

Stupid woman, he muttered to himself all the way to the train station. Stupid, stupid woman.

*

Standing by the gas stove, Oskar put on a pan of milk to warm. He watched the little bubbles rise to the surface and wondered how much pain Gunther had caused his mother. How frail had she become before the cancer sucked the last breath from her body? How frightened must she have been when the curtains finally closed around her?

Bam! Bam! Bam! Oskar jumped, knocking the pan of milk to the floor. His first impulse was to ignore the banging at the front door and mop up the mess, but then he thought that it might be Frau Zwoll overcome by another asthma attack? Or Herr Kozma wanting desperately to talk? Or maybe Frau Miesel, dizzy and disoriented from a spike in her blood pressure?

Oskar grabbed his dressing gown and stumbled down the stairs.

'Not disturbing you, am I?' said a man in a falsetto voice.

Oskar blinked, taking in the shiny black bouncer's jacket.

'Well, actually . . .'

The man took a step forward. 'Remember that letter you received from Herr Krank's lawyer?'

Oskar nodded.

'Well, it seems you haven't taken it very seriously,' the bouncer-man tutted, 'and several villagers have been overheard babbling about your plan to report Herr Krank's business dealings to the Medical Authorities. So that's why we've come up with an alternative arrangement to keep you quiet.'

Oskar swallowed.

'A nice dark cellar, where you can make as much noise as you like and no one will hear a squeak. Of course,' he said, bringing his face up close to Oskar's, 'the other option is to shut your mouth and get the hell out of this village. It's entirely up to you.'

He tapped Oskar's nose with a gloved forefinger. 'And you can forget about telling tales to the police,' he said with a smirk. 'Herr Krank has some pretty influential friends.'

Chapter 27

'Oskar. What are you doing?' Greta was in her pyjamas, holding open her front door.

'I was just passing and I thought . . .' The sound of the wind howling down the high street was so loud that Oskar had to shout.

'It's one o'clock in the morning,' said Greta.

'Yes. Sorry.' Oskar started to turn away, but stopped when he felt Greta's hand on his sleeve.

'I'm awake now. You might as well come in.'

Upstairs in Greta's living room Oskar was shivering by the window while Greta sat on the sofa, with a large jumper over her pyjamas and her feet curled beneath her.

'You'll have to repeat all that, I barely heard a word,' said Greta, pointing to the window, which was rattling from the heavy rain outside. 'Come and sit down.'

Oskar sat down but his left leg was still twitching with nerves. He took two deep breaths, counted to seven then began again.

'It was the part about the cellar,' he said, when he had finished, 'and how no one would hear me squeak.'

Greta placed an arm around Oskar's shoulders. 'I'm sure it's just a threat, but even so, we need to report this.'

Oskar shook his head and repeated what the man had said about Krank's influential friends.

'In which case,' said Greta as she pushed herself up from the sofa. 'We'll have to think of a Plan B, while Herr Krank is still away on business. In the meantime, I'll make you some tea.'

Greta was back on the sofa next to Oskar and both were clasping mugs of camomile tea.

'I'm sorry to have woken you,' said Oskar. 'I didn't know who else to tell.'

'I'm glad you came,' Greta smiled.

The brief silence was broken by the sound of the raging wind.

Oskar shivered. 'I used to be terrified of storms when I was younger.'

'What else scared you?' Greta sipped her tea.

'The dark ... my stepfather ... never really feeling I fitted in.' Oskar stopped, aware that his voice was quivering. 'Oh, and losing my legs from deep vein thrombosis,' he added to lighten things a little. 'I definitely spent too much time with my medical dictionary. What scares *you*?'

'People killing each other ... animals being tortured ... global warming ... all the usual stuff.' Greta eyed him over her mug. 'Oh, and never falling in love.'

Outside, lightning jagged across the sky but inside in the warm living room, all was still.

Oskar set down his mug. 'Greta,' he said, holding her gaze. 'I think I might be in lo –'

But the rest of his sentence was drowned by a thunderclap, which shook the furniture. Dust showered from the ceiling and a clump of plaster fell to the floor by Greta's feet. Seconds later, a large crack snaked down the right hand wall.

Oskar grabbed Greta's hand and dragged her towards the door.

Down on the pavement, shards of flying glass splintered the air. Bricks, broken bottles, dustbin lids and roof tiles littered the high street. The entire front window of the butcher's had been ripped away and the contents of the meat counter were now strewn across the cobbles, three pigs trotters dancing like little marionettes in the shrieking wind.

Still clasping Greta's hand, Oskar stumbled towards the *Bierkeller*, in whose upstairs window he could see a flickering light.

'Thomas!' Standing in front of the bar's locked door, Oskar shouted upwards. 'It's me, Oskar.'

An overturned dustbin was bowling towards them and behind that, what appeared to be a small tree clattered along the pavement, snapped branches waving like severed limbs. Another crack of lightning sliced through an overhead telegraph pole, which toppled down onto the chemist's roof.

'Thomas!' Oskar hollered again and this time the window opened and Frau Fettler's face appeared.

Upstairs in Thomas's sitting room villagers huddled around the fire, shaking with shock. Herr Kozma, wearing just one carpet slipper, clutched his violin to his chest and gabbled to Herr Schlachter and Frau Fettler. Frau Trundel wiped Adalbert's bleeding forehead, while Frau Zwoll sucked greedily on her inhaler. Thomas was nailing some hardboard to a broken window while Oskar peered once again towards the bakery. 'Someone *must* have seen Frau Miesel?'

For the next couple of minutes they all discussed the quickest and safest way for Oskar to get to the bakery. Frau Zwoll suggested using the small tunnel, which ran from the bar to Frau Miesel's basement, but Herr Kozma said that, like the other tunnels running beneath the village and the forest, it was filled with rubble. Either way, said Oskar, he'd prefer to go overground.

Outside in the street, the wind was so strong that Oskar couldn't even stand. So he crawled instead, stopping every few seconds to turn his head away so he could take in some air. *Thwack*! A roof tile smashed into his right shoulder, and he ducked to avoid part of a flying drainpipe. A lone pig's trotter lay in one of the central gutters, next to Herr Kozma's other carpet slipper.

By the time he reached the bakery, Oskar was breathless and bruised but once inside, he leapt to his feet and raced through the downstairs kitchen.

'Frau M!' he shouted when he reached the bottom of the staircase. 'I'll be with you in a second.' Taking the stairs two at a time, he kept calling for Frau Miesel, urging her not to be frightened.

Upstairs on the first floor landing, the carpet was covered in plaster and splintered beams from the roof, which had partially collapsed.

'It's a right old mess up here,' said Oskar, as much to calm himself as Frau Miesel. 'What *have* you been playing at –?'

Craaack! Something hard and heavy hit Oskar's back, knocking him to the floor. A hot knife of pain seared up his legs and the metallic taste of blood swamped his mouth. He tried to roll over but something was pinning him to the ground. A second blow, this time to the shoulders, slammed his forehead against the floorboards. There was a brief fizzing in his ears and then everything went dark.

'Oskar? Wake up!' Oskar was aware of a man's voice in his ear and a hand gently shaking his shoulder.

I'm probably dreaming, he thought, so he ignored it and let himself slide back into that warm sleepy place, where everything was quiet.

'Oskar!' The voice was much louder. He tried to twist his neck to see who it was but another sharp pain sliced down his spine. This time he could sense someone moving around behind him, dragging away whatever it was that had pinned him to the floor.

'We need to find Frau Miesel,' he shouted, fully awake now. He rolled over and pulled himself up into a sitting position, squinting down the corridor into the darkness. 'Is anyone there?'

Through a hole in the landing floor, he thought he saw a beam of light downstairs but when he looked again, it was gone.

'Frau M, can you hear me?' Oskar had finally crawled into Frau Miesel's bedroom and was crouched over her motionless body, feeling her wrist for a pulse. She was lying on the floor, her legs trapped by a beam and her nightdress splattered with blood.

'Frau M?' Oskar waved a hand in front of her closed eyes. 'Please be OK,' he added in a choked whisper.

Oskar had never given anyone the kiss of life before, but having spat on the floor to get rid of any remaining blood from his fall, he filled his lungs with air and pinched Frau Miesel's nostrils together. Then he blew into her mouth as hard as he could and followed up by pumping his hands against her chest.

'You know, when you're up and running, we're going to have such a laugh about this,' he said, trying to keep his voice steady. 'The night I gave you the kiss of life. I mean, much as I love you . . .' He blew once more into Frau Miesel's mouth. '. . . it's definitely more of a mother/son thing.'

Oskar was still pumping away when a gurgling noise rose from Frau Miesel's chest, followed by a long splutter, then a ragged cough.

Oskar whooped and flung his arms around her neck. Seconds later, Frau Miesel's eyes fluttered open, locked with Oskar's and her mouth spread into one of the most beautiful smiles he had ever seen.

Chapter 28

Oskar and Thomas were assessing the damage through the *Bierkeller's* ground floor window the following morning. Many of the houses' roofs had collapsed, tipping TV aerials and chimney stacks down into the muddy street amongst the debris of shattered glass, snapped tree branches and the contents of Herr Schlachter's meat counter.

In the bar, rainwater still leaked down the back wall, staining it dark brown. The parquet floor was a sodden mass of warped wood, where the mud had seeped in under the door. All of the overnighters had left, aside from Frau Miesel who was upstairs sleeping. Although her legs were badly bruised and she was very shaken, otherwise she was remarkably unscathed.

Through the broken windows, Oskar watched the villagers starting to clean up. Sopping sofas, mattresses and armchairs were dragged onto the pavement to air in the morning sun and clothes, curtains and carpets flapped soggily in the breeze on makeshift washing lines looped between the houses. Greta and Herr Kozma were sweeping up outside the chemist's, whose entire shop front had been demolished. Greta had been trying to get hold of Herr Krank but all the masts were down and there was no telephone reception.

Oskar himself was reluctant to leave the bar and go home. His body ached and the bruises on his face and limbs from his crawl to Frau Miesel's were already turning green and purple. But despite all the drama, he'd rather enjoyed the previous night, once she had been rescued. With everyone squashed into Thomas's sitting room, they had all stayed up drinking hot chocolate with shots of brandy, while Herr Kozma played his violin and Greta recited Goethe poems.

By late afternoon when a few lines of communication were open again, news of Keinefreude's plight had spread and offers of help were pouring in. Deliveries of bread, fresh water, milk, meat, eggs and vegetables, along with blankets, boots and warm clothing were sent by the neighbouring villages, most of whom had escaped the storm. On the second day, a group of carpenters from the Carpenters Guild turned up, as well as a man all the way from Italy, who'd seen the news and packed his Fiat 500 with fresh fruit and vegetables, which he distributed from a trestle table outside the bar.

With the deliveries came the TV and news reporters. Even though three other towns in the area had also been hit by the storm, the world seemed most fascinated by Keinefreude. By mutual consent Oskar was nominated to be the spokesman and now he stood in front of the camera for his fifth live broadcast.

'It's a miracle no one was killed,' he said, in reply to the woman from ZDF's opening question. 'And the response has been amazing. So much generosity from complete strangers and such a feeling of community.'

'No!' the woman said crossly, motioning for the camera to stop filming. 'We need to hear how *terrible* it's been. Try and look like you're in shock, as if your whole life has been destroyed.'

'Why would I do that?' asked Oskar.

The woman sighed as if it was the most obvious thing in the world. 'It's what people want to see!'

In the end Oskar agreed to do as they asked and let himself be shunted this way and that. First he stood in front of Frau Miesel's house, telling the viewers how narrowly he had escaped death, then he posed outside the old florist's pretending that his whole business had gone down the pan. Another news team dragged him to the ruined church to make out that that too had been destroyed in the storms, instead of by vandals some twenty years before. All of this he did, while his plan began to take shape.

Of course, all the journalists and news teams needed to eat and drink so it was up to Thomas, Frau Miesel and Herr Schlachter to provide what they could. Thomas, along with a helpful reporter from the *Süddeutsche Rundfunk*, had managed to repair Frau Miesel's oven and she had been baking amongst the fallen debris of her shop. She was even taking orders – fluffy white rolls for the Berlin news team, honey and almond biscuits for the reporter from the *Süddeutsche Zeitung*, and a large apple tart for the portly man from the *Münchener*.

The final live interview was to be the main slot on ARD's six o'clock evening news on the second day. That afternoon Oskar had spent almost half an hour practising his speech.

'Ready?' asked the programme's director as the make-up artist applied the final touches to highlight the bruises on Oskar's face.

'Definitely,' said Oskar.

The director nodded towards the cameraman and began the count down.

Oskar faced the interviewer's furry microphone with his by now well-practised air of resignation.

'How are you dealing with the aftermath of this tragedy?' asked the reporter.

'We're just trying to rebuild our lives,' Oskar replied, with a sorrowful shake of his head.

The reporter smiled encouragingly.

'Everything has been destroyed, our homes, our bakery, even the chemist's . . .' he sighed.

'In view of the unpredictable weather patterns that seem to be occurring worldwide, do the residents of Keinfreude have any advice on how to cope?'

Oskar shrugged. 'We're just hoping that something good comes out of it.' He stared at his feet for a couple of seconds, then with a sudden beaming smile he was off.

'And for us something good already *has* come out of it, apart from bringing the community closer.' He gestured towards the battered cardboard boxes stacked outside Krank's. 'All the stock in the chemist's was ruined, including eight boxes of an antidepressant called Equavol . . .' He took a step closer to the camera. '. . . which is really called Seramax, and is a Grade 2 antidepressant still being sold on the black market, despite having its license withdrawn by the Medical Board.'

Oskar could see the director of the news team shaking his head, but he ignored him, pointing instead to Frau Zwoll who was standing nearby. 'It nearly killed this woman because of her high blood pressure and Herr Kozma over there, blind as a battery chicken after taking it, and Frau Miesel, our village baker – she now suffers from terrible migraines as well as dizziness and nausea. All caused by Equavol.'

The director was making violent sawing motions across his throat. The producer leapt forward and wrenched the microphone from Oskar's hands. But Oskar didn't give a stuff – his job was done.

That evening almost everyone in the village met in the bar to toast Oskar. Two members of the press had stayed behind, wanting to interview him about his former career as the *enfant terrible* of the art world, but Oskar declined. Instead he chatted to Herr Kozma and Signor Paudice, who'd decided to stay in the village and open up a temporary grocery.

Over the next few days, Greta tried to contact Krank to discuss the future of the chemist's, but as predicted, he wasn't answering his phone. So she and Oskar took the chance to gather the final statements from the villagers, which would then complete the evidence against Equavol for the Medical Board.

By Saturday night Oskar was exhausted, so he went to bed early. In fact, it was so early that he woke at 4 a.m. Feeling the urge to gaze at the stars, he got up and went over to the window. It was then that he noticed the black van parked just outside the former spectacle shop.

Buttoning up his trench coat over in his pyjamas, Oskar crept downstairs and out into the street. Nearing the shop, he could see the outline of Krank through the half-open door, standing by the table at the far end of the room and taping up a cardboard box.

Oskar stepped over the threshold and cleared his throat. 'You do work strange hours, Herr Krank,' he said, nodding to the stack of pills packets on the table. 'I wonder why?'

Krank sprung away from the box, dropping the roll of tape.

'You missed all the fun,' said Oskar. 'The storm, the TV cameras, those lovely news reporters . . .' He shook his head. 'Still, I guess you couldn't resist another little free trip from your pharmaceutical friends.'

From across the shop Krank eyeballed Oskar for what felt like minutes. 'You've been a very stupid boy,' he said eventually. 'Telling stupid lies.'

'Not lies, truth,' said Oskar. 'And now that the Medical Board is about to hear what you've been up to, I doubt you'll be able to open a chemist's anywhere, let alone persuade your doctor mate to prescribe any more drugs.'

'How refreshing to be so naive,' said Krank, smiling as he took a step towards Oskar. 'But sadly, no one will get to hear your side of the story . . .'

'Aha, it's my little trespassing friend.' This second voice was coming from behind Oskar by the door and before he had the chance to swing around, he felt a pair of hands grab his shoulders.

'Oskar was so excited to try out his new lodgings,' said Krank, 'that he came over all by himself.'

'Time to check him in then,' said Krank's shiny-jacketed assistant, tightening his grip.

'Get off me,' Oskar shouted, as he was dragged back towards the door. 'You can't –'. But the rest of his words were muffled by the damp cloth that was clamped over his mouth and nose. He briefly registered the sickly sweet smell of ether before he passed out.

When Oskar awoke, he was in the back of the van, which was travelling very fast down a very bumpy road. His head felt thick and foggy and his mouth was as dry as a pumice stone. He tried banging on the metal partition, which blocked the driver's seat from view but the roar of the engine was too loud for it to be heard.

Oskar sat back, trying to cling onto the safety belt attached to the wall behind him. But within a few minutes the van had skidded to a halt and the back doors were wrenched open. Krank's assistant grabbed his legs and pulled him out onto some damp earth in front of a small wooden cabin surrounded by pine trees.

'Welcome to your new accommodation.' Krank laughed as Oskar was pushed through the door. 'Feel free to make as much noise as you like, the sound-proofing is *very* effective.'

Oskar was shoved towards the middle of the room where there was a large hole.

'What's that saying printed on the side of those cockroach

traps?' chuckled Krank. 'You can check in, but you can't check out.'

'NO!' shouted Oskar with all his force as he felt the assistant hoist him into the air and hurl him down into the deep, dark hole.

'Hello?' Oskar rubbed his eyes and coughed. He wasn't sure how long he had blacked out for, but his head hurt like hell and there was a throbbing pain in his left collarbone.

'Are you still up there, Krank?' he called, listening for a few seconds to the echoing silence. Wincing with pain, he stood up and staggered over to where he guessed the cellar steps might be. Then he slowly felt his way around the walls and outwards into the middle of the small space. But there were no steps.

You're going to be OK, Oskar. Just keep breathing. Oskar was crouched on the floor of what he now realised was just a small, deep pit. His voice was hoarse from shouting and his left shoulder felt like someone had cut clean through it with a hacksaw. The air was damp and clammy, clinging to his cheeks and forehead like damp muslin.

It won't be long until morning. Oskar tried to steady his breath, which was coming in short panicky gulps. *Then you can find your way out.*

Think of other things. Things that make you feel happy and safe. So Oskar thought about Greta asleep in her bed, hair fanned on the pillow, head full of dreams. Next he thought about Frau Miesel, who would just be getting up to start the morning's baking. And then he imagined sitting next to Thomas during one of their shared afternoons in the bar. By the time Oskar had pictured the faces of all his friends in the village, he was feeling a little better. He even started to plan the dinner he would cook for them when he got out.

Something flickered in the darkness, just in front of Oskar. He jumped, peering into the ink-black gloom. For a moment he thought he saw a man's face, bloated and bruised, with a gaping hole for a mouth.

'Go away,' shouted Oskar, 'you're not real!' He squeezed his eyes shut and counted to twelve.

When he opened them again, the face was gone. But in its place was a floral headscarf that seemed to be hanging in mid-air.

Why didn't you come back and see me?

Although Oskar knew the voice was coming from inside his head, his own voice still caught in his throat.

'I did come back, Mum. But I was too late,' he whispered. 'I wanted to see you, I really did.'

You broke my heart.

Oskar bent his head down to his knees, as a tear trickled down his cheek. 'I'm sorry, Mum. I know how hard you tried to find me. Herr Hinkel told me. I'm so sorry.'

Come on, Oskar, you can do this. Oskar was standing up now with one hand on the damp wall of the cellar. He had to find a way out. There was so much to do. Not only would there be the court case against Krank, but he needed to see Franz so he could apologise to him face to face and give him the help he would need to get his life back.

Oskar dropped forward onto his knees and despite the pain in his left shoulder, he crawled around the pit's walls, feeling for any gaps. It was a long shot, but if those tunnels beneath the forest that Herr Kozma had talked about on the night of the storm really did exist, then maybe, just maybe, there was one here.

The pain in his left shoulder had spread to his upper body, which felt like it was on fire. He stopped, breathing deeply into it, before forcing himself forward. He was almost back where he had begun, when his hand hit what felt like a large metal grate.

218

Hunched down, Oskar poked two fingers through the grate's small holes and sensed a very slight movement of air in the space behind it. He tried to pull the grate away but it was firmly attached to the wall by two screws. Feeling their rusted ridges, an image of Jonas using a small coin to unscrew the grate on a school outhouse suddenly popped into Oskar's head. Although he had no change on him, he did have the metal buttons of his trench coat.

He wrenched off the top button and slotted it into the first screw, turning it millimetre by millimetre to the right, until it eventually came loose. The second one seemed a little less rusty and within a few seconds, that too had fallen to the floor and Oskar was able to pull away the grate.

The tunnel was small, barely big enough for Oskar's body. But with his heart roaring in his ears, he crawled inside, trying to push away the rising sense of panic.

You can do it, Oskar.

His whole body was shaking and he could feel that head-swimming dizziness. He was eight years old again, sick with fear in that freezing dark drainpipe. Outside he could hear Jonas laughing.

As Oskar inched forward, other memories slid into his mind: Jonas as he stamped his favourite sketchbook into the playground mud; Jonas pushing his head into a wash basin filled with icy water; Jonas cornering him in the junior changing rooms, unbuckling his bronze belt.

But in between these memories, were unfamiliar images, ones that made Oskar shiver: Jonas himself pinned up against a wall, being shaken so hard that blood was trickling from his nose; Jonas being thrown to the floor and kicked in the stomach by a large boot; Jonas curled up in a foetal position on a small bed as a man stood over him.

In that moment, Oskar suddenly remembered all those

times he had seen Jonas at school with a black eye, a split lip, or a bloody nose. He'd always thought that they had come from playground fights. But now, as he remembered the reason for the care home closing down – that one of the supervisors had been found guilty of assaulting two boys – he knew that wasn't true.

With this realisation, a rush of air filled Oskar's lungs and he felt his heart swell to double its size. *I forgive you, Jonas*, he whispered. *You didn't know any better. You were only doing what someone else had already done to you.*

Oskar was still crawling forwards when suddenly his fingers hit a mound of compacted earth and rubble. He tried to burrow through it but it was solid. The tunnel was blocked. He couldn't go forward and he couldn't crawl backwards. Panic pressed down on him like a heavy black blanket and his heart was pounding so hard he thought it might explode. He threw his head back to take a deep gulp of air and that's when he spotted the small disc of light.

It was coming from the top of a thin shaft above him, which in his panic, Oskar hadn't even registered. The shaft was about four metres high, with a width of no more than a metre. He had no idea what lay at the top, but anything was better than this dark tunnel.

With his feet braced on either side of the shaft, and his right shoulder to steady him, Oskar inched upwards towards the light. Several times he lost his footing and slithered back down again, but eventually he reached the top and his fingers brushed something cool and wet. With one final push he levered himself out of the hole and flopped down onto the damp bracken of the forest floor, his eyes squinting upwards through the trees towards the first rays of the morning sun.

Chapter 29

'Fry it,' said Oskar, tugging at the collar of his blue velvet suit. 'That's what I'd do.'

Greta, who was tying an apron over her pale grey silk tunic, wrinkled her nose. 'You fry lamb?'

'Definitely,' Oskar replied, trying not to stare at the silk clinging to the curves of Greta's breasts. This was his very first dinner party and he was determined to act as sophisticated as possible.

Greta shook her head and smiled. 'Move away now.' She pointed to the pile of potatoes on the sideboard. 'You can peel those, while I get on with the grown-up stuff.'

It was the beginning of April, four weeks since Oskar's imprisonment in the pit beneath the cabin and his broken collarbone was slowly healing. But the strain of dragging himself along the tunnel and then hoisting himself up the vertical shaft had torn two ligaments in his left leg, which meant he still walked with a limp.

During that month Oskar had managed to contact Franz. He hadn't said much on the phone, just that he needed to see him in person to explain some things, which Franz needed to know. Franz had sounded delighted that Oskar wanted to visit him. Apparently he'd just started a new job at the local garage and in a couple of weeks would be moving into his own flat. Together they had decided that as soon as Oskar was able to walk without pain again, then he would travel to Füssen.

The village, with the help of the carpenters, was also getting back on its feet. The *Bierkeller* had been renovated, the butcher's had a brand-new shop front and even the bakery was fully open for business. Oskar had painted a new sign for it: *Frau M's Bakery*, featuring a picture of a tray piled high with apricot tarts, cream puffs and *Apfelstrudel*. When he had presented it to Frau Miesel, he pointed out that she was now duty-bound to bake a rich and varied selection of cakes and pastries, otherwise he would report her for false advertising.

Signor Paudice (or Giacomo as everyone called him) was still in the village, renting one of the upstairs rooms in the *Bierkeller*. Every three days, he would collect fresh vegetables and fruits from the nearby farms, which he sold from a make-shift stall in the high street. The previous Saturday he had invited all the villagers to the bar for a supper of pasta with grilled baby artichokes and for pudding a creamy rhubarb and meringue pie.

It was at this supper that Greta had suggested to Oskar they invite both Giacomo and Frau Miesel to dinner, which was why she and Oskar had lugged a table and chairs from the bar to Oskar's that afternoon, and why they were now standing in his kitchenette, awaiting their two guests.

'Am I too early?' Frau Miesel stood in the sitting room doorway, clutching a plum tart in one hand and a carton of apple juice in the other. Her shiny purple waistcoat was matched with a cream shirt, a long purple skirt and a pair of sensible brown lace-up shoes. Her hair was styled in a soft side parting.

'Not at all,' said Oskar, hurrying forward to relieve her of her cargo before hugging her. 'You look beautiful!'

Frau Miesel blushed then pulled from her cotton bag three Heino records, which she handed to Oskar. 'A small gift for giving me the kiss of life,' she smiled.

Oskar inspected the albums and grinned. 'Ooh, *Sing Mit Heino Nr 2*. A classic!'

'Hi,' said Greta, coming over from the kitchen and kissing Frau Miesel on both cheeks. 'I love your hair.'

Frau Miesel smiled shyly and patted the side parting. 'I went to Staufen this afternoon. It's the first time in years that I've been to the hairdresser.'

'Well, it suits you,' said Greta.

'Drink?' said Oskar.

'Apple juice,' said Frau Miesel.

'We've opened some wine,' said Greta.

'No, thank you,' said Frau Miesel.

Oskar had just poured Frau Miesel's apple juice and a glass of white wine for himself and Greta when Giacomo arrived, wearing a blue linen suit. He kissed Frau Miesel and Greta warmly on both cheeks then grabbed Oskar for a manly hug.

The four of them were seated at the table, which Greta had laid with her own crockery and decorated with candles and a jam jar of fresh freesias.

'Yummsky!' Oskar swiped another white asparagus stalk through the melted butter and popped it into his mouth.

Greta grinned at him before raising her glass to Giacomo, from whom she'd bought the asparagus that morning. She'd been helping him out for three days a week, since the chemist's had temporarily closed. Oskar sometimes worked there on weekends, between his shifts of painting the interiors of the village houses that had been damaged by rainwater. The local council were actually paying him a half decent wage, so at least he could afford his rent and living expenses now.

'You like the asparagus?' Giacomo asked Frau Miesel, who was seated opposite him at the table.

Frau Miesel looked up at somewhere over Giacomo's right shoulder and blushed. 'Lovely,' she mumbled.

'Will you be going on holiday this Easter, Frau Miesel?' asked Oskar, keen to keep the conversation flowing. Holidays were a suitable topic for dinner parties, weren't they?

'I'm . . . n . . . not sure,' Frau Miesel replied before slurping at her apple juice.

'I'm not a fan of holidays myself,' said Oskar. 'I've only ever been on one – to Worpswede. Grim.'

Greta burst out laughing. 'Worpswede! You old hippy.'

'And you?' Greta turned to Giacomo. 'Are you going anywhere this year?'

Giacomo shook his head. 'My wife die three years ago and I have no one to go with.' He stared at the remaining lone asparagus on his plate. 'She die of *cancro*.'

'Cancer,' said Greta quietly. 'How terrible.'

'I'm so sorry,' said Frau Miesel, looking forlornly at her fork.

'That's just awful,' said Oskar.

'But tonight is about new beginnings.' Giacomo picked up the second bottle of Franken wine, opened it and began filling everyone's glasses. When he came to Frau Miesel's, her hand was already covering the rim.

'Oh go on, Frau M,' said Oskar, nodding towards the bottle. 'It's good stuff.'

'Just a taste,' said Greta.

Frau Miesel looked over at Oskar, then Greta and finally at Giacomo. After a short hesitation, she removed her hand to let him fill her glass.

'I'll make sure you don't get trolleyed,' said Oskar, giving her a wink.

'Giacomo's not going to bite you,' whispered Oskar to Frau Miesel as they stood in the kitchenette together. He'd beckoned her over there after the first course on the pretext of discussing the pudding. 'But you need to look him in the eye and talk to him.'

'I can't,' whispered Frau Miesel. 'I'm scared.'

'Giacomo is a kind and honest man,' said Oskar. 'And he obviously likes you.'

'Don't be ridiculous.'

'Then why did he insist that you sat next to him at supper last Saturday?' said Oskar, clattering some cutlery to cover their conversation.

A tentative hand fluttered up to her cheek. 'Really?'

'But you need to say something, Frau M. Tell him about what you love – baking, the mountains, *die Schwarzwaldklinik*. Anything.' Oskar squeezed Frau Miesel's arm. 'You can do it.'

The lamb was cooked perfectly as were the braised carrots and roast potatoes and now they were pausing before pudding while Greta told them about the two officials from the Medical Board, who'd visited earlier in the week and spent two hours questioning her about Herr Krank.

'They examined almost everything in his office for evidence,' said Greta. 'Except for the safe, because I still can't find the key.' She turned to Giacomo. 'Assuming they do manage to arrest Krank and assuming he's found guilty, then the old florist's will be empty again. Why don't you use that for your grocery?'

Giacomo nodded enthusiastically, then turned to Frau Miesel. 'You think it is good for me?'

Frau Miesel took another swig of wine and swallowed noisily.

'That's a yes,' said Oskar.

The plates had been cleared, another bottle of wine opened and Frau Miesel was whipping some cream for the plum tart.

Giacomo was inspecting the one remaining canvas on Oskar's wall. All the others including *The Dark Side of Mother* had been thrown away after the storm because they were so damaged by water leaking through the roof.

'This is all I've managed to paint in months,' said Oskar, joining Giacomo in front of the picture of two swallows perching on his window ledge, pecking at *Leibniz-Keks* crumbs.

'I've been a bit blocked,' he added, 'ever since I had an eye test in the spectacle shop last October.'

'Spectacle shop?' said Giacomo.

Oskar pointed across the street to the former florist's. 'It was only here for a week. I wish it could have stayed longer though. The optician, Dr. Sehle, was an extraordinary man.'

Giacomo scratched his head. 'My sister also tell me a story like this. She lives in a village near Bolzano and last November a man open a shop which sell glasses.' Giacomo smiled. 'Only one person go inside for eye test – the crazy man from the gas station. Afterwards he tells everybody that he has seen . . . *Paradiso*.'

'Pudding's ready!' Frau Miesel plonked the plum tart down on the table, knocking over the jar of freesias.

'What did the optician look like?' said Oskar. 'Did he have puckered skin like he'd been in a fire? What happened to the man from the gas station?'

But Giacomo was already hurrying towards the table. '*Che bellissima torta!*' he said, grabbing a napkin to mop up the spillage, before refilling Frau Miesel's glass. 'You have many talents, Frau M.'

Giacomo had refilled the other wine glasses and was now on his second slice of *Pflaumentorte*. Across the table Oskar had tried again to find out more about the spectacle shop in his sister's village, but Giacomo didn't know anything else about it or its owner.

226

'How much longer you stay in this village, Oskar?' asked Giacomo. 'If you cannot paint.'

'I don't know,' said Oskar, glancing at Greta. 'That depends. Apart from everything else, I really need to earn some proper money.'

'You could become a rent boy!' Frau Miesel clapped her hands and laughed before lunging across the table for the wine bottle.

'I'm not sure I'm really cut out for that career, Frau M,' said Oskar, leaning over to gently take the wine bottle from her hand and replace it with the apple juice.

Frau Miesel waved him away. 'Juice is for babies!'

'Music! That's what we need,' said Oskar, desperate to distract Frau Miesel from the bottle. He strode over to the turntable and selected the first Heino album on the pile.

Setting the needle to the second track *Karamba, Karacho, Ein Whiskey,* he beckoned Frau Miesel towards the impromptu dance floor. 'Let's make some shapes, Frau M!'

By the next song, Giacomo had joined Frau Miesel and the two of them were really going for it. Oskar was sitting down again next to Greta, having helped himself to some more pudding as he watched Frau Miesel high-kicking her legs.

'Want to join them?' said Greta.

'Nope,' said Oskar. 'Dancing is the devil's work.'

Greta laughed. 'It might loosen you up a bit.' She grinned over at Frau Miesel, who was belting out the chorus to Heino's *Komm in Meinen Wigwam.*

'Come on, just for this one.' She grabbed Oskar's right hand and dragged him towards the dance floor. 'Otherwise, you'll have to do all the washing up.'

It was difficult to know what dance technique should be applied to *Komm in Meinen Wigwam*. Should he swing his arms around? Should he jiggle his legs? Or should he just go mental and copy Frau Miesel? In the end Oskar opted for some simple old-school moon-walking.

'Do you think she's alright?' he asked Greta, nodding over at Frau Miesel.

'Relax,' said Greta, moving towards him. 'She's fine.'

'I'm just a bit worried.' Oskar tipped an imaginary glass to his lips.

'What can happen? We're both here.' Greta took his hand and folded it into hers.

Frau Miesel galloped past them with Giacomo close behind. When she reached the wardrobe, she came to an abrupt halt.

'*Komm in Meinen Wigwam!*' she giggled, clambering inside and gyrating her hips hula-style in the doorway. '*Komm in Meinen Wigwam! Wigwam!*' she shouted, waving at Giacomo.

Creeeaaaak! The noise coming from behind the wardrobe was loud but only Oskar appeared to hear it above the music. The back panel was pulling away from the wall, tilting the wardrobe forward.

'Frau M!' he called. 'Watch out . . .' But the wardrobe was already teetering on its two front legs. Oskar leapt forward to the sound of splintering wood just as it crashed face-first to the floor.

'Frau M? Are you alright?' Oskar shouted into the missing back panel of the overturned wardrobe. He peered inside but could only see his black silk dressing gown.

Next to him, also on all fours, Giacomo pressed his ear closer. 'Can you hear us?'

'Are you hurt?' asked Greta.

A few seconds later they heard Frau Miesel's trembling voice from inside. 'Where am I?'

'In the wardrobe,' said Oskar. 'But don't panic, we'll have you out in a second.'

The wardrobe weighed roughly the same as a small tractor, but after a lot of puffing Greta, Giacomo and Oskar heaved it upright. The door swung open and there was Frau Miesel looking very pale.

'I think I'd like to go home now,' she hiccuped.

Oskar, Greta and Giacomo escorted Frau Miesel home, with Oskar taking her elbow for support. After a strong coffee and two glasses of water she had sobered up and apart from feeling a bit shaky, she was unhurt.

'Are you sure you'll be alright?' Oskar plucked a mothball from Frau Miesel's hair, as they stood in front of the bakery.

'We can come in if you want us?' said Giacomo.

'I can give you some aconite for the shock,' said Greta.

But Frau Miesel just shook her head.

Oskar squeezed her hand. 'In that case, we'll leave you to it.' He kissed her on both cheeks. 'I'll see you in the morning.'

After walking Giacomo back to the *Bierkeller*, Greta and Oskar were standing out on the street again. Above them, the stars glittered in the blue-black sky and the moon, not quite yet full, pooled its silver light on the cobbles at their feet.

'Are you tired?' said Greta.

Oskar laughed. 'No way! Far too much excitement.'

Greta pointed to the hill just beyond the village. 'Reckon you're up to it?'

Oskar smiled and they started walking.

'My dad and I would walk together in the evenings,' said Greta, as they neared the churchyard. 'After mum died, it was one of the few things he still liked to do.' She tilted her head to stare at the night sky, the light breeze ruffling her hair. 'He used to tell me old folklore stories. My favourite was one from the Middle Ages about a man who lived in the forest around here.

Whenever people were lost, he would appear and lead them home. He had a long wooden staff with the symbol of an eye carved into it, which he would tap in front of him because he was blind.'

'I wonder if that's the same symbol I read about when I was in Jena,' said Oskar. 'According to the *House of Optics*, there's a whole lineage of people, who carried an amber eye symbol to show their dedication to helping others see the world differently,' he paused. 'I have a funny feeling that Dr. Sehle belonged to it.'

They had reached the graveyard, where the scent of the recently planted rosemary bushes filled the air. Oskar linked his arm through Greta's.

'It was my mum who told me stories,' he said, quietly. 'Mostly about the stars. I loved her ones about Orion's Belt the best.'

Greta stopped, her face turned towards Oskar. 'You realise that's the first time you've mentioned your mother?'

Oskar stared in front of him at a nearby gravestone beneath the branches of a large beech tree.

'What's wrong?' Greta whispered.

'Nothing,' said Oskar.

'Liar.'

Oskar rubbed his eyes with his sleeve then twisted his head away so Greta couldn't see his face.

'Talk to me, Oskar.'

It was the tenderness of her voice that triggered it and when it hit, the pain in his chest was so intense that Oskar could barely breathe.

Oskar had no idea how long the words had been tumbling from his mouth. There was no logical sequence to what he was saying, just random snatches of memories as they surfaced: the blanket-soft soothe of his mother's voice as she pointed out the stars on those stormy nights; the sweet apple scent of her hair; the feeling of her arms folded around him. Other memories kept slipping in between: those first weeks in Berlin, wandering from bar to bar, asking for Werner; that moment in the morgue, when he wasn't even allowed to touch his father's face; that long night after he had left the hospital, running through the dark streets, unable to stop crying.

When he finished, Oskar looked straight ahead, willing the storm of emotions to settle. Around him, everything was still: Greta, the beech tree, even the breeze, as if they were all silently contemplating his memories.

They were standing opposite each other, so close that Oskar could feel Greta's breath feathering his cheek. He pulled back a little to gaze at her face and found himself falling once more into the depths of those grey-green eyes.

And then he kissed her.

Chapter 30

Oskar lay on his bed, thinking. It was just after seven in the morning and he was still dressed in his dinner party outfit. He'd spent most of the hours before dawn replaying in his mind that kiss: that first berry-sweet brush of Greta's lips, the velvet crush of her mouth, the silken glide of her tongue. Each moment had left an imprint, a sensory explosion seared for eternity onto the fabric of his soul.

Down on the street, Oskar watched the village waking. Windows were flung open to let in the morning sun, duvets shaken, breakfasts eaten. In the bakery Frau Miesel was pulling a tray of glistening brown rolls from the oven and outside the butcher's, Herr Schlachter unfurled his new red and white striped awning. Suddenly, all of these morning rituals seemed to have acquired an added richness, an innate harmony, like a finely choreographed dance or a perfectly worded poem.

The walk to Greta's house seemed endless, past the bright red geraniums in Thomas's window box, past the old florist's where Giacomo was arranging baskets of broad beans, past Herr Kozma's house from whose windows wafted the first notes of his daily violin practice. And with each step Oskar tried to work out what he would say.

'But first I need some coffee.' Greta yawned and rubbed the sleep from her eyes. They were in her kitchen and she was still wearing her dressing gown with a pair of red knitted socks on her feet.

'Good idea!' Oskar's voice sounded ridiculously bright as he watched her take two mugs from the cupboard. Behind them, the radio was announcing the weather, another fine spring day with plenty of sunshine.

'There you go,' said Greta, handing Oskar his coffee. 'Now what was so urgent that you needed to wake me?' She hopped up on the sideboard, with her chin resting on her right knee.

Oskar placed his mug down next to the sink, so that she wouldn't see how much his hands were trembling. His heart thundered in his chest and time seemed to collapse into one single moment, a moment shining with a dozen possible futures.

He couldn't look at her while he spoke. Instead he kept his eyes focused on the kitchen window and the churchyard beyond.

'Is that really how you feel?' asked Greta, once he had finished.

'Yes,' Oskar whispered.

There was a pause, a silence filled with the fading echoes of those dozen possible futures, all of which he'd just smashed to pieces.

'How do you know you'll do it again?' Greta's voice was as quiet as Oskar's.

'Because that's what I do.'

'But I'm not Bettina or Paula or Sandra.' Greta laid her hand on Oskar's. 'Besides, you've said that you're deeply sorry for what happened, and that you'll do whatever it takes to make amends.'

'That's not the point,' said Oskar, his eyes finally meeting Greta's. 'It's the fact that I was capable of hurting them in the first place.' He shook his head. 'I'm sorry, Greta, I just can't risk doing the same to you, because I . . .' He couldn't even finish the sentence. Instead he slid his hand from beneath hers and without looking back, he walked towards the door.

Chapter 31

Oskar was spring-cleaning. He'd started after breakfast with the outside larder, removing some rancid cheese, a carton of not-so-Long Life milk and a mound of mouldy mashed potato. After that, he'd swilled out some empty meatball tins. Then he'd crawled under the bed and collected fistfuls of Kinder Bueno wrappers. And finally he'd given the floor a thorough mop with his Edvard Munch T-shirt.

He had to keep himself busy and he'd tried all the other obvious ways from listening to Wagner and memorising Goethe poems to attempting to assemble complicated Kinder Egg toys. He'd even gone on a nature ramble.

He hadn't seen Greta since he'd walked out of her house two weeks before. According to Frau Miesel, she was staying for a month in Staufen where she was helping out on her friend's flower stall at the market. She had asked Oskar not to contact her.

'Bored again?' Thomas paused from washing the windows as Oskar entered the bar later that afternoon.

Oskar nodded and went over to the bar to help himself to a *Weizenbier.*

'You're supposed to be an artist. How about painting something?'

Oskar shrugged. 'What's the point?' He slumped down in Thomas's re-upholstered armchair and switched on the television.

'You could give me a hand if you're *that* bored,' said Thomas. 'I know you need the money.'

It was true. Oskar did need the money. The painting jobs were drying up and he was even wondering if he should go back to Berlin and knock out some paintings in his old style, in the hope of finding some buyers.

'Maybe tomorrow,' said Oskar. 'I don't feel too good today.' He stared at the telly, which showed a cluster of derelict houses overshadowed by clouds of thick black smoke. According to the reporter, the village, which was in Romania, had the highest rate of suicide in Europe along with widespread lung disease, impotence and asthma, all linked to the local lead smelting works.

Thomas had moved onto the last window, wringing out the soapy cloth into the bucket beneath him. 'What about an exhibition? We could do it here in the bar.'

'I haven't got anything new to show,' said Oskar, 'apart from a picture of some swallows. Anyway, why are you washing the windows again? You only did them last week.'

Thomas tossed the cloth back into the bucket and walked over to Oskar. 'I'm putting this place on the market so I can move back to Jena. Kensho and I are going to work together again.'

'You're leaving?' said Oskar, feeling a sharp pull in his chest. 'For good?'

Thomas rested his hand on Oskar's shoulder. 'Who knows? But if I don't come back, you'll just have to come and stay with me in Jena.'

When Oskar left the bar an hour later, he didn't feel like going home. Instead he kept walking down the high street, past the empty chemist's towards the church. Unlike most of the buildings, it hadn't been renovated following the storm. Instead, its four crumbling walls were covered with ivy and the thick wooden door in the porch was riddled with woodlice.

Inside, a few pews were still intact along with the organ whose oxidised green pipes were choked with bindweed. A yellowing sheet of hymn music flapped in the draft from a huge hole in the half-collapsed roof. Walking up the aisle, Oskar spotted the four stained glass windows at the far end by the altar. Only one remained unbroken, and washed by the recent rains, it sparkled in the afternoon sun. The picture showed a man standing on the edge of a forest, holding a long staff. Beneath it was a small plaque: *'This window was commissioned to mark the 500th anniversary of the birth of Wilhelm Hochheim, guardian and protector of the village of Keinefreude.'*

Oskar was still staring up at the window, when he heard the creak of the church door behind him. He spun round and there, next to the cracked marble pulpit, was an elderly man wearing a woodsman's hat with fur-lined earflaps.

'Dr. Sehle!' Oskar rushed over and threw his arms around him.

'Hello, Oskar,' Dr. Sehle smiled and hugged Oskar in return. He looked exactly the same as all those months ago, the same puckered skin and broad smile, although his clothes were even more weathered.

'Where have you been?' said Oskar.

Dr. Sehle pointed to his boots, whose battered leather had been completely re-stitched. 'Everywhere!'

'Was it you in that Italian village where Giacomo's sister lives? Were you here during the storm when I was looking for Frau Miesel? And if you were, why didn't you say something?' Oskar was gabbling, giving Dr. Sehle no chance to reply. 'And what about that waxwork in the Jena museum? That was *weird*!

I mean, I may be a bit stupid sometimes, but how could it possibly have been you?'

Dr. Sehle grinned and wagged an index finger. 'Didn't you pay attention in your science lessons? Can you not remember how travelling at the speed of light affects time?'

Oskar shook his head. His brain was so bursting with things he needed to ask Dr. Sehle, that he could barely remember his own birthday, let alone anything that Herr Brugger had said.

'According to the museum's brochure, you died in a fire,' said Oskar. 'But there wasn't a body.'

'You might say that I have died in several fires,' Dr. Sehle laughed, his fingers brushing his wrinkled skin. He nodded towards the stained glass window straight ahead of them. 'Do you know who that is?'

'Only what's written on the plaque.' Oskar stepped forward to get a better look at the man with the staff. 'What exactly did he do anyway?'

'Wilhelm Hochheim was known as the guardian angel of the area,' said Dr. Sehle, still standing behind Oskar. 'Whenever people became lost, he would guide them safely home. On the way he would tell them stories to illustrate how they weren't miserable sinners after all. Instead they, like all humans, were divine beings, and when they learnt to see the world through the eyes of love not fear, they would fully understand this.'

'He sounds like the man from a folklore story that Greta told me about,' said Oskar. 'Except that guy was blind.'

Dr. Sehle smiled. 'Over the centuries there have been many people helping others find their way back home.' He sighed and shook his head. 'Unfortunately Wilhelm wasn't very popular with the church. He was eventually imprisoned for heresy and burnt at the stake. But just before they tied him up, they singed out his eyes with hot coals.'

'Ouch,' said Oskar, instinctively rubbing his own eyes.

At that moment the sun slid out from behind a cloud, lighting up the stained glass to a dazzle of blue, green and gold. The man's eyes glowed an intense fiery amber.

'Can you see that, Dr. Sehle?' said Oskar, facing the window again. 'His eyes look like yours.' He stood there for a few more seconds, soaking up the coloured sunlight that was pouring through the glass. Then, hearing no response, he turned round to face the pulpit, searching for the spot where Dr. Sehle had been just moments before.

'Dr. Sehle?' he called, scanning the pews and aisle, then back towards the pulpit. But the church was empty and the only sound was the sheet of hymn music rustling quietly in the breeze.

Chapter 32

Oskar was doing a bit of comb-work to thicken up his quiff. He was wearing his blue velvet suit and a new shirt that Thomas had given him. Tonight was going to be a big night and he wanted to look his best. It also happened to be his birthday, but he doubted whether anyone in the village would know that.

Initially, when Thomas had suggested an exhibition, he'd said no because he had almost nothing to show for his time in Keinefreude. But over the last fortnight Oskar had worked at his easel for up to fourteen hours a day. Even though he'd only produced two paintings, he still believed people might want to see at least one of them.

All the villagers were gathered in the *Bierkeller* when Oskar arrived. Herr Kozma, wearing a pair of brothel creepers that Oskar had given him, was talking to Frau Trundel and Adalbert. Frau Zwoll and Frau Fettler were helping Thomas fill a tray of *Sekt* glasses. Frau Miesel was setting a big white cardboard box on top of the bar, and Giacomo was arranging jam jars of wild spring flowers on the long trestle table. On the wall at the far end hung Oskar's canvas measuring two metres by two and covered with a white sheet.

The supper table was heaving and included four roasted geese courtesy of Herr Schlachter; bowls of broad beans doused in olive oil, artichokes dipped in *alioli* and fried courgette flowers from Giacomo; and five loaves of rosemary and olive focaccia bread baked that afternoon by Frau Miesel.

Half an hour later all the guests were squeezed around the table, eating, chatting and laughing. Oskar laughed and joked with them, but every so often he glanced towards the door. The place on his right was empty, reserved for Greta, just in case. Both Thomas and Frau Miesel had sent her messages so she knew the party was happening.

The goose carcasses had been stripped, the artichokes and courgette flowers devoured, the focaccia gobbled, and every broad bean had been swallowed. Now Thomas was standing on his chair, tapping his glass with his knife.

'Before pudding I want to say a few words.' He surveyed the guests one by one. 'I'm sure you all know why we're here tonight. Firstly, so I can say goodbye before I return to Jena and secondly, . . .' he said, swivelling to face Oskar. '. . . because this young man has finally painted something.' He pointed to the covered canvas.

'When Oskar arrived in Keinefreude six months ago I'll admit, I didn't like him much. He was, to be honest, pretty irritating,' Thomas smiled. 'But in the last few weeks I've come to see that he's actually one of the kindest and most compassionate people I know.' He coughed and wiped something from his eye.

'And if I had been fortunate enough to have a second son, then I would have wanted a son like Oskar.' Thomas reached for his glass. 'So I would like you all to toast –'

'Wait!' Frau Miesel sprung up from her chair. 'I happen to know that it's quite a special day,' she said, raising her glass high above her head. 'Ladies and gentlemen, will you join me in wishing Oskar a very happy birthday.'

The room resounded to the chinking of glasses and a loud

chorus of Happy Birthdays while Frau Miesel hurried over to the bar. Flipping open the lid of the white box, she lifted out a colossal Black Forest gateau layered with cream and topped with chocolate shavings and shiny red cherries.

'Happy Birthday, dear Oskar,' she said, placing the cake in front of him and kissing him firmly on the forehead.

The cake had been cut and consumed, more wine had been downed and the guests had risen from the table. The raucous conversation and laughter had quietened, and everyone was facing the back wall where the canvas was hung. Next to it stood Oskar, holding the edge of the sheet. With one last look at the door, he gave it a tug and it crumpled to the floor.

The first impression was of a typical Black Forest village on a sunny April morning. The bustling high street was lined with brightly painted shops and outside the windows of each wooden-beamed house hung pots of pink and red geraniums. In the distance, the trees of the surrounding forest glistened a deep dark green beneath the electric blue sky.

On closer inspection you could recognise the faces: Thomas sitting outside the bar, dressed in a clean white shirt as he polished his reading glasses; Greta inside the new grocery, admiring Giacomo's baskets of fresh vegetables; Frau Miesel in the bakery, mixing the dough for her apricot tarts. Further down in the butcher's Herr Kozma, Frau Zwoll, Frau Fettler and Frau Trundel were queuing in front of the counter, casually contemplating the three remaining *Wiener Schnitzel*.

In fact, everything in the village, aside from the figure of Greta, looked exactly as it had done just ten hours ago when Oskar put his signature to the painting. The only difference was the presence of one extra shop between the bakery and the new grocery, in whose sparkling windows hung every sort of spectacle imaginable.

The villagers were still silent, staring open-mouthed. Oskar stared with them, mesmerised by the light that seemed to stream from the canvas out into the room. The more he focused on this light, the more he could feel it spreading within him, filling every cell in his body.

'Have I missed all the fun?' Oskar immediately recognised the voice by the doorway and without even looking, he had an image of Greta in her grey silk dress with her hair falling in loose curls around her shoulders.

'Hello,' she mouthed when his eyes met hers.

'Hello,' Oskar mouthed back.

The party was in full swing. Herr Kozma had brought his violin and was playing gypsy songs to which everyone was dancing – everyone except Oskar and Greta who were still standing beneath the picture, where they'd been since she arrived. Her face had caught the sun and freckles had spread to her cheeks and nose. It took all of Oskar's willpower not to kiss them, one by one.

'So you *can* paint after all,' said Greta, nodding at the picture.

Oskar blushed and took a gulp of *Sekt*. 'It feels like you've been away for ages. I was worried.'

'I'm a grown woman, I can take care of myself,' said Greta, chinking her glass against his. 'So you heard the news about Krank?'

Oskar nodded. The previous week both Krank and his assistant had been arrested near the Swiss border. They were now awaiting trial in Freiburg, at which Oskar and several other villagers would be giving evidence.

'In which case, I can give you your birthday present,' said Greta, pulling out a small oblong package from her bag.

'The morning before I left, I found the duplicate key to

Krank's safe. This was inside.' She handed Oskar the package. 'Happy Birthday.'

Oskar was about to untie the green ribbon when Greta shook her head. 'Open it tomorrow, when you're alone.'

'You know I'm leaving tomorrow?' said Oskar.

'I do,' said Greta. 'Frau Miesel told me. She also said that you might have some work with your old gallery back in Berlin.'

Oskar nodded. He hadn't expected to hear back so quickly after he had sent them an image of his painting of Keinefreude that morning. But just after lunch he'd received a phone call from the gallery owner to say that he had shown the image to a philanthropist client looking for art for his new office. Despite the high price that the gallery had placed on the painting, the client still wanted to commission Oskar to paint a similar picture, but of his hometown. He'd even put down a 25% deposit.

'Will you come back?' asked Greta.

Oskar had been wondering the very same thing since he'd made the decision to go. He looked around the room, his eyes resting on the familiar faces: Frau Miesel, Thomas, Frau Zwoll, Herr Kozma, Frau Fettler, Frau Trundel, Adalbert, Herr Schlachter and finally back to Greta. The lump in his throat made words impossible but he already knew the answer.

Chapter 33

At 6.30 a.m. the next morning Oskar stood at his window, looking down at the village. Behind him on the bed, his suitcase was bulging with two new jumpers knitted by Frau Zwoll, three of Thomas's shirts, two pairs of trousers and an embroidered woollen waistcoat from Herr Kozma. He wondered if he'd packed the right things. After all, he was going to three different climates – first to Füssen then onto Romania via Berlin.

When he'd initially seen the report about Romania on Thomas's television, he hadn't given it much thought. But in the fortnight that followed, he couldn't forget that village cowering in the shadow of the lead works. Two nights before he'd finally decided to go, although he had no idea why the urge to visit the place was so strong – nor what he would do there once he arrived.

The rest of Oskar's belongings were to be sent on afterwards – apart from his new painting, which would hang permanently in the bar. The only canvas he was taking with him was the small portrait of Greta that he had done on the day she left for Staufen, and which was now sandwiched in his case between a book of Goethe's poems and a packet of *Birkel* macaroni.

He walked over to the record player and selected the final

aria from Wagner's *Faust*, where Faust's soul is born heavenward by a host of angels. He'd been playing it a lot recently.

The small package lay on his side table where he had placed it the night before. He picked it up and untied the ribbon before removing the brown paper wrapping. Inside was a dark green leather glasses case identical to the one Herr Kozma had shown him.

Oskar flipped open the lid and there, wrapped inside a cream silk handkerchief, was a pair of round silver spectacles. He walked over to the window and with his eyes firmly closed he put them on. Several seconds passed before he dared open them again and when he did, he saw that the entire village was bathed in the same shimmering light that he'd seen in Dr. Sehle's attic. A feeling of exquisite happiness bubbled up inside him and with it came another feeling; a deep sense of belonging not just to this beautiful village but somehow to *himself*.

Oskar removed the glasses to wipe a tear from his eye. But gazing down at the village again, he realised that the shimmering otherworldly light was still there. This time two phrases echoed through his mind:

Whatever I see is part of me.
Nothing is separate.

Oskar smiled and picked up the handkerchief to fold around the glasses again. As he did so, he spotted the tiny symbol of an amber eye, stitched in gold thread into the top left hand corner.

The street was silent when Oskar closed the front door behind him. He glanced up at the gargoyle. Its scowl was gone, replaced by a smile that seemed to quiver around the carved wooden lips as though it was about to burst into laughter.

———

When Oskar reached the edge of the village, he set down his suitcase and let his eyes linger on the street for one last time. Unwrapping a breakfast Kinder Bueno bar, he took a bite. It was then that the village sign caught his eye. The K in Keinefreude had come unstuck and now dangled from its nail, giving the remaining letters a completely different meaning – *Eine Freude*. A Joy.

Oskar repeated the words to himself as he walked down the road, chuckling at the irony of it all.

Acknowledgements

It's taken a while to get Oskar out into the world and without the constant support and encouragement from my family and friends, the road would have been even rockier. So thank you: Jacqueline, Lee, Sue, Tanja, Fi, Sadie, Lucille, Joe, Mum, Clive, Anna, Charlie, Jamie, Gabriella, Max, Tom, Hugo, Kim, Camilla, Anna K, Dick, Jane, Henry – and Tim. I also owe a massive thank you to Angelika Michitsch for her admirable enthusiasm while combing through and smoothing out endless drafts. And thank you to the team at RedDoor: Clare, Anna and Heather, for making the publishing process such a collaborative and enjoyable experience – again.

About the Author

Hattie Edmonds has attempted many jobs, including junior sales assistant on Separates in Clements (of Watford) department store and chief plugger-in of cables in a Berlin recording studio. For ten years she was the London correspondent for the German pop magazine, *Bravo*, interviewing many, many boy bands. After that, she spent three joyous years as the in-house comedy writer at Comic Relief. Now she writes fiction and non-fiction, and volunteers for a refugee charity.

Find out more about
RedDoor Publishing and
sign up to our newsletter
to hear about our **latest
releases, author events,**
exciting **competitions**
and more at

reddoorpublishing.com

YOU CAN ALSO FOLLOW US:

 @RedDoorBooks

 RedDoorPublishing

 @RedDoorBooks